D0948684

Frederic Raphael

THE GLITTERING PRIZES

Frederic Raphael

THE GLITTERING PRIZES

ST. MARTIN'S PRESS   NEW YORK

First published in America by St. Martin's Press 1977
Copyright © 1976 by Volatic Ltd.
All rights reserved. For information, write:
St. Martin's Press, Inc., 175 Fifth Ave., New York, N.Y. 10010.
Manufactured in the United States of America
Library of Congress Catalog Card Number: 77-76651

Library of Congress Cataloging in Publication Data

Raphael, Frederic, 1931
   The glittering prizes.

   Originally presented as a six-part television series with
the same name.
   I. Title.
PZ4.R217Gl 1977   [PR6068.A6]   823'.9'14   77-76651
ISBN 0-312-32957-1

For Stella Richman
and in memory of David Gore-Lloyd

CONTENTS

An Early Life *11*
A Sex Life *73*
A Past Life *119*
A Country Life *165*
An Academic Life *203*
A Double Life *251*

An
Early
Life

'Hullo,' Adam said, when the girl opened the door, 'it's only me. Anyone at home?'

'Only me,' she said. 'Any news?'

Adam looked blank. 'News?'

'Don't be silly. From Cambridge.'

'Oh from Cambridge!' He went past her into the sitting room. 'Well, they did send me this.'

He was holding out a telegram. Sheila took it from him and read it. When she looked at him again, he was grinning.

'Aren't you a pig?' she said. 'Major Scholarship! You are a pig. "They did send me this!" Pig.'

He tried to put his arms round her, as if he had earned something. She was a pretty, dark girl with green eyes and a very red mouth. In 1952 most girls had very red mouths, but Sheila's mouth had a pout at once sensual and disapproving which gave its redness a particular charm. She wore a tartan skirt with a stainless steel safety pin in it, and a white angora sweater, enchantingly tight. She disengaged herself from Adam and went, awkwardly, to the mantelpiece, where candlesticks and family pictures in silver frames were arranged with symmetrical propriety. 'So,' she said, 'the secret is out. Adam Morris is a genius.'

'It's now official, that's all. It's no news to me.'

'Three years,' Sheila said.

'You know what I'd like to do now? I'd like to drive down to my dear old school in a fleet of limousines – I've now officially left incidentally, as of the aforesaid telegraphic communication – and I'd like to wrap the good news round a large brick and sling it personally through the Headmaster's window.'

'What for? He got you your scholarship, didn't he? What's your grouse?'

'What's my grouse, what's my pheasant, what's my hard-boiled egg? He only did his damnedest to stop me getting anything at all.'

'Why would he want to do that?' Sheila was turning a chocolate round and round in its crinkled paper. There was a little red Venetian glass dish of them on the side table. 'What's he got against you?'

Adam assumed the voice of The Man in Black. 'It all started one winter afternoon, in the School Chapel,' he said.

ii

The sermons on Sunday evenings were always given by a visiting preacher, if possible an Old Benedictine, though Benedict's was not a religious foundation. Its original buildings, in South London, had been confiscated from the Benedictine order by Henry the Eighth and acquired by a merchant adventurer who became pious at the onset of his final illness, when he founded a school to commemorate his name and decorate his not entirely amiable reputation. The school had moved to the Surrey countryside in the nineteenth century and was there housed in what looked like a congeries of overgrown Victorian branch-line railway stations. It was said to be one of the great Public Schools of England.

Adam sat in the pews reserved for members of the Sixth Form. Chapel was compulsory. When Adam's father raised the question with the Headmaster, after Adam had won his entrance scholarship, Mr Charlesworth was succinct. Jewish boys must come to services. 'They are not required to believe, but they are expected to attend.' Adam didn't mind all that much. He sang the hymns, after a fashion, and refrained from bowing his head in the Creed. In large, he conformed. He sat in the Sixth Form pews and yawned like a Christian at the sermons.

On this particular night, the preacher was the Provost of Ipswich, a gaunt man with a gaunt voice who leaned over the Memorial Pulpit and put his hands under the lacy sleeves of his surplice and held onto his own elbows.

'When I think of Him as a young man,' he was saying, 'I like to imagine Christ – or Jesus as he was then – working simply at his trade as a carpenter in his native Nazareth. A man skilled with his hands. And at the end of the week, he would take the work he had finished, be it never so humble, down to the village shop and offer to sell it to the shop-keeper. And the shopkeeper – being a Jew – would give him as little for it as he possibly could . . .'

The Sixth Formers round Adam woke into a guffaw of laughter. It was quickly repressed, but its echoes whispered away down the Chapel and even when it had died out completely, people had to avoid looking at each other in case they laughed again. Adam stared ahead of him, red with rage and embarrassment and fear. When a Benedictine said somebody had jewed him, Adam adopted the same attitude of stiff unhearing. But now that same ugly usage had been endorsed from the pulpit. After Chapel, he sat down and wrote to the Provost of Ipswich. And a week after that, he received a message to go and see the Headmaster.

'Did you write this letter, Morris?'

'Yes, sir.'

'To a guest of the school. Someone whom I personally invited to come and preach. You call him, among other choice things, a – bigot and a – a – I can't read it.'

'Simpleton, sir.'

'Yes, and a – a – a psychotic, which also happens to be misspelt.'

'Misspelt? Is it really? I'm terribly sorry about that.'

'The word, if you must use it, comes from psyche, the soul, and it's spelt with an aitch. You actually go on to call Basil Staunton a fascist.'

'Correctly spelt, I hope, sir, from fasces, meaning a bundle of rods.'

'Your housemaster once had cause to beat you, I seem to remember, Morris, because of insolence.'

'Oh? I wasn't entirely sure of his motives, sir.'

'Do you honestly imagine that this kind of abusive trash is going to advance your cause in the world?'

'My cause, sir?'

'This is hardly likely to recruit Basil Staunton to your point of view.'

'No, sir. I wonder if you would care to give me some advice about what might.'

'Basil Staunton, you may care to know, spent three years in the trenches in the First War. He was also decorated for gallantry.'

Adam stood there, fighting back his rage, and his tears.

'You're your own worst enemy, you know, Morris.'

'History doesn't suggest that, sir, but – May I ask you, sir, quite honestly, did you personally approve of the Provost's sermon?'

'You've elected to live in a Christian society, Morris.'

'Yes, sir, of course. Stupid of me.'

'I want you to write and apologize to Mr Staunton.'

'Apologize to Mr Staunton?'

'Yes. I can tell you one thing, however, and that is that Mr Staunton does assure me that he would never have said what in fact he did say, had he known that there were any Jews in the chapel.'

iii

They were on the cut velvet sofa. They had often been on it before, the girl lying back, with her stockinged feet over the far arm rest and Adam balanced urgently on what was left of the cushions. Sheila sat up suddenly, almost tipping him onto the floor.

'Adam,' she said, 'you're bleeding on me. You're bleeding on me.' There were drops of blood on her sweater. She dabbed at it with a hankie, while he tilted his head back to staunch the blood from his nose.

'It's oddly satisfying, isn't it?' Sheila said, dreamily. 'French kissing.'

'I can think of something that'd be a lot more satisfying still.'

'You're the one who wants to go to Cambridge,' she said. 'I'm never going to get this out. Never. Oh do stop.'

'What's Cambridge got to do with it?'

'I shall be twenty-two. By the time you've finished. Twenty-two. Look at it.'

'Take it off. I wish you would. Take it off, why don't you?'

'It's different for men.'

'I read a story the other day,' Adam said. 'About two people. He was about to go away, join the army actually, in the American Civil War it was supposed to be, and he was engaged to a girl and the night before he was due to go into the army, they rowed out to an island and you know what they did?'

'I can guess.'

'On the contrary. They took their clothes off and all they did was, they looked at each other. And that was it. It was a sort of marriage, and after that he went off to the war.'

She sat there for a moment, looking at the blotted blood on her lovely angora breasts. 'You won't want me when you come back,' she said. 'I'm going to go and change my sweater.'

'I love you,' he shouted at her.

II

Cambridge was wet and cold that October. But to Adam the weather was irrelevant; he had come to the greatest university in the world (that he had once dreamed of going to Oxford was soon forgotten) and he was about to join a community of intellectual equals, an élite – as he did not hesitate to think of it – amongst which, as a scholar, he would have an unquestioned place. Pride and humility jostled among his feelings. Who could not be proud to be armed with such eminence, or humble when he passed for the first time through the fortress gates of a College badged with a famous history? He belonged now among the happy few. Gone forever were the days when Benedict's beefy traditions governed his horizons. Here there was no headmaster to underwrite reactionary ideas, no 'school spirit' to institutionalize enthusiasm or cow the heart. Adam dumped his bags and ran across the street to buy himself a new undergraduate gown. Once he had that in a parcel under his arm, he felt himself truly recruited into the army of the elect.

A College porter, in dark coat and trousers, with a bowler hat on his head, directed him to his rooms in Third Court. He passed other members of the College, second and third year men, who with blasé accents bemoaned their return to 'this bloody hole'. He smiled at their irony. So might angels grumble at the lineaments of paradise.

He found his name bracketed with another, 'DAVIDSON, D. ST J.', clumped up the uncarpeted wooden stairs and heard confident voices inside the rooms. He pushed the door open with a sort of apprehensive arrogance and went in. A middle-aged lady was pouring tea by the gas fire.

'Oh,' Adam said. He knew how to make even the shortest expression very telling when he wanted to, and he often wanted to.

'Do come in,' said the middle-aged lady. She was wearing a hat with a blue veil, and a navy-blue suit. 'You must be Morris A. B.'

'And you, I take it,' Adam said, 'are Davidson D. St J.'

'That's me,' said the tall, fair-haired young man standing by the fire. He was blue-eyed and his pink cheeks gave him the appearance of one who had shaved for the first time that morning.

'Ah,' said Adam, in his shortest and most telling way.

'We were just speculating,' went on the young man's mother, 'on how you and Donald came to be sharing.'

'Are you a scholar?' Adam asked.

The young man shook his head, with good humour.

'Then I can't think.'

The young man's father, who wore a tweed suit and an MCC tie, put down his tea cup and stood up. 'You know, my dear,' he said, 'I rather fancy we should consider moving along. These two young men have things they must do.'

His wife followed his lead with unexpected docility. 'If there's anything you need,' she said to her son, as she gathered her handbag and her gloves, 'you've only to let me know and I'll get Nanny Hedges to pack it up for you.'

Her husband shook hands with Adam. 'Glad to have met you, Mr Morris.'

'And you, sir.'

'Are you walking us to the gate, Donald?' his mother asked. She looked sharply at Adam as she went to the door. 'You weren't by any chance at the Jesuit School in Sussex, were you, Mr Morris?'

Adam looked back at her. 'Hardly,' he said, with one of his special razor-edged smiles.

'Well, goodbye, Mr Morris.'

'Goodbye, Mrs Davidson.'

The navy-blue suit disappeared. Adam went to the door and shut it with abrupt violence. He took the brown paper parcel from under his arm, threw his beastly school mackintosh onto the sofa and, like an emperor coming into the purple, slid his arms into the sleeves of his brand new gown.

ii

'You mustn't mind my mother,' Donald said, as they divided the shelf and cupboard space and began to unpack. 'It's three hundred years of being deferred to.'

'Oh,' said Adam, 'she's three hundred years old, is she?'

'Three hundred and fifty actually. But the first fifty were lived in relative obscurity. Incidentally, she's Lady Frances, not Mrs – hence . . . '

'Oh I'm sorry. I don't know how I was expected to know.'

'You were expected not to know.'

'Your father's Lord Davidson then, is he?'

'No, he's just plain mister. My mama is the daughter of an earl. Not a very special earl, actually, but an earl. One of her ancestors rendered some particularly personal services to James the First. Do you have vices at all?'

'Vices?'

'Smoke. Drink. Things like that.'

'Women?'

'If you like. Only I suppose it's only polite to warn you – '

'What?'

'I tend to pray.'

'Seriously?'

'Flippant prayers aren't particularly encouraged. You're not a Christian?'

'No. But you go ahead.'

'I shall. I shall. Do you row?'

'No. Benedict's was strictly non-aquatic.'

'I was thinking of rowing. You liked it there, I gather?'

'Liked it? I loathed it. What was your place like?'

'Reasonable. You don't mind if I stick this up?' Donald held up a crucifix which he had taken from where it had been carefully packed among his pyjamas.

'Stick it up by all means,' Adam said. 'You really believe in all that, do you?'

'There are quite a few of us, actually.'

'Not as few as there are of us,' Adam said.

Donald showed no sign of understanding what Adam's savage tone might be intended to convey. He hung the crucifix on a nail above his chest of drawers and then went to hang up his dinner jacket. Adam did not have a dinner jacket. Why would one need a dinner jacket?

iii

How quickly paradise became a commonplace! How like Benedict's, in many ways, it turned out to be, after all! Adam was reading Classics and soon he was once again turning out obedient imitations of Ciceronian prose, Euripidean iambics and Ovidian elegiacs. Intellectual adventure was harder to find than he had expected. So was stimulating company. Though he had no real community of interests with Donald, Adam spent much of his time with his room-mate. They went together to the Union, where the pomposities of the speakers were punctuated by the elaborate self-importance of the President, who rang a little bell before rising to deliver himself of apparently hilarious interjections. The motion before the under-graduate parliament was that 'This House views with admiration the achievements of the last government'. Mr Churchill had recently returned to power and one of his Ministers lounged on the front bench, where the guest speakers sat alongside the Officers of the Society, who aped with agile sycophancy the sprawling attitudes of real parliamentarians. How grown-up they all looked to Adam's contemptuously admiring eyes! How easily they spoke and how grandly they dealt with the ritual hecklers! When Gavin Pope rose to speak, a murmur of expectation thrilled the crowded chamber.

'Mr President,' he began, 'we are asked to admire the achievements of five years of Socialist government – '

'Six,' someone shouted.

'Six was it? I must say it seemed like six hundred. Achievements. What achievements? Indeed what government? Was it, after all, for *fricassée* of snoek that we hazarded our courage and our treasure? Was it for whale-meat *schitzel* – '

'*Schnitzel*,' called the usual witless wit.

'That may be what the honourable gentleman had. I know what I had.'

Even Adam, crouched in the visitors' gallery, agreed to smirk at that one.

'Was it for *suprème de merde à la Strachey* that we have weathered a thousand years of battle and adventure – ?'

'On a point of personal information, Mr President, when did Mr Pope last hazard his courage, or indeed his treasure?'

'Mr President, sir,' said Gavin, in a drawl of Churchillian consonants, 'I had the honour of spending two years defending the heights of Caterham whence all but we had fled, and who could blame them? Mr President, sir, the last so-called government was – to conjure up what generosity it deserves – one of the dullest, dreariest, meanest, weakest and most boring – oh Mr President, was it not tedium beyond the dreams of Marxism? – in the whole history of these islands, their dominions and colonies. If that is your idea of an achievement, then vote for the motion by all means. And God save us all!'

The President, Ronald Braithwaite, already large and somewhat bald, rose to his feet, with a ting of the bell concealed in the arm of his throne. 'I am grateful,' he said, 'for the honourable gentleman's permission, but the rules of this Society forbid the Chair to vote except in extreme cases.

And I trust we shall not be driven to extremes tonight.' This standard joke received the standard laughter and applause.

'I'm off,' Adam said.

'Where?'

'First to have a beer and then to join the Communist Party. Coming?'

Donald scrambled after him. 'You ought to join,' he said, 'and have a go. You must admit you know how to talk, if you can't do anything else.'

'Thanks a lot.'

'I meant – '

'I know what you meant, and thanks a lot. Waste my time joining that sort of thing?'

'I suppose it's some sort of preparation,' Donald said.

'Oh of course. That's the whole thing about England, isn't it? Everything's a preparation. A preparation for *nothing*. It's not a preparation, it's a postponement. It's a charade.'

'I rather like charades,' Donald said, as they went into the Baron of Beef. 'And England.'

'I'm sure you do. Bitter?'

'Bass, if you don't mind.'

'I've got better things to do,' Adam said, 'than play at politicians. That man Pope, is he really a Conservative?'

'So is my Pa,' Donald said. 'And my Ma.'

'I never knew anyone of our age could be a Conservative.'

'And I suppose I am, though I never really thought about it.'

'There's no evidence you ever really thought about anything, is there?' Adam said, with a smile. He expected to be liked for saying that sort of thing.

'I'll tell you a club I'm thinking of joining,' Donald said, 'and that's the Judo club.'

Adam found more intellectual company in Bill Bourne, also a Major Scholar, whom he met at a lecture on textual criticism. Bill came from Birmingham, a dark, intense young man with a heavy accent. Adam had never before met anyone who talked in such a voice. Although Bill was evidently very clever, it was all Adam could do not to patronize him. They went together to the University library, where Bill would file notes in an alphabetical index while Adam, head in hands over Jebb's Sophocles, fought not to fall asleep. The library's chairs were narcotically comfortable.

One day, as he left the library alone, on the way to a supervision with Austin Denny, for whom he had been hurriedly writing an essay on Anaxagoras and Anaximander, he heard a shout behind him: 'Ho-hoy, Adam Morris, I say!'

'The voice of the bluebottle was heard in the land,' Adam said. 'Hullo, Ken, how are you?'

'What are you doing here, ex-schoolfellow of mine?' Ken Hobbs' voice had become that of Grytpype-Thynne, another Goon Show character.

'Avoiding ex-schoolfellows of mine mostly,' Adam said. 'What are you?'

'Avoiding them?' Ken was Bluebottle again. 'Why are you avoiding them?'

'Because they all imitate Bluebottle all the time,' Adam said, imitating Bluebottle. 'What're you reading actually?'

'I am reading Geology, Neddy. And I'll tell you something for nothing, it's never going to replace sex.'

'You don't still happen to play poker, do you?' Adam said.

'Poker! You have touched me on a soft spot, you filthy swine. I am potty for it.'

'Only there's a game tonight in my rooms, if you're interested.'

'I feel like it, I feel like it! Only I trust the stakes aren't too high. I hate a high stake.'

'Sixpenny raises,' Adam said. 'It shouldn't break you.'

'And if it does, I can always touch you for a loan, can't I?' Ken said.

'Can you?' Adam said.

A girl on a bright red bicycle was riding towards them. She wore polka-dot slacks and her hair was in a pony tail secured with a rubber band. Ken pointed at her with sudden derision and let out a huge shriek. 'Get you!' he cried.

The girl pedalled past them with a painful smile on her face, wobbling slightly.

'So anyway,' Adam said, 'it's C7, Third Court, St John's. Only I've got to rush.'

'I shall be there, my Captain. I shall not fail thy feast.'

'Don't bother to wear the Old School tie,' Adam said.

'But how will we recognize each other?' Ken called after him.

v

'My first woman was my regimental sergeant-major's wife,' Bill Bourne said. 'I had her in the back of a six-hundred-weight truck on the way home from a mess hop. I'm in.' He threw three matchsticks into the kitty.

'Christ,' Ken said, 'the RSM's wife. The definitive instance of duty beyond the call of courage. Me too.'

'It was a deeply significant and highly spiritual experience. I wouldn't have missed it for the world.'

'If I know anything about sergeant majors' wives, you *couldn't* have missed it for the world.'

Adam said: 'Don, are you in?'

Donald nodded sourly as he threw in his matches. Things were not running his way.

'The lucky winner would like two cards, please,' Bill said. 'And what about you and the two-backed beast, Lieutenant Hobbs, sir? Strictly in the interests of comparative studies, he added quickly.'

'Three cards, please,' Ken said. 'Nice ones. The first woman I ever had was a black lady as a matter of fact. In a place called Entebbe. East Africa.'

'Five for me,' Donald said.

'And the quim *Africaine*, do you recommend it, he inquired delicately?'

'Best thing I ever had that left change out of half a crown,' Ken replied.

'The winner bets two,' Bill said. 'And you, oh scholar of the ancient world, tell us, was your iota ever subscript?'

'I'm in,' Adam said. 'Well, Bill, I haven't had your advantages. Her Majesty has yet to put one of her six-hundredweight trucks at my disposal. Or one of her sergeant-majors' wives.'

'Up six,' Donald said.

'You want to get a bit of service in, son, he asserted sanctimoniously. Up six, did you say? And up another six, brave Donald, he taunted.'

'I don't know what to do,' Donald said, getting up and walking to the window. He opened it and climbed up onto the sill.

'Don't go and commit suicide for the sake of one and fourpence,' Bill called.

The sound of Donald pissing into the Cam, three storeys below, came unmistakably to their ears. The nearest bog was at ground level.

'And up another six,' Donald said, as he returned to the game.

'I'll see it,' Bill said.

'Three kings.'

'From Orient are. Beats two pair,' Bill said, but as Donald reached to gather in the matchsticks, he stayed his hand. 'But not a straight, my dear old Carian friend. Which is what I happen to have. Five, six, seven, nine, eight, he demonstrated gloatingly.'

'What luck!' Donald said. 'What filthy luck! The whole damned evening. *And* it's the third time running. What've I lost this time?'

'Two and fourpence so far.'

'Announced Ken Hobbs, the impassive mathematician.'

'God, I was unlucky!'

'You'd be unlucky at chess.'

'I *am* unlucky at chess,' Donald said, so sincerely that Adam and Bill burst out laughing. 'I'm *serious*.'

'Of course you're serious,' Adam said. 'It wouldn't be so funny, if you weren't. Tell me, are people allowed to play poker in heaven? Or do they just sit around counting their lucky stars?'

'I only know about hell. Do you know the trouble with hell? The noise, my dear, and the *people*.'

'I like that,' Adam said. 'Tell me something else. I've always wondered, is there a separate part of hell for the heathen of various persuasions, or am I likely to find myself sharing rooms with Goering as well as Jean-Paul Sartre, who turns out, of course, to be a Lesbian?'

'My uncle once went shooting with Goering,' Donald said. 'He liked him rather.'

'And afterwards, no doubt, they washed their hands in soap made from their victims and went in for tea,' Adam said. 'I'd sooner commit the sin against the Holy Ghost – whatever kind of spook that may be – than boast of having an uncle who liked Goering.'

Donald walked into the bedroom and slammed the door.

'You go it a bit, don't you?' Bill Bourne said.

'Yes, I go it a bit,' Adam said. 'What do you do?'

'You've got a rough tongue, mate. You want to watch it. Someone might say something to you.'

'He warned self-importantly. Not in my rooms, they won't.'

The game broke up. Adam could never resist showing those on whose company he relied that he did not rely on their company. Donald was in bed when Adam finally went in to undress.

'Did I upset you?' he asked.

'No.'

'Did they? Talking about sex, I mean.'

'I'm a Catholic, not a Puritan.'

'You'll wait, I suppose, till you're married? Before you –'

'It's possible.'

'Who was this uncle of yours actually? The one who –'

'Knew the Reichsmarschall? An ambassador of some sort.'

'Don't misunderstand me,' Adam said. 'In many ways, you know, I really rather wish I was like you.'

'I'm sure you do,' Donald said.

III

Adam went to the station to meet Sheila when she came up to visit him later in the term. He wore his new green corduroys and a school jacket with patched elbows and a College scarf round and round his neck. Sheila looked very pretty as she stepped off the train, but why had she decided to wear a hat? Her pink dress and her gloves and her frilly umbrella made her look as though she had come to a garden party. 'Here I am!' she said.

'In the pink, I see.'

'Don't you like it?'

'I like it, and I like what's in it,' Adam said.

'I hope I haven't come too early or anything. You're

not supposed to be working, are you? Because I wouldn't like to be luring you from the straight and narrow.'

'I can't think of anything I'd sooner be lured from,' he said, taking her arm. 'Are you hungry?'

She looked at him with her usual pretty suspicion. 'Why?'

'Why? Because I am and I hope you are. Do you like curry at all? Because the Cambridge diet is basically curry or curry. Unless you like curry. Or, we could have curry.'

'I'd quite like some curry,' she said.

He squeezed her arm and smiled. Maybe things were going to be all right after all. He took her to the Taj Mahal, which was said to be the smart curry house. The cream of the acting crowd went there between rehearsals. Adam had not dared to go even to an audition for the ADC, though he had done some acting at school. He glanced with disdain at the big centre table where the famous faces of the Cambridge theatre were eating a loud meal.

'So this is the city of dreaming spires,' Sheila said.

'Theoretically that's Oxford,' Adam said. 'This is the city of perspiring dreams.'

Adam looked anxiously to see whether Sheila's naïvety had been noticed, but no one had paid it, or his witty rejoinder, the smallest attention. John Cadman, a rather elegant young man, with curly fair hair and a yellow waist-coat, was holding forth. Since he was the producer of the current *Romeo and Juliet*, he expected to be listened to. 'The theatre, to my mind, should be a place where brilliant things are said and brilliant things are done. I refuse to abandon myself to commiserating with the misfortunes of peasants and spud bashers. The common man has, I am perfectly sure, a great deal to be said for him. And as far as I am concerned, every single word of it has now been said.'

'How thoughtful of him to say it all at dictation speed!' Adam said. 'Did you get my letters? You didn't write much.'

'I did write.'

'Yes. I've missed you. I bet you haven't missed me.'

She looked at him. 'Not a bit,' she said.

The door of the restaurant burst open and a flamboyant young man, in a black cloak and carrying a silver-knobbed cane, flung into the room. 'I thought as much!' he cried. 'The gaiety's all here and shriekin' its livin' 'ead orf as usual to the embarrassment of ordinary decent folk. I do apologize for my friends.'

'Friends?' said Cadman. 'I've never seen this fellow before in my life.'

'It's all right,' Sheila said.

'The lady,' said the newcomer as he hung his cloak near Sheila's head, 'the lady, who is as witty as she is beautiful, says it's all right. Never seen me before, he says. The jewels I lavished on that boy! The last of the archduchess's emeralds; satin slippers crammed with caviare, not to mention the emperor's Fabergé capote and now . . . Rejection! Canst wonder that I weep? Master Clode, move up this instant and make room for your betters.'

'There's no room, Denis. Sit over there.'

'*Toujours la polizei!*' said Denis. 'What would your dear mother say? She never turned anyone away! A wonderful woman and the cynosure of her ancient profession. I should do something about those spots, dear, if I were you. Of course clean living's the only real safeguard. Unfortunately. I've tried everything else.'

'Who are they? Sheila whispered to Adam.

'Actors.'

'She fancies me,' Denis said, nodding in the direction of Adam and Sheila.

'Which one?' Mike Clode said.

'Outrageous!' Denis pouted at him. 'The shepherdess,

of course, bless her pretty little Dresden tail, and her alabaster breast.'

'Have you done any acting?' Sheila asked.

'I can't stand those sort of people,' Adam said.

'You *should*,' she told him. 'You'd be good. You used to do a marvellous Bluebottle.'

'*Everyone* does a marvellous Bluebottle. Anyway they wouldn't want me.'

'You always think people don't want you. I bet they'd have you like a shot.'

'Would you?' Adam said.

'You know you'd enjoy it,' she said.

'Enjoy what?'

'Acting. Once you got in.'

'The problem is getting in, isn't it?'

'You always can if you really want to, can't you?'

'Promise?'

'Of course you can. You ought to act. You ought to meet people.'

'Don't worry,' Adam said. 'I'm very happy as I am.'

He was listening with half an ear to the conversation at the main table, where the girl in polka-dot trousers at whom Ken had shrieked was giving her opinion of the characters of Romeo and of Juliet, whom she was playing. She was small and dark and had a low, confident voice. 'They've both chosen an impossible love, haven't they?' she was saying. 'The whole play's anti-romantic basically, that's how it seems to me.'

'There's certainly an element of doom,' Cadman said. 'Almost wilful self-destruction. I agree with you there, Anna.'

'Mike, don't you think I'm right?' Anna turned to the tall, watchful actor on her left, who was playing Mercutio. 'Romeo has to die because otherwise all that can happen is that things go off the boil. You've got this funny thing with Romeo, the name I mean, that we talk of people being

Romeos, that is going from one woman to another, when Romeo himself dies rather than live without Juliet. I mean, that's rather fascinating and suggestive, isn't it?'

Mike smiled. 'I'm sure it'll get you your First, Anna, if that's what you mean, when the time comes.'

'Oh I'm not worried about *that*,' she said.

'And,' Mike went on, 'if it alters the angle at which you lean over the railing in the balcony scene, I'll be very surprised.'

As the others laughed, Cadman said: 'I suggest that we return to the *champ de bataille*. I told them forty-five minutes. Shall we – ?'

'You can't see them happily married exactly, can you?' Anna said as they all added their contributions to the bill.

'Romeo and Juliet?' Denis said. 'Highly unsuitable! Unless he gets a steady job, of course.'

'Denis, you are maddening sometimes.'

'So my uncle, the general, always used to say when I put grapenuts in his caviare.'

Mike Clode loitered with Anna as the others went out. 'You can't expect them to take in an idea like that,' he told her. 'All John Cadman cares about is "letting the verse do the work". Actually, I think you're bang right about the psychological context.'

'I'm sure I am,' the girl said.

'I'm sure you are! But for the moment, I should just – '

'I talk too much, right?'

'Not too much, too well. You want to watch that. Because people are going to be jealous enough of you as it is.'

'And how is it?' she wanted to know.

'You know damned well. You really have exceptional technical skill for someone who's never acted professionally – '

'I think it's mainly a question of brains, acting, don't you? Most things are if it comes to that.'

'So do I, Anna, so do I. But don't ever tell anyone, because – ' He smiled into her eyes and she glanced away to see Adam looking at her.

'Goodbye,' she said.

'Goodbye.'

'She knows you,' Sheila said.

'Well, I did have a short story in *Varsity* last week,' Adam said.

'Did you really? Jolly good for you.'

'Who the hell was that?' Mike Clode asked Anna as they left the restaurant.

'Haven't the faintest,' she replied.

ii

After lunch, Sheila wanted to see the sights. 'After all, that's what I've come for,' she said.

'Oh, is that what you've come for?'

She gave him her sideways look. 'I jolly well want to see everything there is to see.'

He considered her with a cocked eyebrow. 'You're sure you're not cold? We can always go up to my rooms.'

'I want to see the colleges,' she said. 'I want to see King's.'

'There it is. King's.'

'I want to see inside. Come on. Oh, it's all so lovely. No wonder you're happy. I wish I'd worked harder. You could have helped me.'

'I did help you. I translated half Livy for you, in case you've forgotten.'

'I never got a question on the bit you did.'

'Next time I'll set the papers as well.'

'Don't start being sarcastic again.'

'Again? What do you mean again?'

'Everyone knows how sarcastic you are.' She leaned on

the parapet of King's bridge and looked round. 'Golly, you're lucky.'

'Now you're here,' he said. 'Tell you what, why don't you stay the weekend? Go back on Monday. Do.'

'I hate hotels,' she said.

'Who said anything about hotels?' Adam said. 'You can stay in College, you can stay in my rooms. No one will ever know.'

'What would your room-mate say?'

'A few Hail Marys, I expect. He won't mind disappearing. He's a Catholic, not a Puritan.'

She smiled. He hardly dared to breathe.

'I promised I'd go home,' she said at last.

'Did you know,' Adam said, as they started walking again, 'that the Spanish anarchists once passed a resolution saying that any woman who excited a man's desire had a moral obligation to satisfy it?'

'Oh, that'd just suit you, wouldn't it?' the girl said. 'A law making it illegal to deny Adam Morris what he wanted. And what about women?'

'Women can have anyone they want now,' he replied.

'Oh can they?' she said. 'Can they just?'

They visited six more colleges, the Union (which Adam had joined in order to use the library and play billiards) and the Senate House. Only when Adam had convinced her that the Sheldonian was in Oxford would Sheila finally agree to come up to his rooms for tea.

'Have you seen Gerald Lewis at all?' she asked him as he went to answer the whistle of the kettle. 'Because he's at Cambridge.'

'So are a lot of people I don't see.'

'Only don't you go to the Jewish Society? Because he's hon. sec.'

'No, I don't. I don't want anything to do with religion. Kosher or otherwise.' He came back with the tea and offered her a plate of Fitzbillies' cakes. 'These are probably the best in the world. It's all lies, She. All of it. Religion.'

'That's your opinion.'

'It's not a question of opinion. It's a question of fact.' On Bill Bourne's suggestion, Adam had been going to lectures on philosophy. His tone imitated the hesitant fervour of the professor who had succeeded to the Chair once occupied by Ludwig Wittgenstein and whose manner-isms of speech and hand movement Adam's generation was eagerly acquiring. 'None of the propositions of religion can be proved,' Adam went on. 'Not like the propositions of natural science can be proved – or indeed disproved. Surely you can see that?'

Sheila munched a chocolate-coated madeleine. 'Not really,' she said.

'There's a gas fire in this room, true or false?'

Sheila considered the obvious cautiously. 'True?' she asked.

'Of course it's true,' Adam said. 'And how do you tell it's true? By empirical observation.'

'I just looked.'

'Now: "God is in this room." True or false? Have a good look round. You can't be too careful. Any signs?'

'You don't look for God like that.'

'Precisely. And why don't you? Because he's non-sensical, literally non-sense.'

'I don't agree,' Sheila said.

'You *have* to agree. I'm telling you something. It's fact. All these ideas we live by and die by and kill by, they're all based on nothing. They have absolutely no foundation in anything we can touch or see or observe in any way at all.'

'A lot of people don't think the same way you do.'

'Take something else. Take – take not making love until you're married. Where does that come from, an idea like that? It's all nonsense. When two people love each other, that ought to be it.'

'*If* two people do.'

'I love you.'

'You're too clever for me,' she said.

'Nothing has to happen,' Adam said.

'Happen?'

'No. You know,' he moved next to her on the narrow sofa. 'Stay here tonight. She, do. Nothing will happen. I promise.'

'You don't really want me,' she said.

'Oh Christ Almighty,' Adam said. 'I want you more than anything in the world. I want you even more than the elimination of metaphysics. There!'

'You'd never forgive me,' she said. 'I know you.'

'Forgive you if what?'

'If we got married now.'

'Who's talking about getting married? You talk as if marriage was the only alternative. Don't you ever *listen*?'

She picked up her gloves. 'I have to go home,' she said, 'honestly.'

'According to what logic do you have to?'

'Because I have to.'

'That's a mere tautology.'

'And because I want to.'

'That's not logic, that's autobiography.'

'All you care about is words,' she said.

'Words are loaded pistols,' he quoted. 'We use them at our peril.'

She straightened her hat. 'Are you walking me to the station?'

'Well I can't ride you, can I?' Adam said.

'Clever!'

'Two and a half years of telling her I love her,' Adam said, as he lay in bed the next morning, watching Donald getting dressed to go to Mass, 'and I've never even seen her breasts. I have felt them a few times, I mean I know she's definitely got them, but I've never ever seen them. Christ. Or Jesus as he was then. What're you doing after your devotions?'

'I thought I'd read the pictures in the *Sunday Graphic*.'

'You might bring the heavies when you come back. I wouldn't mind seeing what Messrs Powell and Lejeune don't like this week. *Sunday Graphic!* You can look as long as you don't touch, can you?'

'I like the emphasis they put on the spiritual side,' Donald said.

'Have you got money?' Adam said. 'Because you'll find some . . .'

'I'll short-change the collection,' Donald said.

'Don't do that,' Adam said. 'I wouldn't like you to endanger your chances of eternal bliss.'

'I shan't, don't worry. I'm not missing a thing like that.'

'What will it actually be like?'

'I'm promised an eternity of sexual ecstasy. At least according to some authorities.'

'Sounds interesting. Maybe I ought to come along.'

'Too late! I'm off.'

'Confess nicely.'

'They don't like it when you're nice.'

'Give him a touch of the Sunday graphics then.'

'I'll see you later,' Donald said, on his way. Church and chapel bells were ringing all over Cambridge. Adam winced.

'Sunday,' he said. '*Christ.*'

Adam was eating cornflakes and reading *Brideshead Revisited* when Donald returned from Mass. Donald dropped the *Observer* and the *Sunday Times* onto the table beside him. 'Sunday lunch,' he said.

'How was your Father Whichart?' Adam inquired.

'Paternoster you mean?'

'That's the Johnny. Good form?'

'Yes, thank you.'

'You're now pure in thought and word and deed, are you?'

'That's the general idea.'

'Until the next time.'

'Presumably.'

'I must say it's a very comfortable doctrine you people have,' Adam said.

'That's probably why it's caught on, don't you think?'

'I honestly envy you sometimes.'

'There's no subscription, you know.'

'Your credulity.'

'I suppose it is somewhat enviable,' Donald said.

'I don't really envy you in the slightest,' Adam said. 'I pity you, if you really want to know.'

'Ah,' Donald said.

'Oh, by the way,' Adam said, flipping a shilling across the room, 'with the compliments of the heathen. Mustn't short-change the Trinity, must we? They have an excellent accountant, I'm told. The recording angel never misses a trick, does he?'

'There's no record of it,' Donald said.

'Very good. Very good.' Adam read the paper. 'How I hate the Sunday papers! All right, so the Russians may have got the bloody A-bomb, why no Arsenal report? No sense of proportion. Do you feel like a game?'

'When I've finished,' Donald said, adding more corn-flakes to his bowl.

Adam started moving the furniture. They had evolved a version of Fives, played with a pingpong ball against the wall of the sitting room between the bedroom door and the fireplace.

'Best of five, OK?'

'Right,' said Donald, removing his coat to reveal red braces.

'For service. Ready?' Adam threw the ball up and they started to play. 'Have you never had any doubts? About your religion, I mean?'

'Why should I have?'

'You could be anything you wanted and you choose to be a slave. My serve, OK?'

'My religion suits me very well,' Donald said. 'And it doesn't interfere with anyone else.'

'Have you ever heard of the Holy Inquisition by any chance? That was out.'

'No, it wasn't. Have it again. The Spaniards always were a bit extreme. It's probably the climate.'

'Well, that certainly was. One-nothing. Ready?'

Donald nodded. Adam served. 'Sorry,' Donald said. 'I wasn't ready after all.'

'You nodded.'

'I thought I was, but I obviously wasn't.'

'Two-nothing. Ready?'

'That's not fair.'

'It may not be fair, but it's the game. Look, either play or don't. OK? What never ceases to amaze me is that you can go on believing in something that quite simply isn't true.'

'Good heavens!' Donald exclaimed in mock amazement. 'When did you hear this?'

'It's common knowledge,' Adam said.

'I hate common knowledge,' Donald said.

'Blast,' Adam said. 'Your point. One-two. Your service.'

'I wasn't ready,' Donald said when Adam won the next point.

'What do you mean not ready?' Adam said. 'You're bloody serving.'

'That's what I mean.'

'Rubbish. Four-one. If this was Graham Greene, you could pray for a miracle and then when it was granted you could give up the game. You'd probably be well advised.'

'My mother thinks Graham Greene's a heretic.'

'You've seen one Jansenist you've seen 'em all.'

'She prefers Georgette Heyer.'

'Five-one. You do at least meet a higher class of sinner.'

'Exactly her point.'

'Look, are you trying? Six-one.'

'I'm trying, I'm just not succeeding.'

'Perhaps Holy Communion disagreed with you. I hope you didn't eat something indigestible. In future I should insist on white meat or nothing . . .'

Donald had finally been goaded enough. He jumped on Adam and wrestled him to the floor. Adam was strong, but Donald was angry and determined. It was all Adam could do to get Donald onto his back long enough to offer a rather guilty truce. 'Shall we stop this? Because I'd hate to hurt you.'

Donald took a deep breath and suddenly arched his back and twisted out from under Adam and reversed the situation.

'Time you learned to control your tongue,' Donald said.

Adam said: 'I'm sorry if I offended you – '

But Donald was not appeased. He sat on Adam's chest. Adam thrust his hand in Donald's face and pushed, hard, against his nose. Donald gasped and toppled sideways.

'What the hell's going on in here?' The door had opened and Bill Bourne was standing there.

Adam and Donald got to their feet, panting and sheepish.

'We were just having a slight philosophical discussion,' Adam said.

'Only I was going for a beer,' Bill said, 'and I wondered – '

'A better plan than going for each other, eh, Mr Davidson?' Adam said, playing the Vicar.

'You bloody made my nose bleed,' Donald said, 'you – '

'Say nothing irrevocable,' Adam advised. 'The friends you make at university will last you all your life. If you're very unlucky.' He bent and picked up the buckled pingpong ball. 'Christ! Look what you bloody did!'

'It was mine in the first place.'

'I know. But look what you bloody did.'

'Look what you bloody did, if it comes to that.' Donald showed him the blood on his handkerchief.

'I have a strong objection to people tearing my arms out at the roots,' Adam said. 'Sorry about that.'

'A plaque on both your houses, say I.'

'And not for the first time,' said Adam.

'Why did I ever come up here in the first place?'

'Because you didn't want to have to buy the second round yourself, I presume.'

'Adam's in a filthy mood today,' Donald said.

'I didn't notice anything different,' Bill Bourne said. 'Look, they're going to shut in a minute.'

Adam held out his hand to Donald. 'Sorry, Don.'

Donald bowed and shook Adam's hand. 'OK,' he said, 'for the moment. When I have black belt, I kill. Until then, apology accepted.'

'He's funny, Adam,' Bill said. 'He always hurts people and then he apologizes.'

'I've never hurt you, Bill, have I?'

'No,' Bill said.

'Then shut up,' Adam said, 'and mind your own business, will you? Oh sorry! Sorry, Bill! Look, perhaps you and Donald had better go to the Mill; I'll stay and wrestle with the *Theaetetus*.'

'Don't you feel like coming?' Donald asked.

'No,' Adam said, 'I'll – I'll stop here. You two go.'

He heard them laughing as they went down the stairs and went gloomily to where he had left the Sunday papers. He was sure they were laughing at him. The *Theaetetus* could wait. If only Sheila hadn't been such a frigid cow. He sat down and wrote her a letter saying how much he loved her.

She never answered the letter. A week before the end of term he received an invitation to come to her engagement party. She was going to marry somebody called Michael Sachs.

v

Every Sunday morning Donald's alarm went off in time for him to go to early Mass. The same thing happened on the last Sunday of term. Adam surfaced reluctantly from under his bedclothes and called across the bedroom. 'Oy, Don, for God's sake, wake up and turn that bloody thing off – '

'I am awake,' Donald said. 'The thing sticks.'

'Then chuck it out of the window or something.'

'It's OK now,' Donald said. 'I say, did you know that over thirty per cent of American men have their first sexual experience with another man?'

'Where the hell did you get that from?'

Donald held up a large volume. 'The Kinsey Report.'

'You'd better go and see what Father Carson has to say about it. You're going to be late.'

'And almost one in two has a homosexual experience of a genital order at some time in their lives.'

'In his life,' Adam said. 'Even in the face of the un-believable we can still try and be grammatical.'

'And only a fraction of one per cent of men below the age of twenty-five fail to have an outlet at least once a week.'

'An *outlet*?'

'That's the term he uses.'

'How the hell did you get hold of that? You might leave it behind when you go to Mass. Or are you going to read it on the way? In which case I'll walk along with you and take over as you hit consecrated ground. You'd better hurry up, incidentally.'

'I'm tired.'

'Been reading all night, have you?'

'I think I'll give it a miss for once,' Donald said.

'Give Mass a miss!' Adam said. 'Whatever next?'

'You realize this includes priests, don't you? It must.'

'I realize, of course. But do *you* realize? Statistics are, I understand, no respecters of the Cloth.'

'I mean, *priests*,' Donald said. 'It really makes you think.'

'Oh you don't want to do *that*,' Adam said. 'You end up being burnt at the stake that way. Entirely for the good of your immortal soul, of course. Of which more in our next.'

'It does make you think,' Donald said.

'Well, after you with it,' Adam said.

IV

Donald went home for Christmas; Adam went home for Chanukah. On the first Friday Adam was home, his father returned from the office before dusk, when the Sabbath officially began, and changed from being an amiable, old-fashioned English solicitor into a skull-capped Jew draped in a prayer shawl. He joined his wife, Estelle, in the dining room where the fresh *chola* lay under its white napkin, next to the unlit candles.

'Where's Adam?'

'Adam,' Estelle called. 'He's coming. Derek'll be home next week. And we'll all be together again.'

'Yes,' Lionel said. 'Is he coming?'

'Adam?' Estelle called again.

'I'm here,' Adam said, coming in.

'Didn't you hear your mother?'

'I'm here,' Adam said, putting the traditional skull-cap on top of his longish hair. 'OK?'

Lionel opened his prayer book and Adam watched his parents with tactful irony as they proceeded with the ancient ritual which ended with Estelle lighting the candles. They then sat down to dinner.

'Guess who's coming in after supper,' Estelle said.

'Certainly not,' Adam said. 'Who?'

'The Millers. Their daughter's just got into Oxford.'

'Really?' Adam said.

'I said she should come. It's not easy for a girl, is it? Getting in?'

'She's a Classic too,' Lionel said.

'Ah,' said Adam. 'Look, um, I may have to go out later.'

'Friday night,' Lionel said. 'Since when do we go out Friday night?'

'Look, Dad – we – '

'The first Friday of the holidays.'

'Vacation,' Adam said.

'Where are you thinking of going?' his mother asked.

'I said I might meet somebody, that's all.'

'Anybody we know?'

'No.'

'Who exactly?'

'Someone I met at Cambridge as a matter of fact.'

'Oh,' said Estelle. 'A fellow student?'

'Why not have him come here?' Lionel said. 'Your mother likes you at home Friday nights.'

'And here I am. I said I might go out a bit later, that's all. I didn't know the Millers were coming. It seems *they* go out on Friday nights.'

'They live two doors away.'

'Look, Dad, we've been through all this. I don't want to make a big thing out of it.'

'But it is a big thing.'

'I'm in to supper, aren't I?'

'There's a principle involved.'

'Your principle, not mine. Do we really have to pretend – ?'

'Pretend what?'

'That God's in his heaven and all's right with the world. He isn't; it isn't.'

'That's your opinion.'

'That's my opinion. And I am, as they say, entitled to it.'

'You're turning your back on five thousand years.'

'I sometimes think that's the only sensible thing to do with five thousand years. Five thousand years of superstition, humbug and mumbojumbo.'

'That's what you think of your people.'

'Oh let's not have a quarrel, his first weekend home.'

'That's what you think of your people,' Lionel said.

'Dad, I'm going out for just a couple of hours. *That's* what I think of my people.'

'And what am I going to tell the Millers?'

'That we had a philosophical disagreement.'

'I think you'll be surprised at Tessa,' Estelle said. 'She's become a very interesting young woman. I know she'd love to talk to you.'

'That's the kind of build-up that puts paid to most conversations,' Adam said, with a smile.

'Couldn't you go out tomorrow night?' Lionel said.

43

'No, she – no. It's – it's just that it's the last opportunity before Christmas, you know – '

'You'd better go then,' Estelle said.

'I'm going,' Adam said.

'I'd be glad if you'd arrange to be in next Friday,' Lionel said. 'Your brother'll be home from school and – '

'You don't want me leading him astray.'

'It would be civil if you didn't.'

'Look, I – I might see them when I get back. I shan't be late necessarily.'

'See whom?' Lionel said.

'The Millers, of course.'

'Oh,' Lionel said, 'I shouldn't worry about the Millers.' He threw down his napkin and went out of the room.

'Try not to quarrel this holidays,' Estelle said.

'Believe it or not,' Adam said, 'I *was* trying not to.'

'Is it serious?'

'Is what serious?'

'This – this girl.'

'Girl? Serious? No. Of course not. I'm not – she's not – '

'What?'

'There're going to be other people. It's a sort of party, that's all, and I said I might go along.'

'Is she – ?'

'It's not serious. Is she what?'

'Jewish.'

'I haven't asked her.'

'Can't you *tell*?'

'You mean has she got a big nose and a cavalry moustache? No, she hasn't.'

'Adam, your father – '

'Don't worry, Mother, if she turns out not to be Jewish, I'll make sure she goes and cuts her throat. I told you: don't worry. It isn't serious, as you put it. I'm going to a little party, that's all.'

44

He had met her with absurd ease. Her name was Barbara Hughes and she was a student teacher, spending a year in a school in Cambridge. She had been there all term and he did not meet her until the last week. They had been Christmas shopping in Joshua Taylor's and both reached at the same moment for the same thing, and found each other. They laughed, they had tea. They went to the cinema, they went to supper and two days later, as if it were the most natural thing in the world, they went to bed. She was, of course, not Jewish. Had she been, he might not, would not, have been so reckless in his seduction of her, a seduction in which, equally of course, she had made more of the running than she allowed him, at first, to believe. She had brown hair and she was beautiful beyond all reasonable expectation. He could not understand how she came to be free, and he did not press her to explain. There had been someone, no doubt, and he had gone away. She was twenty-two and she had no virginal anxieties. She gave herself to him, which was nice, but she loved him, which was better, and was not afraid to say so, which was best of all. He was prompt to love her, not merely because he could not believe that he could continue to go to bed with her unless he did (though that reason was not absent from his thinking), but also because her directness and her easy laugh released him from a thousand fears of rejection and suspicion. She was going up to her parents, in Leeds, for Christmas. She had one night in London, that Friday night, and she was staying in the flat of a friend. It was half past three before Adam went home. They had made love four times, five if you included a preliminary disaster. She had been naked under her silk robe when she opened the door and Adam was not used to that kind of a welcome. He loved her, he loved her, he loved her. And she loved him.

V

'Donald?' Adam looked round. Was Donald not there? They had agreed to meet and go to the Moral Sciences Club together. An Oxford theologian was due to be roasted on the slow spit of Cambridge linguistic ingenuity. 'Don? Shit, where is the man?'

Adam went into the bedroom. Donald was lying on the bed.

'Are you all right?'

Adam's eye went to the wall above Donald's dresser. There was no longer a crucifix hanging there. Nor had Donald gone to church this term. He had taken to coming to philosophy lectures with Adam and Bill Bourne.

'If you're coming, you'd better come. We're going to miss the auto-da-fade out.'

Donald stirred and sat up. 'What's going on?'

'This meeting, and we're going to miss it.'

Donald rose groggily to his feet and shook his head. 'I must've fallen asleep,' he said. 'I didn't mean to. I felt a bit queer and – I came in here – and – I must've dropped off. I'm OK now.'

'Are you sure? You're not ill?'

'Of course I'm not ill. I played hockey this afternoon and – well, I probably overdid it.'

'Hockey,' Adam said.

'I like hockey. Well, if we're going to this meeting, we'd better brace, hadn't we?'

'Better brace! I never thought I'd hear that expression again. You're really all right, are you? Because I'm not carrying you home. I'm no fireman.'

'Look, shut up. I said I was OK.'

'Then we'd better brace,' Adam said.

'I didn't think too much more about it,' Adam said, 'but then a week later, he passed out while I was actually in the room. I suppose you could say that he just fell asleep, but it was a pretty abrupt way of falling asleep. Bang. Like that.'

'Get him to go to the doctor,' Barbara said. They were having Saturday lunch at the Taj Mahal. They saw each other nearly every day. They made love in Adam's narrow bed, with the oak sported and Donald tactfully elsewhere. They were almost indecently happy. 'I suppose he hadn't been boozing or something had he?'

'The way it happened,' Adam said, 'I really think he's sick. Really sick. Oh I don't know. Doctor Morris speaking. I don't know. Perhaps it's nothing. Perhaps it's the shock of discovering that priests have nocturnal emissions. If they can wait that long. He's sick, Ba, I'm sure he is.'

'Perhaps you should write to his mother,' Barbara said.

'His mother is very superior. She'll probably resent it.'

'Then mind your own business for a change,' the girl said. 'He isn't going to die.'

Adam pushed his plate aside. 'You know,' he said, 'I sometimes wonder whether curried blanket necessarily represents the full flower of Indian cuisine.'

'One day we'll go and find out.'

'What are you doing tomorrow for instance?'

'And have days and days all to ourselves.'

'And nights and nights.'

'And those.'

'God, I'm lucky,' he said.

'God, you are,' she said.

'I love you.' They both said it together.

Two weeks later, Adam and Barbara went up to the rooms after their Saturday curry and met Donald coming out with his suitcase.

'Oh hullo,' Adam said, 'are you on your way?'

'How did you guess?'

'Hullo, Donald,' Barbara said, uneasily.

'Hullo. You wrote to my mother.'

'I was worried about you.'

Donald gave them a reproachful glance. 'Rather unnecessary,' he said.

'I hope so,' Adam said. 'Very much. Look, um, when will you be back?'

'Monday.'

'Well, let's – let's all go to the pictures, let's go and see *The Bad and the Beautiful* and *The Good and the Ugly* and things like that.'

'Fine,' Donald said.

'And, um, I'll see if I can get that girl from Pop Prior's for you again.'

'Helga. Will you really?' Donald departed with a less reproachful expression. Adam shut the oak outer door and turned to see Barbara's sweater over her head.

'Poor Don,' Adam said, undoing his belt. 'Never even had a kiss.'

iv

There was a letter in Adam's pigeon hole in the J CR the following Tuesday morning. It was on beige, deckle-edged stationery.

'Dear Mr Morris,' it said, 'Donald will not be coming back to Cambridge this term. The doctors want to perform various tests on him and it's more convenient if he stays at home. He is very disappointed and I am writing to ask whether you would care to come and visit us in the country during the Easter vacation. I know that Donald would be particularly pleased if you would. Yours sincerely, Frances Davidson.'

'Lady,' Adam said.

VI

Donald came to Little Gifford station in a Morris Minor to meet Adam. He wore grey flannels and a yellow-white cricket sweater.

'Hey, you look fine, you swine,' Adam said.

'I'm in quite good nick actually, so the Doc says.'

'I was expecting a Rolls Royce, you know. This is a bit of a comedown.'

'The gardener's using it,' Donald said. 'This is mine. Present from my old mum. At least it goes. Sometimes.' He had stalled backing out of the yard. 'Um, did you tell Helga what I asked you to tell her?'

'I told her and she was duly gratified. She – she sends you her love and she says she'll see you next term.'

'I've thought rather a lot about Helga,' Donald said. 'She's rather an unusual girl.'

'Yes,' Adam said, 'she is.'

They drove along a road pinched between huge chestnut trees and turned between wrought-iron gates up a drive with a picket fence on either side. Black and white cows foraged under more chestnut trees. At the top of the hill, behind box hedges, was the house. Gifford's End was of red brick and had the twisted chimneys that declared Elizabethan origins. If it was not quite a stately home, it was certainly a stately house.

'Been in the family long?' Adam asked.

'Well – longer than I have,' Donald said.

'What's that?' Adam asked. 'Over there.'

'Oh that. That's the private chapel. I always hid out there when I was small and Nanny Hedges was in a bait.'

'With a direct line to God, no doubt?'

'No doubt. We always used to have our own private priest as well. We've still got one actually. My uncle. He's coming over tonight. I told him an enemy of Mother Church was coming to stay. He couldn't wait.'

ii

They dined by candle-light at a Jacobean table with tall-backed chairs. The china was Haddon Hall, the silver was sterling and the temperature of the room was decidedly low. Adam sat next to Lady Frances, with Donald's sister, Francesca, next to him. Francesca was seventeen, with long fair hair and the face of a Florentine virgin. She was small and watchful and eloquently silent.

'At least,' said Lady Frances, once they had been warmed up by the kidney soup, 'at least we've got a decent government at last. I've never actually felt that Winston was *safe*, but at least he's English.'

'I always thought Mr Attlee was English,' Adam said. 'What was he if he wasn't, Lady Frances?'

'The last government was the greatest tragedy in our history since Henry the Eighth. Detestable man.'

'At least it enabled me to make a few bob out of my mining shares,' Father Kenneth Follett observed. 'I never thought to see a penny and then along came compensation. Salvation!'

Lady Frances looked sharply at her brother, who sat opposite Adam. 'The Welsh ruined the mines,' she said. 'There was nothing intrinsically wrong with the shares.'

'Come, Frances. Our father – the one who isn't in heaven, to our knowledge at least – had the worst eye for investment of any man you could ever hope to meet.'

'You obviously don't know what actually happened,'

Lady Frances said. 'Some solicitor put him into them. Probably in order to do some fellow Hebrew a good turn.'

Adam stood up. 'If you don't mind,' he said, 'I think I'll go. Or even if you do.'

'Go?'

'Home,' Adam said.

'Have I said something?' Lady Frances asked.

'You know you have, Ma,' said Donald.

'You said that Mr Morris was agnostic, I believe. What is my offence exactly?'

'I believe our young friend has every right to be indignant,' said Father Follett.

'I'm not your friend, Father,' Adam said. 'You have no friendship for me whatsoever.'

'I assure you – '

'While six million Jews were being murdered,' Adam said, from the doorway, 'the Roman Catholic clergy preached sermons against them every Sunday from virtually every pulpit in Europe. If the Germans had made it to England, you would have greeted them very gladly and you'd have preached exactly the same sermons in Westminster Cathedral or wherever the place is.'

'I will not be accused of treason in my own house.'

'Not treason, Lady Frances. Not treason. Just murder. There's no need for indignation. Now I'll go.'

'I'll come with you,' Donald said.

'It's much too late to go anywhere,' said Donald's father, from the far end of the table. 'I think we should change the subject.'

'Change it by all means,' Adam said. 'Once I've gone, you can talk about me.'

Adam was halfway up the stairs, under the eyes of some dark ancestral portraits, when Donald's father came out of the dining room and called to him. 'Mr Morris. Please wait.'

'Is there more?'

'Please. If you'd just spare me a minute.'

Henry Davidson opened the door of the library and his manner, at once dignified and somehow imploring, brought Adam down the stairs again. They both went into the library.

'My wife can be very foolish,' Mr Davidson began.

'I don't think she's foolish, sir.'

'It's Donald, you see.'

'What is?' Adam asked.

'I thought she wrote you.'

'She asked me to come and stay. God knows why.'

'To please Donald. He likes you very much, you know. And – he's going to die, you see.'

Adam said: '*Die?*'

'Yes. That's what we've been told.'

'He said he was fine,' Adam said. 'He said it was nothing.'

'If you could possibly see your way to coming back and having a glass of brandy, I'd be extraordinarily grateful. Do you think you could?'

'He said it was nothing,' Adam said.

'Yes, well, it's not. Not that he knows, of course. Or that he should.'

Adam opened the door of the library for Donald's father. 'I had no idea,' he said as he followed him back into the dining room. The brandy was excellent.

iii

The next morning, there was tennis on the hard court behind the old chapel. Father Follett, very sharp at the net, partnered Francesca against Adam and Donald, who specialized in lobs of an eccentric trajectory but showed no signs of the mortal disease with which he was said to be stricken. Francesca, with her neat body and her smart boarding-school coaching, played a surprisingly good game. Adam had begun by serving her gentlemanly spins, but soon exerted his full, if erratic, power against her. One of his best services struck her hard on the thigh.

'Terribly sorry. Are you OK?'

She nodded briefly. The game went on. Adam finished the set with a powerful smash which Francesca touched but could not return. The ball flew over the netting off her racket.

'Well played. I'll get it,' Adam said. 'I saw where it went.'

Her expression did not alter. She followed him towards the long grass where the ball had gone. Donald and Father Follett hesitated and then walked towards the house.

'I hope I didn't hurt you,' Adam said.

The girl was cuffing the long grass with the side of her plimsoll. 'You've hurt us all,' she said, without looking up.

'I have?' Adam said. It was, he realized, the first time that she had actually spoken to him. 'How? What have I done?'

'You've seduced Donald.'

'Seduced Donald? How?'

'You've taken him from his family,' the girl said, 'and I hate you for it.'

'Got it,' Adam said, picking up the ball.

'It's all your fault. Everything.'

'Look, don't be silly. I haven't seduced anyone.'

'Why do you think Uncle Kenneth is here? Because Donald is ill and he's in danger.'

'I know he is, but –'

'And it's your fault,' the girl said. 'Jew.'

iv

'Here I am,' Adam wrote to Barbara, 'in one of the most beautiful places I have ever seen, part guest, part prisoner, part friend, part enemy, welcome and unwelcome, protected and exposed. I want to leave and yet I feel obliged to stay. I hate them and I also pity them. I would gladly see them in hell, and yet if I could sacrifice myself to earn their good opinions, I do believe, God help me, that I'd do it. I have no place in this country as they have one. My only place is between your legs, that's my only country. The only place I can plant my flag and feel at home.'

He was writing his letter in the library, a handsome room smelling of floor polish and old leather and the fine dust which rare books dispense. Father Follet came in and went, with tactful directness, to one of the shelves. 'Don't let me disturb you,' he said.

Adam found it difficult to continue with a love letter while there was a priest in the room. He turned in his chair. 'Do you think I'm wrong to stay here?' he asked.

'Wrong?'

'Should I go?'

'How can I say what you should do?'

'I thought that was your office,' Adam said.

'Hardly,' said the other. 'Hardly.'

'Lady Frances certainly seems to wish I wasn't here. Do you?'

'She envies you,' Father Follett said. 'You're going to live.'

Adam said: 'Isn't there always the life everlasting?'

The priest looked at him as if Adam might regret having said that. Adam found a new tone. 'Francesca thinks it's all my fault, you know,' he said.

'Does she?'

'Yes. Do you?'

'That what is your fault exactly?'

'She thinks I've seduced Donald from the path of truth and he's been given – whatever he's got – as a punishment.'

'Leukaemia. Does she really?' The priest had found the book he was looking for and was checking a reference.

'Are you never going to tell him?' Adam said.

'It's not for me to tell or not tell him,' Father Follett said.

'Why not? Why isn't it?'

'Forgive me,' the priest said, 'but I begin to feel that you blame me for Donald's illness no less than his sister blames you.'

'I wonder why it is you never hesitate to tell people things which cannot be proved, things you call truth, and yet you're so tactful about – about the actual truth.'

Father Follett came and sat near Adam, on the window seat. Behind him, the double cherry blossom was beginning to burst against a blue sky.

'What would be gained by devastating Donald prematurely with a cruel and inalterable revelation?'

'*Prematurely*,' Adam said. 'I see. May I ask why exactly you're here?'

'I'm here because I was invited.'

'You're here to persuade him back into the fold, aren't you?' Adam said.

'That's not a sin, is it?'

Adam looked at Father Follett, signed his letter and thrust it into an envelope. 'And at what point,' he asked, 'are you going to spring the news on him and gather his soul like a ripe gooseberry?'

'I have no intention whatever of behaving as you imagine.'

'At least not prematurely,' Adam said. 'You never hesitated to tell him all the other crippling, degrading, superstitious "truths", all the castrating claptrap of the Church. Why this sudden tact?'

'I don't think the Church has anything to do with this.'

'I think it has everything to do with it, you see, so there we are. I'm sorry. I'm sorry. I must go to the post. I shouldn't have said what I said.'

'But you said it,' Father Follett said. 'I think I prefer you angry to apologetic.'

'Well, there's lots more of that if you want it,' Adam said.

'I'll walk with you. May I?'

'After you,' Adam said. 'Father.'

They walked across the gravel and down the drive between the thickening chestnuts.

'Why does God condemn Donald to die and allow me to live?' Adam asked. 'Doesn't that honestly make you wonder?'

'I fancy it makes you wonder more than it makes me,' the priest replied.

'Don't you wish it was the other way round? Honestly.'

'No. I have no such wish.'

'Oh come,' Adam said. 'Isn't that the God you really want, one that cracks down hard on Jews and atheists and the rest of the subhuman rabble? Isn't that the big, muscular God you'd really like to believe in? One that stopped sitting on the fence and moving in a mysterious way his wonders to perform and really came in with the big stick and the black Mercedes? Of course it is.'

'How evil you want us to be! That wouldn't be my God at all.'

'That *is* your God,' Adam said, 'only you won't recognize it.'

'And what is yours?'

'I have no God.'

'And what will you put in his place?'

'Oh no, Father, I'm not falling for that one. One does not replace a lie, nor does one need to have a replacement in order to show that it is one. Nonsense is not replaced, it is simply eliminated.'

'Like the Jews,' Father Follett said.

'Oh what masters you are! What masters! There isn't a cheap trick or a false analogy you're afraid of trying out, is there? Who threatens you? Who breaks your children's heads against the wall? Who drowns your old men in shit? Who skewers your unborn babies on bayonets? Who gasses you?'

It was a few seconds before Father Follett responded. 'Tell me,' he said, 'what will you do in life, Adam?'

'I honestly haven't any idea.'

'Preach?'

v

When they returned from the village, Donald was waiting for them. 'I was wondering where you'd got to,' he said.

'What the hell's that? If you'll forgive the expression, Father.'

'I've heard worse,' Father Follett said, indicating that he was going back to the library. 'Thank you for the walk, and the conversation.'

'Pleasure,' Adam said. 'Your old pram or something?'

'That's exactly what it is,' Donald said. 'I was going to show you the family sport.'

'I think I have some idea what that is,' Adam said.

'The Cresta run,' Donald said. 'Haven't done it for years, but I thought you'd like to see how the upper classes break their necks.'

He led the way past the tennis court towards where two huge oaks overhung a steep slope that went down towards open meadows. The path was rubbed bald by winter rain and summer drought. The roots of the oaks ribbed it on either side.

'Nanny Hedges wouldn't let us do it if she could help it.'

'She sounds a very sensible woman.'

'A neighbour of ours broke his neck and she locked it in the old stables.'

'Donald, I have absolutely no desire to break my neck.'

'Well, at least it's quick,' Donald said. 'I'll make the first run. You grab the stop watch and bugger off down to the bottom of the hill, OK? Go on, a bit further. Bit more. Right. Now, when I shout "go", press the tit.' Donald lowered himself onto the frame of the old pram and manoeuvred himself to the verge of the slope. 'Go,' he shouted, and thrust himself forward. The pram went hurtling down the slope, racketing back and forth between the humped roots; it straightened out and plunged towards Adam. Donald's face was transformed, the eyes bulging, the mouth wide open, a strange yell of terror and triumph bursting from it. Donald flashed past, the pram swivelled and toppled and there he was lying on the edge of the green meadow beyond Adam.

'Don? Don, are you OK?'

'What did I do?' Donald asked. 'What time did I do?'

Adam looked down at the watch in his hand. The seconds were still ticking by. He had forgotten to press the knob. 'God, I forgot!' he said. 'Are you all right?'

'Why do you keep asking me?' Donald asked, levering himself to his feet. 'I'm fine. Your go now.'

'You're skilled,' Adam said. 'I shall break my neck. Where's he buried, this neighbour of yours?'

'Oh he's not dead,' Donald said. 'He just has to wear a concrete necklace for the rest of his life.'

'Oh fine,' Adam said, as he hauled the pram back up the slope. 'Off we go then. Good heavens. I'm not really very keen, you know.'

As he reached the top of the run, he was conscious that someone was standing there. It was Francesca. 'Hullo,' he said. She called to Donald over his head: 'It's lunchtime.'

'Why the hell do we do things?' Adam said, as he lowered himself onto the pram. Francesca turned and walked back towards the house. Yet, he thought, as he pushed himself to the edge of the drop, it was for her that he was doing it. 'Go,' he shouted and plunged forward.

'Twenty-two seconds,' Donald said. 'Not bad at all. Not bad at all.'

Adam felt a great hunger. He started back up the slope

hurriedly, before Donald could suggest another attempt on the record. When he reached the top, he turned and saw that Donald was still there in the patch of sunlight at the edge of the meadow. Adam half-ran, half-slid back towards where his friend was standing. 'You look a bit rough,' he said.

'It's these bloody pills,' Donald said. 'I wish they didn't make me feel so piss awful.'

Adam said: 'Do you think you can make it back to the house?'

'Oh, I'm OK,' Donald said. 'Probably hungry.'

'I know I am,' Adam said. 'Look, um, can I help you or anything?'

'Help me?' Donald said. 'Whatever for?'

vi

Lady Frances was arranging pressed flowers on a black velvet background with a pair of tweezers when Adam went into the drawing room later that afternoon. 'Oh hullo, Adam,' she said. 'Are you all right?'

'I'm fine,' Adam said. 'Donald's asleep. I just wanted to tell you that I think I ought to be going. Soon.'

'Ought you? Why?'

'I fancy you've really had about enough of me,' Adam said.

'And are you thinking of taking Donald with you?'

'No. No, I wasn't.'

'He very much wants to come back to Cambridge next term if possible. How do you feel about that?'

'Feel about it? I hope he does, obviously. Very much.'

Lady Frances did a delicate placement with the tweezers. 'Do you have a place in town?' she asked.

'In London? A place? I live with my parents. I don't have a place.'

'For entertaining, I meant.'

'My parents are quite civilized,' Adam said. 'I'm allowed to entertain people at home.'

'You have a young lady, I understand,' Lady Frances said. 'Only we have a *pied à terre*, you know. In Cadogan Square. I was wondering whether you'd like to have the use of it for a few days.'

'No, thank you.'

'I gather Donald has a girl too, is that right?'

'Has he?' Adam said. 'Good.'

'Perhaps you could persuade him to come with you when you go back to town. And then you could use the flat. Both of you.' She looked up from the dead flowers. 'Helga, isn't it?' she said.

'Yes,' Adam said. 'I believe so. Unfortunately – my girl, as you put it, is up north with her parents. But if the idea is to get me to take Donald off your hands for a few days, I'll certainly do so. I don't need to be offered any consolations for spending time with him.'

'How nice of you!' Lady Frances said, picking up her tweezers once more.

'He fears that he's hurt you very much,' Adam said.

'Does he? By doing what?'

'By his new attitude to the Church.'

'He has *grieved* me very much,' Lady Frances said, 'not hurt me.'

'And this is your way of revenging yourself, I presume? Wishing him out of your sight.'

'When will you be going, do you think?' Lady Frances said.

'As soon as possible,' Adam replied. 'When he wakes. As soon as he wakes. Don't worry, Lady Frances, I'll take him away, if that's what you want.' He turned and quit the room. Lady Frances continued to work, until Adam was safe from embarrassment. Then she unclenched her face and two tears fell onto the dry flowers.

VII

They sat in the Morris Minor observing the prostitutes in Curzon Street. One of the more splendid of them was wearing a lurex trouser suit and wedge sandals. Her cleavage was accentuated by the unsubtle upthrust of her breasts. Her hair was piled on her head in snakey coils which would have discountenanced Medusa. 'What's the average price roughly, do you think?' Donald asked.

'Hard to say. About three quid, I'm told.'

'Look at her,' Donald said. 'She's rather sumptuous, don't you think? She looks so marvellously *like* a tart. How much do you think she'd want just to take off her clothes?'

'They don't like doing that,' Adam said.

'Only thirty-three per cent within the upper price bracket actually undress entirely without extra charge, I know. I'd like to just talk to her really.'

'Unfortunately she's not in the talking business.'

'Eighteen per cent of American males have their first genital experience with prostitutes, did you know?'

'The gospel according to Kinsey.'

'It would be interesting to ask her a few questions, wouldn't it?' Donald said. 'A lot of things I'd like to know.'

They watched while a man approached, raised his hat and sought some information.

'I've got two pounds ten,' Donald said.

'She's not really worth going to hell for, Don, is she?'

'Has my mama commissioned you to be my spiritual mentor, or something?'

'On the contrary,' Adam said.

'So it's just being in love that makes you so infernally prim, is it?'

'In love? Who said I was in love? Ah there they go! Too late now, Don, I fear. She's got a passenger.'

'With Barbara, aren't you?'

'Am I? Yes, I suppose I am.'

'I say,' Donald said, 'I'd rather like to wait and see how long it takes her to be back on the beat. The average client seems to get about eight point two minutes.' He opened the glove compartment and took out the stop watch with which he had timed the Cresta run.

ii

Donald came back to Cambridge for the summer term. Did he seem better? Certainly he seemed no worse, which was much better than Adam had feared. May was brilliant with sunshine. They sat on the Mill bridge with their tankards and their Players' Number Three and talked of doing some serious work the next day. They lay on the Backs with their books face down on their chests and promised themselves that relaxation was the best way to prepare for an approaching examination. One day they took a punt and went, with Barbara and Helga, up to Grantchester for tea. Donald punted rather well, his shirtsleeves rolled up to just above the elbow, while the girls lolled in the bottom of the boat, Adam facing them. Adam was an anxious man with a punt pole; he was happy to allow Donald to do most of the work.

Eventually they came to the famous meadows. 'Stands my cock at ten to three,' recited Adam, 'and are there hormones still for tea?'

'I don't follow,' Helga said.

'Follow, follow, follow, the merry, merry paps of pun,' cried Adam, grabbing at an overhanging bough and pulling them towards the Grantchester bank. 'Here we jolly well are. To the Finland Station, driver.'

Donald stepped ashore, with perilous agility. 'I'll buzz and get the teas,' he said. 'Coming, Helgie?'

'I stay here,' the girl said, one hand in the water. 'And take the sun.'

Donald nodded and went off alone. Barbara gave Adam a look which reflected on Helga and stood up, tottering. 'Hold on, Donald. I'm coming.'

Adam said: 'Don't you like him?'

The blonde girl shrugged. 'He's O K. Why does he call me Helgie?'

'Because he thinks you like it,' he said. 'He thinks a hell of a lot of you, you know.'

Helga looked straight at him. 'And what about you?' she said.

'I think you're very beautiful,' he said.

She leaned forward and put her arms round his neck and kissed him on the mouth. When she had finished, she leaned back again and looked at him. He shifted his legs.

'Helga,' he said, 'will you do me a favour?'

'Depends,' she said.

'Be nice to him,' Adam said.

Helga said: 'I am nice to him.'

'Look, I do have a reason for what I'm saying.'

'You have no right to ask me,' she said.

'I wouldn't ask otherwise,' he said.

She pouted. 'I don't follow.' She really did pout.

'Trust me,' Adam said. 'Please. It wouldn't hurt you.'

'What do you want me to do?' she said.

'Be nice to him,' he said.

Donald was running across the meadow from the tea shop towards them, with a heavily charged tray supported on one hand above his head. 'Have you never seen the sprinting waiters of Samarkand?' he cried. 'My dear, you haven't *lived.*'

'Hold on!' Barbara was trying to keep up, but she was laughing so much it was difficult.

'You see?' Helga said.

'No,' Adam said.

'Of course you do,' she said.

He hated her so much he could hardly keep his hands off her.

Donald came running and laughing up to the bank and then, rather slowly, he seemed to trip. The tea tray described a parabola, in the best silent movie tradition, sailed past Helga's head and splashed into the water. Scones and cupcakes and cucumber sandwiches floated in the stream. Helga hugged herself with laughter. Donald was prone among the cow parsley and the nettles. Adam leaped ashore. He and Barbara looked at each other and at the unconscious Donald, while Helga fished for cupcakes.

iii

'I promise you I'm OK,' Donald said. 'I tripped. I'm OK. I promise.' He had recovered quite quickly from the attack. Adam punted them home as fast as he could and he and Barbara had got Donald to bed. Helga had had to go to a class.

'Shouldn't we at least call the Doc?' Adam said.

'I'm not going home.'

'No one's suggesting that, but – '

'I couldn't see Helga if I went home. You know this Italian trip you were talking about, you and Barbie?'

'I do wish you wouldn't call her Barbie,' Adam said. 'What about it?'

'What if I asked Helgie and we made it a foursome? It's only a suggestion, but we could take the rusty wagon.'

'It would be nice to have a car,' Adam said, 'but I don't know – '

'I think she'll make a hell of a good wife, don't you, Helgie?'

'Wife?' Adam said. 'What do you want a wife for?'

'I think it's the pills that make me feel rough,' Donald said. 'I've a good mind to pack them in. You won't tell anybody about this afternoon, Adam, will you?'

64

'Who would I tell?'

'We wouldn't get in your way, and if we came, you'd at least be mobile. And I rather reckon with seeing the Eternal City.'

'It'll be bloody hot, I'm warning you.'

'Did you know that there were still officially licensed brothels in Italy? Be interesting.'

'I thought you were in love.'

'Purely from the point of view of statistical research,' Donald said. 'You wouldn't give Helga a call, would you? I expect she'll be worried about me.'

Adam called her. She agreed to meet him for a drink at the Baron of Beef.

'I'm not asking you actually to come to Italy,' Adam explained to her. 'I'm just asking you to say you will.'

'I should be honest,' Helga said. 'I don't like to deceive people.'

'I appreciate that, but I'm telling you, it's never going to happen. No one's going to keep you to anything. So why not let him believe you care for him? Please. Let him believe we're all going to Italy together. I'm doing it; why can't you?'

'It's not honest,' she said.

'Oh come on, Helgie. Helga. How many men have you had since you came to Cambridge, or before, if it comes to that?'

'Don't be horrible, please. That's got nothing to do with it.'

'If you took your bloody clothes off and got into bed with him, it wouldn't kill you, would it, frankly?'

'Now you're being horrible.'

'No, I'm not. Would it? Oh God, honestly, I admire your attitude. I wish more girls had it. You're someone who does what she wants. I think you're terrific. You know I do.'

'I like Barbara very much,' Helga said.

'Be nice to him, please. I'm not suggesting – '

'Yes, you are,' she said.

'No one's going to hold you to anything,' Adam said.

'I know what you're doing,' Helga said. 'Don't think I don't.'

'Me?'

'Of course.'

iv

'I'm sorry,' Lady Frances said. 'My train was late.'

'At least they haven't nationalized the Savoy yet,' Adam said, 'so we can probably still get some tea.' He was waiting in the lobby where she had suggested they meet.

Lady Frances was wearing a pink hat with a white veil and a cream linen suit. 'Donald doesn't know you've come to town?'

'He thinks I'm with Barbara – with my girl friend.'

'Is she well?' Lady Frances asked, as they sat down at one of the little tables. A waiter came promptly. 'Bring us two Indian – Indian, Adam? – yes, Indian tea, please.'

'She's fine,' Adam said. 'Lady Frances, you have a very brave son.'

'The attacks are getting worse, are they?'

'And more frequent.'

'And Italy's not going to be possible, is that it?'

'I'd like to think it was, but – '

'He's told me about your plans. They seem to have been quite detailed.'

'Oh yes, yes we've talked a lot about it,' Adam said. 'The problem is, apart from anything else, Don's the only one of us who can drive. And – if – '

The waiter brought the tea.

'Adam, suppose I gave you the money to go by aeroplane. Sugar?'

'Please. Lady Frances, I'm afraid he really is now too ill to – for us to really – '

'I'll take the responsibility. Even if it's only for a few days – '

'Apart from anything else, he believes this girl – '

'Helga – '

'Yes. That she's in love with him. I'm afraid she really isn't. I don't honestly even believe that she'd be willing to come – '

'He told me quite definitely that you were going à quatre.'

'That's what she's agreed to *say*, but – '

'Perhaps you can talk to her, Adam. Persuade her. You're very persuasive.'

'I have tried. And God knows, I'm willing to try again. But, forgive me, aren't you carrying this a little far?'

'What?'

'Surely he ought to be with his own people when – when things get worse. Not with me, not with – people who – '

'Not if he's happier with you,' Lady Frances said.

'You really – ' Adam shook his head. 'How can you not want him with you just because – ?'

'Just because of what?'

'Because of what happened with him and the Church.'

'Do you seriously think I don't want him because of that?'

'Well, isn't it true?'

'I want him with me every moment of the day,' she said. 'Not a day, not an hour passes when I don't look up the trains to Cambridge, when I don't think of bringing him home. And as for the Church – ' Lady Frances passed the sandwiches. 'I don't give a damn,' she said.

'I do,' Adam said. 'I rather do. I rather wish he'd – well, rejoin – '

'Well, perhaps he will. I hope so, but – if not – '

'And you're not going to tell him what – what's wrong – Not even . . .?'

'Adam, Donald's friendship with you, and with this young woman, has really made him happy for the first time in his life. Do you suppose that I shall ever let him imagine that it was pity and not true affection that was responsible for it?'

'It wasn't,' Adam said. 'It wasn't. I'll stay, if you like, I'll stay in England this summer and be with him. I don't mind. Happily.'

'There'll be nothing you can do,' she said. 'And it's not going to be at all nice.'

Adam said: 'Look, perhaps we still could all go to Italy. Or just the three of us. I'm willing. If you – I'd like him to. We both would. Barbara and I. Truly.'

'Thank you, Adam,' Lady Frances said. 'That's very Christian of you.'

'Or we can stay in England. As I said – '

'No,' she said. 'No. Whatever happens, Adam, you're not to alter your plans. If you did, he'd know. And he mustn't. He really mustn't.'

VIII

Adam took his exams, obediently serving up Latin prose and Latin verse, Greek verse and Greek prose, and the Long Vacation began. Barbara was working a longer term and he returned to London without her. Not until July did they travel down to Gifford's End together. Lady Frances met them in the Sunbeam. Donald's car was in the garage. He was too weak to drive. He lay in bed, his face the colour of unbaked dough. The change in him was marked, and terrible.

Adam and Barbara were due to leave for Italy three days later. As far as Adam's parents knew, he was going with

Bill Bourne. If his mother suspected the truth, she was wise enough to remain silent. Lionel Morris believed his son's lies, not surprisingly, since they were devised to please him.

Gifford's End was painfully beautiful those July days. The chestnut trees were huge with their summer foliage. The rose garden was dense with multicoloured perfume. The raspberries that Nanny Hedges picked were as big as grapes. They played croquet in the late afternoons with Donald's father. Lady Frances made excellent conversation with Barbara. Only Francesca remained apart. She was riding in a gymkhana at the weekend and spent the day exercising His Majesty.

Adam dreaded and looked forward to their leaving. He and Barbara had separate rooms, of course, during the two nights they stayed at the house. They had never spent whole days and nights together. He could not wait to leave, that was the truth, though he felt a traitor when it came to doing so. They loitered at Donald's bedside while Lady Frances waited tactfully in the car at the front door.

'Bloody shame about Helga's father being ill like that,' Adam said.

'Yes. Thanks for the message anyway. She'll be there next term though, won't she?'

'Oh sure. Sure, she will.'

'These bloody pills,' Donald said. 'If it weren't for them – '

'Well, let's hope they do some good in the end.' Adam looked at his watch. 'Listen, Don, we'll – um – be back, you know – '

'Enjoy yourselves,' Donald said.

'We'll do that,' Barbara said.

'You might bring me a sliver of the true cross if you get the chance.'

'And a stick of the rock of ages,' Adam said.

'Cleft specially for me!'

'Would we forget?' Adam said, as they went to the door. 'See you when we see you then. OK?'

'When else?' Donald said. 'In logic there are no surprises.'

They grinned and waved and finally closed the door.

'I suppose there can always be a miracle,' Adam said, as they walked across the hall and out to where Lady Frances was waiting. A couple of men were unloading oxygen cylinders and other medical supplies from a van.

Barbara looked up towards Donald's window. There were tears in her eyes. She looked at Adam and squeezed his hand. 'Three whole weeks,' she said. 'Three whole weeks.'

'Come on,' he said, 'we don't want to be late for them, do we?'

They crossed to the car.

ii

Of course they thought about Donald. Of course they talked about him. And of course they forgot about him. For whole days and nights they forgot about him. They trekked from one hot place to another, shared their first Motta ice creams, ate *pasta* in shaded *trattorie* and looked at more churches and pictures and Roman sites than they could number. Barbara got terrible blisters in Pompeii and Adam got the runs in Naples. Barbara cried and cried one night after they had made love and Adam could not get her to tell him why. When he could not comfort her, he hated her. But it was not too long before she was comforted. In Rome she told him why she had cried and why she had said she hated him. Because she loved him and she was afraid. Afraid of what? He knew. That he would leave her. Why would he ever do that? She was beautiful. When she took her clothes off, he could not believe his luck. When she kissed his body, he thought he must die with the pleasure of it. The mosquitoes swooped and whined and made a meal of their naked flesh, but even to caress her mosquito bites was an act fraught with ecstasy. How could people ever not be happy? How could life ever not be marvellous?

They had saved Rome till last. From there they would take the long train back to London, and temporary separation. They were in the Piazza San Pietro, catching the spray from the blown fountains, when Adam saw English newspapers on sale under the Bernini arcade. 'Must see what the Test score is,' he said. He didn't get that far. The deaths column was on the front page. Among the names was Davidson, Donald. The paper was a day late. The funeral was that very day, at Gifford's End. No flowers.

Adam walked back to where Barbara was waiting in the square. He walked past her towards St Peter's, the Banco di Roma, he had called it a few minutes before. Barbara came after him, trying to ease her shoe; she still had a blister on her right heel.

Adam stood in front of the Michelangelo *Pietà*, the drooping body in the Madonna's arms. Was he moved or did he want to be moved? Was it the expression of the inexpressible, or was it too wishful to be true? He turned away and went into one of the side chapels, where 100-lire candles were burning. The smell of incense hung sickly on the air. He sat down on a wicker-seated chair and leant his face on the high back of the pew in front of him. He closed his eyes. Was he praying?

'It gives me the shudders,' Barbara said, looking round at the plaster piety.

Parties of tourists clattered past. Priests hurried by with a swish of self-importance. The organ began to play. In the dome, on some scaffolding, workmen were hammering discreetly. Adam stood up and took Barbara's arm, almost angrily. They walked towards the door.

'The noise, my dear,' Adam said, 'and the *people*.'

A
SEX
LIFE

How could three years which passed so slowly be gone so soon? Here they were, the best and the brightest of the Cambridge actors, already finishing the last performance of the very last production in which they would appear on the stage of the Dramatic Club. In a few weeks they would take their Final Examinations, attend their last interviews at the Appointments' Board and face, with a sort of arrogant anxiety, the challenge of a bigger world. The Golden Age of Mike Clode, as Adam Morris had not failed to name it, was coming to an end with a *fin-de-siècle* production of *Much Ado About Nothing*. Adam had come late to the Dramatic Club, but he had at least achieved an entrée into that smart world which he satirized so scathingly in his weekly column in *Varsity* and amongst whose starry personalities he was so eager to twinkle.

The scene was set in an Oxford college of the 1890s and the cast was dressed in blazers and boaters and garden party dresses. Barbara Ransome, as Hero, looked particularly delicious in a daring yellow dress, while Anna Cunningham, as Beatrice, wore a lace dress and a wide hat and high boots over dark blue stockings. Dan Bradley was Benedick. He wore a floral suit with a green carnation and carried a silver-topped cane. Alan Parks, as Claudio, sported a rowing Blue's blazer and white flannels. Denis Porson, wearing the scarlet robes of the Master of the College, camped out-rageously as Don Pedro; he toyed suggestively with Benedick's carnation and several times stopped the show with his buffoonery. The performance ended with a tango staged with no little ingenuity, during which Adam, in the invented role of a court photographer, came on with a tripod and loosed off a magnesium flare, before becoming entangled with his apparatus (Denis Porson's description) and having to be carried off stage by a couple of College servants. The curtain fell to enthusiastic applause. Mike Clode had done most of the productions during the year, but this was his triumph.

'Producer,' they cried from the auditorium. Mike shook his head in the wings. He blew thank-you kisses to the cast, a big man who might have been a rugger player and to whom the genial gestures of the theatre seemed always to come uneasily. The cast looked into the wings and signalled to him to join them. He shook his head with renewed fervour, but the nearest of the extras, imagining his reluctance to be feigned, grabbed hold of him and bundled him to the centre of the stage. 'Amateurs,' he mouthed at them, before turning with a large, helpless smile to acknowledge the applause. He was quick to take Anna's and Dan's hands and pull them and the rest of the company forward. 'Bravo, bravo,' cried the audience.

'And I think they're absolutely right,' Mike said, as the curtain finally fell. 'Well done, everybody.' He kissed Anna. 'Wonderful, darling. Best ever. Sensational.'

'I wasn't bad, was I?' Anna said. 'Except I mucked the business with the gloves.'

'It didn't show a bit. You were tremendous. Dan wasn't bad either. For Dan.'

'I mucked it twice. Dan was lovely.'

'And he wasn't bad either. Daniel, you were terrific.' Dan Bradley, whose good looks rendered his reticence eloquent, bowed and said nothing. 'Barbara, my Barbara,' Mike said, embracing the yellow dress, 'you were never lovelier.'

'Should we not have called you on?' she asked.

'I don't think directors should take calls,' Mike said. 'Personally.'

'Just leave them with the credit,' Alan Parks said, 'and they're quickly satisfied.'

'You be careful, young Master Parks, or we'll have to ship you back to sheep-shaggers' land! Bloody Aussies, coming over here – '

'You and who else, sport?' Alan said. 'I thought you said this was your last production, didn't you? Once you've given up the throne, it's no use calling out the guard, my friend. They're likely to cut your throat.'

'What a pleasant little lad it is, to be sure!' Mike said.

'A little peasant lad, did I hear?' Denis Porson appeared from the wings with a tray of bubbling glasses. 'Not from Shropshire *again*, I trust? Rhyming rustics I've *had*. Shampoo anyone?'

'Is it really?' Barbara said.

'Shampoo substitute, dear lady, but just like the real thing, unless you've had the real thing.'

'And you're never likely to do that, Denis, are you?' Alan said.

'Have a care, sir,' said Denis, 'or I shall strike you lightly across the mouth with my kid glove. The choice of weapons will be yours, but I'd advise against the rapier. It's a gentleman's weapon.'

'Well,' Alan said, 'I'd better go and look for my woman. She said she was coming to the party – '

'You were really saying something, weren't you,' Anna was saying to Mike Clode, 'about the whole aesthetic movement – weren't you – as well as – ?'

'You saw it,' Mike said, 'and I saw it. We're in a club of two.'

'I often think those are the nicest ones,' Anna said.

'Do you really? So do I, darling. So do I.' He kissed her and in the same movement stepped away towards the wings. 'Back in a minute.'

Adam went to Anna with a glass of whatever it was. 'You were terrific tonight,' he said.

'Thank you,' Anna said, her eye on where Mike had joined a middle-aged man in the wings. 'I made a mess of the business with the gloves.'

'It didn't show,' Adam said. 'Did you see what I wrote about you in *Varsity* this week?'

'I never read *Varsity*.'

'I said you were the female egg-head of the year. And you didn't even see it? What's the point of being rude to people if they don't take the trouble to read what you say?'

'Mr Lazlo,' Mike said. 'What a marvellous surprise!'

'You invited me,' Bruno Lazlo said. 'I came.'

'And it was very nice of you,' Mike said. 'Look, um, if you don't mind, I won't bother to introduce you to everybody – '

'No, no. Let them enjoy themselves.'

'Are you staying in Cambridge overnight?'

'I have to get back to town unfortunately,' Lazlo said. 'I have to fly to California on Monday – '

'Oh really? Hollywood. What a ghastly thought!'

'I like California,' Lazlo said. 'It's where they sign the cheques.'

'Look, at least let me take you for something to eat – '

'Dan,' Barbara Ransome said, 'I don't think much of this, do you? Let's go round and see if David's at home.'

'I thought he'd gone to London,' Dan said.

'That's what I thought,' Barbara said.

Alan Parks came up from the green room as Mike and Bruno Lazlo were going out of the stage door. 'Mike, you haven't seen Joyce, have you, anywhere?'

Mike shook his head. Alan looked closely at Lazlo, knowing the producer's face, but Mike did not introduce them. 'Bloody woman, I must say,' Alan said.

'No one here!' Barbara said, as she opened the door of the house in Portugal Place.

'Good heavens,' Dan said.

'I think he must have gone to London.'

'That's amazing,' Dan said. 'Tell me, how did you know where to find the key?'

'I read it in the Stephen King-Hall Newsletter,' Barbara said and kissed him with urgent lips. 'I've been wanting to say that all evening.'

'When I first saw you,' Dan said, 'I thought you came from Harrods.'

'I like Harrods.'

'The cooked meat counter.'

'We could stay all night if we wanted to,' Barbara said, unzipping the yellow dress. 'I can't wait to get out of this.'

Dan said: 'Look, um – '

'It's all right,' Barbara said.

'Aren't you organized?' Dan said.

'Daniel, Daniel, Daniel,' she said, 'you looked fairly organized yourself.'

iii

When Dan came in, just after midnight, Mike made some coffee. They shared rather elegant rooms in King's Parade. (There was a piano in the window, and a record player.) Mike brought Dan a Festival of Britain mug and sat down on the arm of his chair.

'Dan, do you trust me?' he said.

'No, of course not,' Dan said.

'Because you know something, don't you? We haven't really started yet.'

'Oh?' Dan said.

'What's Cambridge, after all? A bunch of amateurs who

can't cross the stage without laddering their tights. We're only just beginning, Dan. It's a kindergarten. Baby's got to walk now.'

'He liked you, did he?' Dan said.

'Trust me and I'll make you the biggest star on the English stage. You see if I don't.'

Dan did his Richard Dimbleby imitation: 'Here we are on the pinnacle of the temple! The devil is whispering in his ear ... I can just see the Cities of the Plain spread out in front of him ...'

'I'm serious, Dan. London's what matters now. That's where we've got to prove ourselves. As soon as the next couple of weeks is out of the way, we're really going places.'

'I just hope they're places I want to go,' Dan said.

'They will be,' Mike said. 'I come from suburbia, Dan, personally, and I don't ever want to go back. It's the one place in the world that's further away than anywhere else. OK, your old man was a country schoolmaster, you weren't exactly raised in the lap of luxury. But at least you lived in a recognizable place. Because try SW13. If you went back, at least someone would know you. At least you had a tree to carve your initials on. No one carves their initials on Key Flats. My father's gone round the same bloody round for twenty-five years and he's still known as Mister Um-er. The shops he goes into, they still don't call him by his name, some of them. That's not ever going to happen to me. By God, they're going to know my name before I've finished with them. And yours, Dan, and yours.'

'That's very nice of you, Mike,' Dan said.

'Nice! Don't let Cambridge turn you into a snob, Dan. The theatre is a business. Films especially.'

'Oh, he wants us to make films as well, does he?'

'Eventually, on our own terms, obviously.'

'Obviously.'

'Meanwhile, I know some people in London, Bruno told

me about. I can raise some finance. We can take a theatre, start our own company – you, me, Barbara – he thought she was stunning – stunning – '

'And Anna?'

'Goes without saying. Obviously. We're going to be one hell of a team, I promise you. You and me. Believe me – I know.'

'I know too,' Dan said. 'Mike Clode and Mr Um-er.'

'Trust me, Dan. Trust me, kid.'

Dan grinned and nodded. 'Trust you,' he said, and unleashed a John Wayne punch to Mike's stomach. Mike doubled up, as if the punch had not stopped short, and swung a haymaker at Dan's jaw. Dan toppled backwards over the sofa, lashing a foot at Mike's groin as he disappeared. Mike reeled backwards into an armchair. The routine, at which they were extremely expert, continued until an angry banging from next door rang the bell on it. Mike lay panting in his chair. 'I want a hundred per cent from you, Daniel,' he croaked. 'You're only giving me ninety. I want a hundred.'

'You be careful,' Dan said. 'Or you'll damned well get it.'

'Daniel, Daniel, Daniel,' Mike Clode said.

iv

Denis Porson in frogged pyjamas and Moroccan slippers stood stirring the cocoa which he had just made for himself. On his chest of drawers, in a triple frame, were photographs of the Queen, in her coronation robes, of a Victorian general in full fig and of a middle-aged woman in a floral hat, her face a smudged smirk as a result of being photographed out of focus. Denis held his cocoa in both hands, closed his eyes before these familiar ikons and appeared to mutter a short prayer. He then got into bed.

'Goodnight, Banks,' he said, though there was no one

else to be seen in the small room. 'Goodnight, your Grace,' he answered, 'will that be all, your Grace?' Denis nodded. 'Yes, thank you, Banks,' he replied. He drank his cocoa, turned out his light and went to sleep.

II

'How was it supposed to help,' Alan Parks said, 'not seeing me?'

'It helped,' Joyce Hadleigh said, 'because it avoided this.'

They were sitting in Alan's rooms, unpoured tea and uneaten cakes on the table between them. On the wall was the oar he had won with his College boat in his first year. Joyce looked round as if she had never seen the room before, or never expected to see it again. She had long fair hair, large blue eyes and a decisive jaw. In the sunshine that poured in through the leaded windows, she looked very pale.

'I suppose you are sure,' Alan said.

'Positive,' she said.

'You might have told me,' he said. 'I've been worried sick.'

'Well, I've told you,' she said. 'How do you feel now?'

'Worried sick,' he said, giving her the old smile. He sat forward, seriously. 'It's just something we're going to have to face together, that's all.'

'I thought you'd be angry,' she said.

'Angry? Why should I be angry? Good heavens, I got you – into this.'

'That's why,' she said.

'You don't really know me at all,' Alan said, pouring the tea. 'God, why does life have to be so bloody predictable though? It's all so bloody predictable – this isn't – this just isn't the kind of situation – it's so – so *obvious*.'

'I'm sorry about that,' she said.

'I'm not blaming you.'

'You always said it would be all right,' Joyce said.

'Oh I see: you're blaming me.'

'Talk about predictable,' she said. 'The truth is, you don't love me. You said you did, but you don't.'

'I *did* do a lot of talking, didn't I?'

'*Didn't* you?'

'Well, you'd never have made the supreme sacrifice otherwise, would you? You'd never have allowed me to have my wicked way with you otherwise, would you?'

'Probably not,' she said.

'It's not as if you *enjoyed* it, after all, is it? I mean, I had to give up having a shower after squash with Dan because of the scratches on my back. He might have thought I was sleeping with a cat. I expect that was while you were trying to haul me off, wasn't it?'

'I wish you wouldn't be disgusting.'

'I wish you wouldn't be a bloody hypocrite. That's one wish each so far. How many more do we get? Why *did* you go to bed with me?'

'You were so bad-tempered when I wouldn't.'

'I thought that was probably it.' Alan grinned and offered the cakes. 'Well, now you've really given me something to put me in a good humour, haven't you? Have a sticky bun. Go on.'

'I don't want to get fat.'

'It's a bit late to think of that,' he said.

'With any luck I won't show till well after Tripos,' Joyce said.

'Not love you! You know damned well I love you,' he said. 'Why do you think I've been looking all over the place for you?'

'Because you haven't had it for a week presumably,' she said.

'That's nice,' he said, 'I must say. That's really nice. It's also perfectly true of course.'

'It wouldn't matter who it was really, would it?'

'Not really. As long as it wasn't Hester Michaeljohn.' He grinned again and took her hand. 'It's just bloody bad luck, that's all. Let's not let it foul things up – it should have been all right.'

'Just because withdrawing worked for the Asquiths,' Joyce said, 'doesn't necessarily mean it works for everyone.'

'I won't let you down, Joycey,' he said.

'We don't have to do anything about it until after Tripos,' she said. 'I mean, let's get our degrees, OK? That way, we can always teach.'

'After Tripos? Isn't that leaving it a bit?'

'No one'll notice,' Joyce said, munching her sticky bun, 'provided I wear the right things. And don't come to tea too often.'

'I meant from the point of view of – '

'Point of view of what?'

'Well – getting rid of it,' Alan said. 'Isn't that what you meant? Why are you looking at me like that? Christ! You don't want to *have* the bloody thing, do you?'

Joyce stood up. 'I don't ever want to see you again as long as I live.'

'OK,' Alan said. 'We'll get married.'

'You don't want to get married.'

'What the hell's that got to do with it?' he said, putting his arms round her.

'Do you know anyone?' she said.

'In what sense?' he said.

'In what *sense*? Anyone I can go to, of course. Anyone who'd get rid of it for me. That's what you want, isn't it?'

'I don't want anything.'

'Well, you're going to have something, if you don't wake your ideas up – '

'I don't exactly have anyone in my address book, do I?

82

I can ask around. I did hear about someone in Kennington vaguely.'

'You'd better get the address,' she said, 'and find out how much it costs.'

'About fifty quid, I think. I believe he's quite a decent fellow. Do you know Stanley Webb?'

'And then we shall have to raise fifty quid,' Joyce said.

'It'd be cheaper to get married,' Alan said, with the old grin. 'That only costs three quid and a kiss for the registrar. Come on, Joycey, it's not the end of the world. That way we'd have forty-seven quid left to buy a house with. And a pram.'

'Get me the name,' she said, 'and I'll go up to London on Saturday. I can revise the Eastern Question in the waiting room. Do abortionists have waiting rooms?'

'Listen, I know a medic who could probably get us some pills. I know one girl took them and they did the trick bloody well. At least *try* them. Then, if they don't work –'

'I can go to Kennington.'

'Or we can spend the rest of our lives together!' He pressed her against him. 'Christ, I could take you to bed right now.'

'Yes, well, I wouldn't advise you to try.'

'No risk of your getting pregnant, after all. And you never know, it might shake something loose. It does happen sometimes.'

'Where *do* you get all your information?'

'Out of the gutter, of course. I wouldn't dream of looking anywhere else. What do you say?'

'You've got your gall, haven't you?'

'Never go anywhere without it!'

'You damned well don't, do you? I can see you're going to be a real success in life.'

'Why do you look so absolutely marvellous suddenly?

One minute you're steamed jam roll incarnate and the next – ' His hands were under her sweater and working nimbly on the catch of her bra.

'I must be mad,' she said.

'Wait till you see the etchings,' Alan said, leading her towards the bedroom. She looked towards the door to the landing. He had already locked the oak when he went to make the tea.

ii

'There are some days,' Anna said, 'when I think that there's only one thing in the world worth being and that's a literary critic. I'm not really an actress, you know.'

'Come here and give me a kiss,' Mike Clode said.

'If only I could take D. H. Lawrence a little more seriously, I would stay. Unfortunately I find it very difficult to think of myself as a valley of blood.'

'Fortunately, you mean,' Mike said. 'I need you, Anna, and you know it. You take direction better than anyone I've ever met. For instance come over here and give me a rather nasty, perverted, opportunistic kiss.'

She got up from her revision and went over and did as he asked.

'Not bad,' he said.

'Effing good, thank you very much.'

'You're quite right,' he said, 'you're not really an actress. Unless you feel like trying it again.'

'Have I got the looks?' she said, as she sat on his knee and kissed him again.

'Look at some of the reigning Dames for God's sake.'

'In other words, no.'

'Literary critic! Of course you have.'

'I haven't got much up here, have I?' she said.

'What was foam rubber invented for?' he said.

'Aren't you nice? Aren't you *nice*?'

'I wouldn't want you in London if I didn't think you were worth it.'

'You've worked it all out very neatly, haven't you? The future.'

'What do you mean?' Mike said. 'I'm just a slave of fortune, Anna, like everyone else.'

'And I'm a valley of blood.'

'You and I are a couple, Anna, and that's all that matters.'

iii

'I was keyed-up,' Alan said. 'It doesn't mean anything. I'm sorry.'

'My fault just as much as yours. We were both keyed-up.' She put on her shoes and picked up her tote bag. 'You'd better get me that address.'

'I thought we were going to get married,' Alan said.

'Don't worry,' Joyce said. 'We don't have to get married just because you made a cock of it just now.'

'And you talk about love,' Alan said.

'You were the one who talked about love.'

'I was the one who talked about everything, wasn't I?' Alan said. 'Joyce, when am I going to see you?'

'I don't know. I don't know.'

'Look,' he said, following her to the door, 'do you want that address or don't you? Joyce – for God's sake – ' She clattered down the stairs without a word. 'Bitch,' he said, softly. '*Bitch.*' He went back into the room, his face contorted with anguish and reproach. He sat down on the sofa, hunched with misery, and finished Joyce's sticky bun.

III

'What are you accusing me of, John, exactly?' Mike asked.

John Cadman and Denis Porson had called unexpectedly at the rooms in King's Parade where Mike and Dan were revising for their imminent Final Examinations.

'It's not a question of accusing you of anything,' Cadman said, 'but as Senior Treasurer, I have to approve the club's accounts, that's all, and at the moment it seems to me there's been a great deal of expenditure – '

'We've done four productions this year,' Mike said. 'Of course there has.'

'There also seems to have been a good deal of entertaining.'

'There has also been a good deal of entertaining.'

'Take this man the other night,' Cadman said. 'There's a bill from Miller's. Eight pounds. Tell me, was that authorized by the committee?'

Mike said: 'You're so bloody jealous, John, aren't you, you can't stand up?'

'Three hundred pounds is a lot of money.'

'You're really enjoying this, aren't you?'

'On the contrary.'

'That's your middle name. Look at the coverage we've had in the national press, critics down from London – we've played to eighty, eighty-five per cent houses – did that ever happen in your day, in the days when you let the verse do the work? Did it? The money I've spent, I've spent for the good of the club – '

'This gentleman the other night, what good did he do the club exactly?'

'My goodness,' Mike said, 'you've really got me there, haven't you? Edward Marshall Hall, aren't you? Well, the gentleman the other night just happens to be interested in arranging an American tour this summer. As soon as exams are out of the way. *Much Ado* and *Miss Julie* – we might even make it to Broadway. You probably don't think that's worth eight quid. I rather do.'

'And the committee's approved this idea, has it? There does also happen to be another three hundred odd pounds that needs accounting for.'

'I've slaved my guts out for the bloody club. I shall probably fail my Tripos on account of it.'

'Three hundred and seventeen pounds is missing from club funds,' Cadman said, 'and I need to have a proper account of them – '

'I'll write you a cheque for the whole bloody amount.'

'No one's asking you to do that – '

'I'll write you a cheque, OK?'

'All we're asking – '

'Oh, you are asking for *something*, Denis, are you?' Mike said.

' – is a slightly more, um, well, more detailed account of – er – what happened to the – the – the, well, the money – '

Suddenly, and with excellent timing, Mike turned out his trouser pockets. A few heavy copper coins chimed on the floor. He shook his jacket upside down with terrific violence. Keys, handkerchieves, pens and a cheap lighter fell out, together with a wallet whose emptiness Mike flapped in Cadman's face. 'Made my bloody fortune, haven't I?' he said. 'Christ, I didn't even want to do this last production. *Much Ado*. I never even wanted to do it. I wanted to work. I haven't got my future nicely sewn up in the Foreign Office.'

'The exam is open to all,' Cadman said.

'Many are called,' Mike said, 'and we know who gets chosen. How much profit has the club made this year? At least a thousand pounds. That's a lot of money, don't you agree?'

'So's three hundred.'

'And if it comes to that, that's just about what the club lost, I seem to remember, under your Presidency.'

'Our motive was not profit,' Cadman said. 'One doesn't stage *Samson Agonistes* for profit.'

'One doesn't stage *Samson Agonistes* at all,' Mike said, 'if one has any sense whatever.'

Cadman said: 'These people you brought down haven't come from London to see the club perform. They've come to see what Michael Clode has done. And the club's paid their fares and filled their bellies. Frankly, Mike, your self-importance and self-advancement – '

'I take exception to that, John,' Dan said, without looking up from the book in front of him.

'Sorry?' Cadman said. 'Exception to what?'

'More or less everything you've said,' Dan said, turning at last to face the others. 'The truth is, Mike's shagged himself out during the last year. He's probably torpedoed his chances of getting a First and if he has, well, O K, it's not been entirely for the sake of others, but there are a lot of us who'd be nothing but awkward amateurs if it weren't for what he's done. I went up to London with him once – we went through costumes in some airless loft the whole damned day. I nearly stifled. If that's embezzlement, there must be easier ways of making three hundred quid.'

Cadman, pink and white with repressed anger, was disconcerted.

'Dan,' Mike said, 'Dan, thank you. But John's right really. John, you're absolutely right. We've got to get these accounts straight for the end of the year. I lost my temper just now. I'm sorry. I shouldn't have.'

'Forget it,' Cadman said.

'Will *you* forget it?' Mike said. 'I was stupid. I was uncontrolled.'

'It's forgotten,' Cadman said.

'Not least about your *Samson*,' Mike said. 'It was tremendous.'

'The temple didn't exactly fall down,' Cadman said, 'but – '

'You don't happen to have the cheque stubs with you, Denis, I suppose? Because – '

'Oh I wouldn't carry anything like that in the *street*,' Denis said. 'You never know when Mavis will stop you and search you, do you?'

'*Mavis?*' Cadman said. 'Who's Mavis?'

'Mavis. The *Polizei*, dear. Mavis *Polizei*. The girls in blue. Oh never mind.'

'Look,' Cadman said, 'I must go and take a supervision, I'm afraid. I'll leave you two to sort out the details.'

Denis said: 'Is it really true about Broadway? You *are* a clever, I must say.'

'It may only be Boston,' Mike said. 'Keep your knees crossed. And Denis, if you get a chance to look at the cheques before we go through them, I'm sure some of that money went on props and stuff like that. I mean, I was a bit pushed when I wrote some of them and – '

'See you in lights,' Denis said, with a wink. 'Don't worry about a thing. *Quelle bagarre*, I must say, about *rien*, *nesspah?* Gentlemen, your servant.' He bowed and went out. A moment later his head was round the door. 'I thought she'd never go!' he said, and went.

'Thanks,' Mike said.

'Forget it,' Dan said.

'I probably will,' Mike said, 'but thanks all the same.' Dan did not see Mike's outstretched hand. He had gathered his books and was going to the door. 'Where are you off to?' Mike asked. 'Something wrong?'

'Nothing,' Dan said, 'I'm going out.'

'Dan?' Mike put a restraining hand on Dan's shoulder.

Dan dumped his books and suddenly whacked in a phantom punch to Mike's solar plexus. Mike grinned and grunted and retaliated to the point of the chin. Another of their famous Hollywood fights, punctuated with furious bangs from their neighbour, also revising for Finals, was soon in progress.

'You're a smart punk, Clode, but you fight a little dirty,' Dan said.

'Can you think of a better way?' Mike said, putting the sofa on its feet again.

Dan tucked his fist under Mike's jaw and they smiled at each other. Then he picked up his books and started on his way once more.

'Going to read to Barbara, are you?' Mike said.

Dan feinted to the jaw and nudged Mike in the belly. He raised a finger in amiable warning and went out. Mike grinned and rubbed his belly as though he had had rather a good meal.

IV

The examiners had done their worst; the candidates had done their best. Tripos was over. The results would not appear for a few weeks. Meanwhile there was nothing to do but enjoy oneself, assuming (as the Footlights' naughty lyrics put it) one couldn't find anyone else to enjoy. Mike was on the Ball Committee of his College May Ball and swung a few tickets (£7 a pair to those without influence) so that the cream of the Cambridge theatre would be able to have a last dance on the doomed vessel of their youth.

The College never looked so romantic, though crusty Dons might grumble at the meretricious glitter of fairy lights strung along the bridge and between the marquees where Nat Temple and Cyril Stapleton and Edmundo Ros, either in person, or in delegated bands, entertained the dinner-jacketed undergraduates and their partners. Since there were never enough Newnham and Girton girls to go round, many of the females had come up from London and elsewhere, excited and apprehensive, some of them, since everyone knew what was supposed to happen when the night had worked its magic on adolescent inhibitions, such as they were. For once in a while, it was not a crime to have a girl in your rooms, or in rooms you had borrowed or purloined, should their owners have been kind enough to absent themselves. Meanwhile, to the tune of *The Sunny Side of the Street*, as heard over the wireless from the American Forces Network, and *Slow Boat to China*, more routine appetites were satisfied at the buffet. Rationing was scarcely a distant memory and the prospect of all that food, capped with strawberries and cream, was not the least of the sensual joys of the evening.

'The dress looks terrific, Joycey,' Alan found an opportunity to say. 'Terrific. Straight.'

'You mean you can't actually see me sticking out,' she said.

'Promise,' he said.

'In that case, you almost certainly can,' she said.

'I am looking forward to married life, I must say. Based on mutual trust and affection. It should be a knock-out.'

'No one's forcing you into it,' Joyce said.

They arrived back at the table as the rest of the theatricals were imitating the sentimental tones of the last chorus of the Footlights' May Week Revue, to which they had gone before the Ball. 'How does one do hollow laughter?' Alan said. 'Dan, you're the actor, do you know how to do hollow laughter?'

'Dan is now strictly a *professional* actor,' Mike Clode said. 'He doesn't do hollow laughter unless his contract calls for it. And then only if I think it's the right thing for him to do.'

'Ahahaha,' said Dan.

'Do I detect hollow laughter?' Alan asked.

'I want to do the Valeta,' Barbara said.

'Well,' Alan said, 'I'm sure there must be places one can go.'

'We've come to the Ball and we're jolly well going to dance.'

Mike said: 'Barbara is without doubt the most aggressive as well as the sexiest centre forward in the whole history of Cambridge hockey.'

'Shut up,' she said, 'or I'll break my stick over your head. Daniel, I want to do the Valeta.'

'Cold duck and ice cream is really remarkably good,' Alan said. 'It's an acquired taste, of course – '

'So's sheep-shagging,' Mike said, 'but once you get the hang of it, there's nothing to beat it, I'm told.'

'That's what the sheep say,' Alan said. 'Dan, are you taking up your option on the Valeta or not?'

'It makes me seasick.'

'Barbara, will you do me the honour?' Alan said, rising. 'And failing that, will you do me the Valeta?'

'You're really remarkably civilized tonight, Alan, for you,' Barbara said, as they went towards the music. 'You haven't broken anything, you haven't hit anybody – '

'Six hours to go, Barbara. I'll be amongst the scorers yet.'

Dan said: 'You're sure this is a dinner jacket you borrowed for me, and not a straitjacket, aren't you, Mike?'

'You look very slim and elegant, Dan. Pretend you're a relaxed man of the world. Imitate Noel Coward. God knows everybody else does. Those Footlights! Ham, ham, ham!'

'Who did the shirt belong to?' Dan said. 'It wasn't Nessus by any chance, was it?'

Anna gave a sudden blurt of laughter.

'Ah,' Mike said, 'Anna's woken up. You should have worn your father's old cassock and dog-collar, Daniel. Then you would have been comfortable. Who's Nessus?'

'The shirt of Nessus,' Anna said, 'for God's sake, Mike, surely you know that?'

'I did get it actually,' Mike said.

'You hadn't got the smallest idea what he meant,' Anna said.

'Have some fruit cup or something, Anna,' Mike said. 'With any luck the orange segments might go to your head. Or do you want to come and dance?'

'I thought you'd never ask,' she said, as they went off.

Dan said: 'Aren't you going to eat anything?'

'I seem to have been eating all evening,' Joyce said. They were left alone at the table.

'These occasions are much overrated, aren't they? They're really intended to help spotty young Freddie get freckled young Felicity between the sheets without her ever knowing – '

'Which she probably wouldn't anyway,' Joyce said. 'Do you find it hot in here?'

'In this particular shirt, I'd find it hot anywhere. Do you want to get some air?'

'I hate to be dreary, but I do feel a bit – '

'Fragile? Mind if I bring my strawberries?'

They went out through one set of doors as Mike and Anna returned through another with Alan and Barbara.

'We did two steps – ' Anna said.

' – in different directions – '

'And the music stopped. How was the Valeta?'

'A very worthwhile human experience,' Alan said, 'wasn't it, Barbara?'

'I was swept off my feet.'

'The referee awarded a penalty, you can't ask for more.'

'I wonder where Dan and Joyce've gone.'

'Well,' Mike said, 'they can't have eloped. It's not time yet.'

'Why are we all getting married?' Anna said. 'Has anyone seriously thought about that?'

'Because,' said Mike, 'we've all picked out the brightest and best of the sons and daughters of the morning and we want to make sure of them before we get out into the rough seas beyond the breakwater and someone else tries to make a grab. Speaking purely for myself, of course,' he added, kissing Anna's bare shoulder. Over it, he spotted John Cadman entering the tent. 'John, my dear fellow,' he called, 'come over and try a drop of the smooth, the blushful Hippocrene. It's been a particularly good year for Hippocrene.'

'It's rather a nice ball, don't you think?' Cadman said. He was wearing tails. 'Do you remember my aunt? Marigold . . .'

'Of course. How are you?'

'I was at the first night of your *Much Ado About Nothing*,' Marigold said. 'Tremendous stuff.'

'Barbara,' said Alan Parks, 'I feel this overpowering urge to do another Valeta, but at once, if not sooner – '

'So do I. Isn't it funny? Will you excuse us?'

Cadman said: 'What's the latest on this American tour of yours, Michael?'

'Not too sure at the moment. You've let me down, John, backing out – '

'Unfortunately the Foreign Office insist. I'm being posted to Caracas.'

'Won't he make a funny-looking parcel?' Marigold said.

'I'm sorry?' Mike said. 'Oh. Oh, yes. Posted. Very good. No, you've really rather messed things up. I mean, you know very well you're our best all-weather, all-types-of-wicket actor – '

'You do me too much honour,' Cadman said.

'There's no one to touch you in high comedy. I don't honestly know what's going to happen. We may have to do something in London first just to keep some sort of company together – Seriously, I really feel very let down about America.'

Marigold leant over to Mike. 'I bet you're a really good foxtrotter,' she said, 'am I right?'

'I haven't trotted a fox in years, Aunt Marigold.'

'I was a bronze medallist,' she said. 'If you can believe it.'

Mike stood up and took Marigold's arm, with some gallantry. 'I can believe it very well,' he said.

Cadman drew his chair closer to Anna. 'You know, Anna,' he said, 'I sometimes think you and I really belong together.'

'How very exciting. How often?'

'I once dreamed about you. A very nice dream.'

'Did you really?'

'However, Mike seems to have staked his claim rather decisively.'

'What a nice way you have with words!' Anna said.

'Shall I tell you something rather disgraceful?' Cadman said.

'Oh I wish you would.'

'Marigold isn't really my aunt at all.'

'Not your aunt? That's the most disgraceful thing I have ever heard.'

'She's actually my second cousin.'

'This is outrageous.'

'You're laughing at me.'

'Why on earth do you say she's your aunt if she isn't?'

'To avoid compromising her, of course,' Cadman said. 'You won't tell anyone, will you?'

'But who on earth would care?'

'I do have a certain position in the College,' Cadman said. 'I only told you because – well, I have a very great respect for your intelligence – I knew you'd understand – and after all, it is the truth. You do deserve to know the truth.'

'Thank you,' Anna said, touching his hand for a second.

'In many ways, you see, if things had been different – ' He looked into her eyes. 'I want to ask a favour of you, Anna, something I have no right to ask – May I?'

'Depends what it is,' she said. 'Doesn't it?'

'I wonder if you could possibly spare an afternoon between now and when you – when you go down – to come up to my rooms – I should very much like to show you something.'

'Well,' Anna said, 'I – '

'It's some research I've been doing,' Cadman said, 'into seventeenth-century sermons and – '

'Research into seventeenth-century sermons!' Anna said. 'Of *course* I will.'

'I was really afraid to ask you,' Cadman said.

'You shouldn't have been,' Anna said. 'I can't think of anything nicer we could do together.'

'Do you mean that?'

'Of course I do.'

'You've made me very happy,' Cadman said.

ii

Joyce and Dan were sitting on the bridge. The Cam was purple beneath them, badged with the reflections of coloured lights like angelica.

'I went to this address,' Joyce was saying. 'Some beastly place near the Oval. The cricket ground – I got muddled with the buses – they said a number seven, but it wasn't a seven, it was a number thirty-seven, I think it was, and I was late for this beastly appointment. Then I couldn't find the road. There was a Victoria Road and a Victoria Crescent and then Victoria Avenue was some-where else altogether. I ran and ran – '

'Nightmare,' Dan said.

'Nightmare. I found Victoria Avenue eventually and I thought, well, this is it. I was frightened. I was just so frightened. Sick.'

'He didn't come with you?'

'Alan? I would have had to look after him. I was better

on my own. I thought. Well, I walked along the street –
Avenue – and I know it sounds ridiculous – '

'You saw a pram,' Dan said.

'No, not a pram. Sillier than that. Eight bottles of milk
on a step. I don't know what they were doing there, but
I saw these eight bottles of milk and I started to cry. It
wasn't – it wasn't his house or anything, this – doctor's, I
just saw these bottles and, well – that was it. I turned
round and went back to the bus. Spent the morning in the
National Gallery.'

'Why the National Gallery?'

'The bus went there.'

Dan leaned and kissed her, gently, on the cheek. 'How
does Alan feel about it now?'

'Me still being pregnant? He's taken it quite well, for
him. He's sullen and resigned – really quite pleasant for
him. Oh, he's being all right.'

'I hate to break this up,' Barbara said, coming out of the
darkness.

'As the bull said in the china shop,' Dan said.

'Where's Alan?' Joyce asked.

'The last time I saw him,' Barbara said, 'he was being
taught how to do a chassis reverse by Aunt Marigold.'

'*Eheu, fugaces!*' cried Denis Porson, swooping on them
in a black opera cloak lined with crimson. 'To name but a
few. How goes the festive eve, good friends?'

'I didn't think you were here, Denis,' Barbara said.

'A view taken by many dear lady, yet here I am. Large
as life or so the biologists tell me.'

'You're looking very splendid. Have you got a partner?'

'I'm looking for a paratrooper, but the buffet doesn't
seem to stock them. I am, as they say, passing through.
Since this is, after all, my college – at least until Wednesday of next week – I thought I would don me duds and
enjoy the amenities. Are you going to the cabaret? They've
got this brilliant young man who does Bertrand Russell

singing *La Traviata* with Dame Nellie Melba. Apparently it's extremely droll, especially if you were at the original performance. He also impersonates the days of the week. I'm dying to see his Friday. I'm told it's a hoot.'

'Denis, you're a bitch,' Joyce said.

'So I am. Shall we dance?' He hooked his arm in hers and levered her from the bridge.

'I'd sooner see the cabaret,' she said, as they went towards the appropriate marquee.

'The story of my life!' Denis lamented.

Barbara said: 'Do you want to see the cabaret?'

'Not much,' Dan said, 'but if you do –'

'I'd sooner see you,' she said. '*I* thought as everyone else was going to be giggling themselves silly we might go up to your rooms and make our own entertainment. What do you say?'

Dan said: 'I'm at your service. As always.'

'Always is when I like it,' Barbara said.

iii

The cabaret comedian had imitated most of the programmes then current on the wireless and television and ended with Bertrand Russell singing 'I'm Looking Over a Four-leaf Clover' while dancing the Can-can.

Barbara and Dan came in during his final fling.

'Don't tell me we've missed it,' Barbara said.

'Where the hell have you been?' Alan said. 'Of course you've missed it.'

'I felt a little faint.'

'Better now?'

'Like new.'

'In that case, may I offer you a touch of the light fantastic?'

'Ay don't maind if ay do,' Barbara said. Joyce watched them go.

Dan said: 'Are you dancing?'

'Not particularly,' Joyce said.

Denis Porson gathered his cloak about him. 'I think I shall hie me to my lonely bed,' he said, 'since nobody else's is available. Goodnight, Aunt Marigold – goodnight, Sir John. Next time I'm in Caracas, I shall be up to the embassy for a baked-bean sandwich like a shot.'

'Goodnight, Denis,' Barbara called.

'Your servant, ma'am,' Denis said. 'She should be so lucky!'

'Poor Denis,' Anna said. 'What's the latest about America?'

'Looks bad,' Mike said. 'I told you. Too many people peeling off.'

'Because he can be wonderful.'

'I don't want particularly to have people like Denis round my neck forever.'

'What about his Malvolio though? Wasn't it marvellous?'

'Marvellous. In a Cambridge context. Let's dance. What we need to kick off with is a West End production. Professional through and through. Forget Cambridge.' They went past where Dan and Joyce were standing by a bowl of strawberries, talking and helping themselves.

iv

Denis turned the light on in his room and there was an alarmed sound from the bedroom. He opened the door and saw two startled faces looking at him from his own pillow. 'Out,' Denis said.

'Gosh, I'm sorry, I – '

'Out! Or are you not aware of the consequences of *lèse-majesté*?'

'Sorry?'

'Clean living is the only safeguard. Out. And never – *never* – darken my sheets again.'

'You said he wasn't here,' the girl said, pulling up her dress. 'You said – '

'He wasn't – '

'Take your rose with her pathetically bedraggled petals and begone this instant,' Denis said, 'both of you, before I give you in charge.'

'Look, I'm terribly sorry about this – '

The girl said: 'You're behaving exactly like Mummy said you'd behave – '

'Mummy is a very perceptive lady,' Denis said. 'Kindly go back to the dance floor and say ha ha to the trumpet with my personal compliments. At once.'

'Mummy said it would be like this,' the girl said, 'and that's exactly what it's like.'

'That's a bit of a tautology actually, if you don't mind my saying,' her partner said, as they scampered from the room. 'Pompous old pansy,' the young man shouted, when they were clear.

'Old!' Denis said to his reflection. 'How dare she?' He straightened the covers with infinite disgust. 'I'm sorry about this, your Grace,' he said at last. 'That's all right, Banks. Don't let it happen again.' Denis bowed to himself. 'No, your Grace. Will that be all, your Grace?' He looked round the room and nodded. 'Yes, thank you, Banks. Goodnight.'

v

'This is the life.' Mike held a match to the cigar he had just given Dan and then lit his own. 'Isn't Barbara looking marvellous tonight?' he said.

'Isn't she though?' Dan said. 'She really is.'

'Lucky sod you are.'

'Mike,' Dan said, 'I've been thinking.'

'Tell me.'

'I'm not going to be an actor.'

'Stars don't have to act,' Mike said, making important smoke. 'Just twinkle. Not going to be an actor?'

'We were never ever really going to America, were we, Mike? Broadway – '

'America! I wish the place had never been invented. I really did hope for Boston, but it just didn't come off.'

'You just said all that to get John Cadman off your back over the money business, didn't you?'

'Dan, you can be a bit of a bore over things,' Mike said. 'You're a great bloke and you can be a bit of a bore over things.'

Dan grinned. Mike grinned back and that was when Dan punched him, hard, in the stomach. Mike looked at him for a moment with agonized astonishment, and then sat heavily in the fruit salad. 'Steady, Daniel,' he said, 'over-acting now – ' He stood up, panting with pain and self-control. 'Easy, pardner, or you might do some damage you can't repair.' He grinned. Dan grinned and hit him again, same place. Mike fell back, but this time he grabbed a bowl of strawberries and flung the whole thing in Dan's face. 'What the *hell's* got into you?'

'Hey, what are we missing?' Alan Parks said. 'It seems to be cabaret time.'

'Everything's fine,' Mike said. 'Everything's under control.'

'Mike and I were just saying goodbye,' Dan said.

Barbara looked at him. He had strawberries stuck to his shirt front. 'Dan, are you drunk?'

'No,' Dan said. 'I've simply changed my mind about something, that's all.'

'I'll leave him to you, darling,' Mike said. 'If anyone can bring him to his senses, you can.' He went quickly, tight-mouthed, to the door where Anna and John Cadman were standing.

'What I feel about Donne,' Anna was saying, 'is that you can never really understand him unless you compare him with St John of the Cross – '

'Exactly right,' Cadman said, 'exactly right – and how few people see it!'

''Ullo,' Anna said. Mike gave her a bleak look and walked straight out of the marquee.

'Did you actually *hit* him?' Barbara was saying.

'Yes,' Dan said. 'Actually I did.'

'What's the matter with you?'

'With *me*?'

'Hitting Mike.'

'What's wrong with hitting Mike?' Dan said. 'He isn't God. Is he?'

'Is he upset?'

'You'd better ask him,' Dan said.

'What's the shindig all about?' Alan said. 'Anything I can make a bit worse?'

'Leave this to me, Alan, will you please,' Barbara said.

'On the word of command!' Alan saluted and turned away. 'Ah, Joycey, perhaps you can explain – '

'Alan, there's something I've got to say to you,' Joyce said.

'My fly buttons are undone? Sorry, but it sounded as if that was what it was! What's the matter?'

'Dan, I love you,' Barbara said. 'Don't you realize – ?'

'Barbara, I want you to understand one thing,' Dan said, gently. 'I want to lead a very dull life. The dullest possible.'

'But what *for*?' she said. 'After all Mike's done, surely the least you can do is – '

'I want to lead a quiet life,' Dan said. 'A life of complete ordinariness.' He stubbed his cigar in a saucer of melted ice cream. 'I don't want to see my name in lights. I don't particularly want to see *anything* in lights. I want to live a very dull, ordinary, commonplace life.'

'What *have* you been eating?'

'The fatted calf,' Dan said, 'and I think I've had enough. I want to have a home and children and – '

'And what about me?'

'In what way?'

'In what way? In what way? We were – we were – what were we doing up in your rooms about twenty minutes ago?'

'What you wanted,' Dan said. 'Weren't we?'

Barbara said: 'You *have* been thinking, haven't you?'

'That's right,' Dan said.

'A quiet life.'

'Is what I want.'

'And how do you know I don't?'

'You don't,' he said. 'And anyway, it doesn't matter.'

'I want to have children too, if it comes to that. Doesn't *matter*?'

'I'm going to marry Joyce,' Dan said.

vi

'I don't believe it,' Alan said.

'There's no law against it,' Joyce said. 'People are still allowed to marry each other.'

'You're going to marry me,' Alan said.

'No, I'm not,' she said. 'You don't want me to. I don't want to. And I'm not.'

'It's my child,' Alan said. 'It's my child.'

'Predictable. Isn't that what you said? "Why does every-thing have to be so bloody predictable?" Well, here's something you didn't predict. Aren't you pleased?'

'It's my child,' Alan said.

'You don't want to spend your life with me,' Joyce said, 'so why pretend?'

'And I thought we were going to have a terrific evening.'

'You still can,' she said. 'There are several hours left.'

'I'll kill that bastard.'

'You'll have to creep up on him,' Joyce said. 'He's quite strong.'

'Then I'll creep up on him,' Alan said. 'Joycey – '

'You're such a humbug,' she said, taking his hand.

'Do you love him?'

'Yes,' she said. 'Why shouldn't I love him?'

'He was shagging Barbara during the cabaret, do you know that?' Alan said. 'They went up to his rooms and they were having a right old shag. Are you aware of that?'

'Aren't you pitiful sometimes?'

'And you say he loves you!'

'Conventional as they come underneath, aren't you?'

'It's my child, woman.'

'Alan, Dan and I are going to get married,' Joyce said. 'The child's mine. You gave me the right to flush it down the lav. I decided to keep it. It's mine.'

'Dan! Of all people. When did it happen? How long's this been going on?'

'About an hour or so,' Joyce said. 'Since we neither of us wanted to dance.'

'That long!' Alan said. 'And you're going to marry him? Is that really what you want?'

'It's what we both want,' Joyce said. 'We suddenly discovered – '

'Nothing like sudden discoveries when you're playing pirates,' Alan said. 'Come on, Joycey, be honest for once – is it worth it? Just to hurt us? Is it?'

'Us?' Joyce said.

'Barbara and me. Oh come on – '

'We never mentioned you and Barbara. You never occurred to us,' Joyce said. 'Dan makes me feel like a grown-up, Alan. That's what it's all about.'

Alan said: 'Will I ever be able to see it? The kid.'

'I don't know,' she said.

'Because I'd like to.'

'I don't know.'

'Is that very childish of me?'

She shook her head. In the light of the coloured bulbs, her eyes were now starred with tinted tears.

'Be happy,' Alan said. 'You're probably quite right.' She walked quickly away. He loved that tight behind of hers. 'Bitch,' he said.

vii

'Are you terribly upset?' Anna said, her arms round Mike's waist.

'About Dan?' Mike shook his head. 'The thing about Dan, finally, was that, in spite of everything – and God knows he knew how to move – he didn't always get the chat quite right – there was something just slightly amateur about him – here!' He pointed to the corner of his mouth. 'There was a muscle somewhere in there he couldn't control. He probably recognized that himself deep down somewhere.'

'Will it matter?'

'Dan? To us?' He shook his head. 'I believe in travelling light. Deep down Dan was always disloyal to me. He knew how much he owed me. That never helped anybody.' Anna snuggled against his chest. He was wearing black pearl evening studs. Mike grinned over her shoulder at John Cadman, ashen with exhaustion as the indefatigable Marigold whirled him into his third straight quickstep.

viii

Dan threw the soiled dinner jacket and trousers on the sofa. He had put on a pair of corduroy bags, a turtle-necked sweater and a donkey jacket. Joyce had changed for the ball in town and had an overnight bag already packed.

'So much for the shirt of Nessus!' Dan took both her hands in his. 'Came the dawn,' he said.

'Are we mad, do you think?' Joyce said.

'Sane,' he said. 'Sane.'

ix

Barbara and Alan were leaning against the buffet, playing slow draughts with the spilled strawberries and eating their captures. 'He must have been out of his mind,' Alan said. 'Christ, from where I sit – '

'He wanted a quiet life,' Barbara said.

'Out of his mind,' Alan said.

'I don't know,' she said, sipping old champagne, 'I want to do things.'

'And you're just the kind of thing I want to do,' Alan said.

'Go to Paris and places,' she said. 'Live a little.'

'And First Class, am I not right?'

'Hullo,' Marigold said. 'What a splendid evening it's been, hasn't it? I've danced my feet off and I'm still full of beans.' She waved gay fingers and waltzed – one, two, three – over to where Anna was asleep on Mike's lap. Mike was not asleep, but he closed his eyes as Marigold approached. 'Not dancing?' she said. 'Don't tell me you're tired!'

Alan looked at Barbara with earnest severity. 'You have beautiful breasts,' he said. 'I've been looking at them.'

'Thank you,' she said.

'Thank *you*,' he said, and popped the last strawberry between his lips. She giggled and leaned forward and bit it and left her mouth there.

John Cadman cocked an eyebrow. 'A Mike Clode Production?' he asked.

Mike shook his tired old head, but the gleam in his eye said 'could be'. He was not a man to refuse the credit for anything.

V

'There you are then,' Mike said. 'What did I tell you, darling? You've got your First.'

'*Starred* First,' Anna said. 'We must be accurate.'

'I knew I should never have done that sodding production of *Much Ado*,' Mike said.

'What's wrong with a 2.1?' Anna said.

'Nothing a First wouldn't put right,' Mike said. 'Well, I'm not standing here looking at the bloody results all day or someone'll come along and ask me what I got.'

'I think I'll hang around,' Anna said, 'in that case.'

'In that case,' Mike said, 'bang goes your lift to London.'

'Coming,' Anna said. 'Well, at least Dan got something. A third's not all that bad.'

'Enough to get him into ICI as a pen-pusher,' Mike said, clambering into the green MG. 'Quiet life. He'll have one of those all right.' Mike made a lot of noise accelerating down King's Parade. 'I hope you and Bruno get on OK. He's a bit of a hoot, of course, but he can get things done.'

'If you want me to like him,' Anna said, 'I'll like him.'

'London isn't Cambridge,' Mike said.

'I know,' Anna said. 'Pity.'

ii

'Mr and Mrs Adam Morris have moved into their smart new Chelsea home,' Adam said. 'Unfortunately the last tenants, a Mr and Mrs Cockroach, have not yet moved out. Always marry a Jew if you want the big life, Mrs Morris, diamonds, champagne, basement flats, cockroaches – '

'This is the last time,' Barbara said, 'that I propose to laugh at that particular joke. Ever. Ever, ever, ever.'

'Pity, because it's unlikely to be the last time I ever make it,' Adam said.

'Any more paint in your tin?'

'A mouthful.'

'Then drink it,' Barbara said.

'My love,' Adam said.

'Because I am *not* going to be your private detachment of the Arab Legion, so you can just stop sniping, OK?'

'Thanks to you,' Adam said, 'my family doesn't talk to me any more. You can't be all bad.'

'They'll come round,' she said. 'In due course – '

'We are *not* having any grand-children,' Adam said. 'You may be old enough; I'm not.'

'We shall have to eventually.'

'Right,' Adam said, 'and that'll be quite soon enough.'

There was a ring at the bell.

'Grief. A visitor. A *visitor*. Ba, our first visitor. Aren't you going to say something?'

'Probably a wrong number,' Barbara said.

'Denis!' Adam said. 'This is an outrageous intrusion. I've sent the red carpet to be cleaned. How are we going to get you in? Darling, it's Denis.'

'Hullo, Denis.'

'Hullo, Bra dear,' Denis said. 'How are you? Bearing up?'

'To what do we owe the pleasure?' Adam said. 'Sit down. There's no extra charge.'

'Connubial bliss. I trust. I'm sorry to bust in – '

'Something wrong?' Barbara said.

'It is a bit,' Denis said.

'You are looking a bit white,' Adam said. 'You haven't gone and got yourself pregnant again, Denis, have you?'

'It's the dicks,' Denis said.

'Sorry?'

'The *Polizei*.'

'Christ,' Adam said.

'He pretended to be,' Denis said, 'but he wasn't.'

'When was this? What happened?'

'I was at a party which turned out to be rather enjoyable at the time, but unfortunately . . .'

'You bloody fool.'

'More than like,' Denis said. 'However, we don't all have your advantages.'

Barbara said: 'Do you want a Scotch, Denis?'

'I don't know how you guessed, dear.'

'Have they charged you with anything?' Adam said. 'Have you got a solicitor?'

'I haven't got anything, dear.'

'You haven't *admitted* anything, have you?'

'There were witnesses. One of the Guardsmen spilled the beans. Messy.'

'You must have a solicitor.'

'I've got no mun, dear, either. Your friend Denis Porson is *emmerdé jusqu'au bout*. If not further.'

'I'll call my father,' Adam said. 'He knows people. What about your family? Surely with your connections . . .?'

'Ducky, ducky, ducky!' Denis said. 'My family . . .'

'Look, I'm going to call my father.'

'They'll send me to the galleys, dears,' Denis said. 'I know they will. Unless I die while the jury's out. Which won't give me a lot of time, I shouldn't imagine.'

'Denis,' Adam said. 'You ass. You *ass*.'

'Have you ever been lonely?' Denis said.

'Are you going to call your father?' Barbara said. 'Because if you are, you'd better.'

'On my way,' Adam said. The phone was on the floor in the hallway.

'God, I was happy in Cambridge, Bra.'

'I know.'

'Lotus-time, dear. A three-year lease on paradise. Time's up. Nowhere to go.'

'You should've come to see us,' Barbara said.

'I know, but – well, perhaps they'll slap my wrist and

tell me not to be naughty again. They won't. Mavis never does. Not Mavis.'

'Shall we come with you to – to wherever you're going? The station.'

'And see me off?' Denis said. 'Pet, would you?'

iii

The blonde secretary with the drying fingernails put her head round the door of Bruno Lazlo's office. 'He'll be ten minutes longer,' she said, 'and then he'll be right there.'

'For the third time,' Anna said.

'Well, at least it's given you a chance to look at the script. Rather tactful of the old villain. What do you think?'

'You can't possibly do it,' Anna said.

'I can if you can,' Mike said.

'I can't. She's American for a start.'

'You did an American in *Desire under the Elms*.'

'That was a Classic,' Anna said. 'This is garbage.'

'It's garbage,' Mike said, 'that's going on in London. It's a foot in the door.'

'It's a foot in the mouth,' Anna said. 'Look, I've really got to go. I said I'd see Helen Hoby at the B.M. at three.'

'Helen Hoby knows how to use the Reading Room without your help,' Mike said. 'These little old lady dons are tough as old boots.'

'I promised,' Anna said. 'You do know it's garbage, don't you?'

'It's a light comedy,' Mike said. 'It doesn't pretend to be anything else.'

'It better hadn't,' Anna said. 'Look, you can handle Mr Lazlo without me. I only embarrass him. Anything you decide – '

'Comedies can still say something sometimes,' Mike said.

'Of course they can,' Anna said. 'Only not this time.'

'What're you going to wear to this party tonight?' Mike said.

'What I've got on, I thought. And me new tits.'

'Only some people may be – you know – dressed up,' Mike said.

'I'll see you this evening,' Anna said. 'O K?' She walked to the door.

'What's the matter?' Mike called.

'Matter? Nothing.'

'Only you're walking rather strangely.'

'No different from usual,' Anna said.

'It suddenly struck me. Slightly . . . Listen, I'll see you tonight. Six-thirty at the flat, O K?'

'I'll be there,' Anna said. 'You don't mind me buggering off, do you?'

'Not if that's what you want to do,' he said.

Bruno came in a couple of minutes later. 'So sorry. Am I late?'

'I made myself at home,' Mike said, from behind Bruno's desk.

'Terrible traffic, I must say. I saw your fiancée on the stairs.'

'She had to go to the British Museum.'

'Very intelligent,' Bruno said. 'I must say. Did you give her the play to read?'

'She didn't think much of it. I have to be honest.'

'She's got excellent taste. The play is a vehicle, that's all. For the girl.'

'Which Anna doesn't really think she can do.'

'I admire her intelligence very much,' Bruno said. 'She could never do it.'

'Which leaves us where?'

'We need a star. Not a big star. But a personality. We need a personality. Which is why I want you to meet Jill.'

'You don't think Anna could do the girl-friend perhaps?' Mike said.

'A dumb blonde? Your fiancée? I must say I think it would be an insult.'

The intercom buzzed. 'Miss Peterson is here, Mr Lazlo.'

'Ask her please to come in.' Bruno squeezed Mike's shoulder. 'You tell me honestly what you think.' He went to the door and took both Jill Peterson's hands in his. Mike stood up and burst out laughing.

'Knockout,' he said. 'I'm sorry, but sometimes – '

'You see what I mean?' Bruno said. 'Jill, how are you? How was the journey?'

'From Claridge's?' the girl said. 'A little dull. You have to be Mike Clode. Am I glad to meet you!'

'If only because you've heard so little about me, I know.'

'Bruno thinks you're Jesus Christ.'

'Rumours, rumours! I've admired you for a long time.'

'Not *too* long, I hope.'

'Seriously. From afar. There's nowhere further than where I've admired you from.'

'Well, here we are!' she said. 'Bruno, I read the play. I think it's a bunny. I really do. Don't you, Mr Clode?'

'With the right casting,' Mike said. 'Especially with the right Tina Hernandez. Someone like – say – Jill Peterson, if we could ever get her – '

'I like him,' Jill said. 'He's so forthright.'

'He can be a bastard as well, I promise you.'

'I hope so. Am I really going to take a bath on stage?'

'It's an essential part of the plot, don't you think?'

'Oh but I do, absolutely.'

'Look,' Bruno said, 'I have to make a couple of calls in the other office. I leave you two to discuss the psychological motivation.'

Mike and Jill sat with the script unopened between them. 'I'd like to talk just sort of generally,' Mike said. 'If that's all right with you. Getting-to-know-you time.'

'Can't wait,' she said, crossing her long American legs.

'I fought and fought,' Mike said. 'I fought like hell. I was all set to walk out. I actually *did* walk out at one point.'

'And then you walked in again,' Anna said, 'right?'

'If it had been my personal decision, I would have said I wouldn't do it unless you did.'

'I *couldn't* do it,' Anna said.

'That's the point,' Mike said. 'You know and I know that nothing could be more catastrophic than to have you in something that wasn't you and then went phut.'

'You never stop thinking about me, do you?' Anna said, unzipping her new dress.

'What's going on?' Mike said.

She reached in and pulled her padded bra out of her neckline and threw her warm new tits at Mike. 'At least I won't be needing these any more, will I?' she said.

'Anna, you said yourself – '

'I did indeed. And I meant it. I meant it. I really meant it.'

'How was Helen Hoby?'

'She was lovely,' Anna said. 'She's researching into the influence of Peter Ramus on English educational theory after 1688. Fascinating.'

'Sounds it,' Mike said, tying his black tie. 'Sounds it. Anna, listen, if you want me to give up the play, I will. If you want me not to do it, I certainly won't.'

'Of course you're going to do it.'

'Could you possibly play the girl-friend, do you think?'

'No, and don't worry about it. I'll be fine. You're going to be late for the party.'

'You're right,' he said, 'we'd better go.'

'I'm not coming,' she said. 'Don't be silly.'

'Not coming? Bruno expects you. He'll be disappointed.'

'Disappointed! I've told him all I know about Verlaine

and he's told me all I ever need to know about Real Madrid. I think we've given each other all we can.'

'Anna, we're going to be late.'

'You don't need me,' Anna said. 'You've got a girl, for the play. It's garbage, but you'll do it well and it'll be a big hit. Lovely. And there'll be six girls wanting to be in the next one. And a dozen the time after that.'

'I need you.'

'I'd sooner go and help Helen Hoby prepare her material for the Third Programme. I shall enjoy that. She's doing a four-part programme on early English printed books.'

'They'll be queueing round the block,' Mike said. 'Are you *serious*?'

'Goodbye, Mike.'

'I thought you loved me,' he said.

'Even if you don't respect my intelligence as much as you say you do,' Anna said, 'at least don't assume I'm a complete fool.'

'You realize you're breaking my heart?' he said. 'You realize that, don't you?'

'Poor Mike,' Anna said. 'Take it to wardrobe. They'll put a stitch in it for you in no time.'

She went into the bedroom and shut the door. He stood there, gazing in the mirror at his grief-ravaged face with a certain interest. He put Anna's falsies on the table, sighed, sighed again and then shrugged and looked at his watch. If he went now, he'd get to the party just about twenty-five minutes after it had started. Everything was working out rather well.

VI

'What do you think?' Adam said. He was doing a mural, in pastels, on a section of white wall. Barbara was laying four places at the new round table they had bought from

Heal's with some money he had got for editing the manu-
script of an Admiral whose many medals did not, luckily,
include one for punctuation. 'The roofs aren't bad, are
they?'

'San Gimignano, I presume,' Barbara said.

'San Jim,' Adam said. 'Let's not exaggerate. It isn't
finished yet.' He caught Barbara's arm and turned her to
face him. 'It isn't necessarily the end,' he said. 'He can still
appeal.'

'You know it won't make any difference,' she said. 'I
hate them. That judge. That prosecutor.'

'Prosecuting counsel,' Adam said. 'Dry as that sod in
Catullus who shits pebbles. Denis Porson, what harm did
he ever do anyone?'

'I don't think I ever felt less like having people to dinner.'

'We did everything we could,' Adam said.

'Which was nothing.'

'What could we do? As the Germans said when their
neighbours were taken away. Change the world? I will if
you will.'

'We should've said he was here with us.'

'He'd already admitted it.'

'I *hate* them.'

'And I love you. For being so – so *right*, you know?' He
kissed her. 'By the way, have you read what I wrote today?'

'I've been cooking,' she said, 'and – '

'I know. Only it's there.'

The door bell rang. Barbara was appalled. 'They're
early.'

'I did say any time.'

'But they're early. You'll have to entertain them – it's
only seven-fifteen!'

'I'll get the sherry. Don't worry – ' The bell rang again.
Barbara ran into the bedroom, while Adam opened the
door. 'Anna!' he said. 'You found it.'

'We had to ask three times,' Anna said. 'You know Ken, don't you?'

'Ho-hoy,' said Ken Hobbs. 'Hullo-ee, how are yee?'

'I am very well, my Captain,' said Adam.

'Ann,' Barbara said, as she came to meet them, 'how nice.'

'Ann*a*,' Adam said.

'Here we are then,' Anna said. 'Do you know me husband, Ken?'

'Hullo,' Barbara said. 'I don't think I do.'

'It's a great pleasure to meet you,' Ken said.

'The correct Old Benedictine in person,' Adam said.

'Congratulations,' Barbara said.

'Oh yes,' Ken said, 'thanks. Sorry you couldn't come to the wedding. Bit of a rush job.'

'That's life, isn't it?' Barbara said.

'Talking of which – ' Anna was holding up the evening paper. There was a big picture of Jill Peterson and Mike Clode coming out of a register office under a white hail of pelted good wishes. The caption read: GOING PLACES. 'So,' Anna said, 'that takes care of everybody's sex life, roughly, doesn't it?'

'Denis Porson got two years,' Adam said. 'Talking of that.'

'And we've got life!' Ken said. 'Maybe he got off lightly.'

'We were very fond of him,' Barbara said.

'Ken, I *love* you,' Anna said. 'I've got a job with the BBC, did I tell you? On the permanent strength. And Ken's my permanent weakness, so there we are, all taken care of!'

'Clever Anna,' Adam said. 'But then you are, aren't you?'

Barbara said: 'Are you going to do the sherry, Ad?'

'Sherry, yes, absolutely. Everyone?'

'I'm so glad I've got you,' Anna said, hanging round Ken's neck. 'He loves me.'

'What are you doing these days, Adamovich?' Ken said.

'Ghosting the memoirs of the dullest Admiral who ever lived and, on the intellectual side, I'm doing introductions for Doris Day's programme on Radio Luxemburg. The big time. Oh, and a novel for light relief.'

'Well, here's to it. A rosy future.'

'Joyce had a little boy,' Anna said. 'Did you hear?'

'Everybody's doing it,' Ken said.

'Are they?' Adam said.

'Or trying,' Anna said. 'I'm going to have eight.'

'Here's to them,' Barbara said, raising her glass.

'Happy days,' Ken said.

'Here's to going places,' Adam said, mostly to Anna.

'Yes indeed!' Barbara drained her sherry and went towards the kitchen. 'Food in five minutes, children,' she said.

A
Past
Life

In the early summer of 1961, Lionel Morris had a hernia operation. He had scarcely spoken to his son since Adam's marriage over five years before. Adam had spoken quite frequently to his mother, but the silence between him and his father grew longer and longer, without either of them ever quite acknowledging its length or admitting that he wished that it would end. When his mother telephoned to tell Adam of the operation, he was almost glad. He was worried, he was concerned, but he was almost glad. He did not want to go and see his father, but he was glad to be able to go, armed with a good excuse, a bunch of grapes and an advance copy of his new novel. He hesitated outside the door of his father's hospital room, hearing within a familiar voice, that of Olive Wise, the mother of his first serious girl friend, Sheila.

'Two years,' she was saying, 'they told me there was nothing the matter. I went to every doctor in London. I went to Johnny – he says rest; I went to a man in Harley Street – more rest; I went to a man Harry heard about, in Devonshire Place – he had a brilliant idea: maybe I should get some rest. It got so I turned over in bed, I thought I was overdoing things. The end of that year, I worked it out with Harry, I'd been on my back twenty-two weeks. Twenty-two weeks. I thought he was going to leave me. I wouldn't have blamed him. What use is a wife to a man, when she's on her back?'

'Hullo, Dad,' Adam said. 'Hullo, Mrs Wise, how are you?'

'Adam!' Mrs Wise said. 'I don't believe it. He's a man.'

'Yes,' Lionel said.

'And married I hear?'

Adam looked at his father. 'Yes,' he said, 'I'm married.'

'And where are you living?'

'Holland Park,' Adam said. 'Well, Shepherds Bush, really.'

'You've got your own house?'

'We have our own very small flat.'

'Only I have to have all the news to tell Sheila.'

'How is Sheila?'

'Happy! I can't tell you how happy. Married to a wonderful man; can't do enough for her, thinks the world of her. They've just moved into a beautiful house, not too far from me, between Mill Hill and Hendon.'

'And you're a grandmother?'

'Only twice over,' Mrs Wise said. 'James and now Emma Kate. And her husband's just been made a joint managing director, thirty-two years of age and he's a joint managing director.'

'How is it, Dad?'

'Not too bad,' Lionel said.

'Lionel, it's been so nice seeing you.' She went and kissed him and helped herself to a peach. 'I wish I could stay, but I can't – I said it'd have to be a flying visit, I've got a function Wednesday. I haven't ordered a thing.' She looked up at Adam. 'Do you support Israel?'

'I have quite enough trouble trying to support myself at the moment,' Adam said.

'You should. They're doing wonderful things out there. So anyway, Lionel, lots of love to Estelle – I sent her a card about Wednesday, so tell her no excuses – and as soon as you're out, we'll have to have a partnership. The cards I've been holding, count your blessings you're in hospital, but anyway – I must go.' She put the peach stone in the ashtray. 'Don't eat too much fruit all at once, the first day or two, Lionel; remember – easy does it. No unnecessary pressure on the bowel before you're ready. Any message for Sheila, Adam?'

'Well, give her my love.'

'A married man! Lionel, that surgeon of yours must be a very clever man. You look wonderful. Don't tire your father now, Adam.'

She went out. It was a relief for Adam and his father to have something in common to smile at.

'I didn't know there *was* anything between Hendon and Mill Hill,' Adam said.

'She's inclined to be what Gerald Gerson would call "a rather talkative witness".'

'Anyway I brought you these,' Adam held out the bag of grapes. 'And also my book.'

'*A Promised Land.* They've done it nicely.'

'We shall have to see what the critics say. If anything.'

'I'm sure they'll like it very much.'

'I'm not sure you will,' Adam said.

'We shall have to see,' Lionel said.

'It's been a long time,' Adam said.

'Yes. Yes, it has.'

'I've wanted to see you, several times, but – '

'Adam, I think I'll have one of those grapes of yours, if – '

Adam took the grapes to the basin and washed them under the tap.

'How – how's your wife?' Lionel said, over the sound of the running water.

'She's fine. She's fine. She hopes you're better.'

'Under the anaesthetic – '

'What?'

'I dreamt she came to see me.' He smiled. 'Not, of course, at my invitation.' He took one of the grapes. 'Anyway, she's made you happy?'

'I understood how you felt,' Adam said. 'I didn't like it, but I understood it. We both did.'

'Tell me, what did they pay you for the book?'

'That's my business.'

'And how's business?'

'Don't ask. The old jokes are the best, eh?'

'Well, they're certainly the oldest,' Lionel said. 'Your wife's working, I gather.'

'Yes, she's working.'

'She's a very tiresome woman,' Lionel said. 'Olive Wise. She's a very tiresome woman indeed. An unnecessary pressure on the bowel.'

'Yes. I hate all that.'

'All what?'

'All that.'

Lionel frowned. 'So do I,' he said. 'Adam, when I'm out of here, you must – you must come to dinner. Both of you, I mean.'

'You'll like her, you know. Barbara. If you let yourself.'

'I don't doubt it. She doesn't mind eating our sort of food? If you come to dinner.'

'I do,' Adam said, 'she doesn't. You still really believe it's all crucially important, do you? What we eat, who we marry?'

'I don't think it matters all that much whom we marry.'

'But what we eat!'

'Let me have another one of those grapes,' Lionel said. 'Adam, I never wanted it to happen,' he said, 'what happened.'

'You made that very clear.'

'Not – the marriage,' Lionel said, 'the rift.'

'The rift,' Adam said.

'Never. I – occasioned it, I recognize that; of course. But I never wanted it.'

'You always were a great one for tradition,' Adam said. 'Dad, um, look – I've got something to tell you.'

'Have I guessed?'

'Probably. We shan't be calling it Emma Kate, I can promise you that.'

'Or Moishe, I presume.'

'Or Moishe, you presume.'

'When – when is this likely to happen?'

'December roughly,' Adam said. 'Around the 25th. First Coming, Second Coming, what does it matter as long as it's the Messiah? I don't know exactly. Months yet anyway.'

'What will you do when she can't work any more, your wife?'

'Dad, her name's Barbara, OK? I shall do some ghosting or a bit of TV or something. If I'm lucky! I do earn a bit, you know, on my own. We shall survive.'

'Have you told your mother the news?'

'I thought *you* could.'

'Get her to phone mummy,' Lionel said. 'Get – Barbara.'

ii

Adam got into the lift with a woman who was crying. Tears were running down her cheeks. She made no effort to staunch or dry them. They dripped onto her polka-dotted dress. Some of them fell on the modernized floor of the lift. Adam watched her, kindly, with observant pity. At the second floor, they were joined by another visitor to the hospital. He shot Adam a sharp glance, to which Adam replied with another of the same.

'I thought it was you,' Alan Parks said.

'I thought it was you.'

'And it was,' Alan said. 'Someone was talking about you only the other day.' He pointed accusingly. 'You've written a book.'

'I heard someone talking about you as a matter of fact,' Adam said.

'Nothing good, I trust?'

'No, no; you don't have to worry! Bitch, bitch, bitch.' They reached the ground floor and waited politely for the weeping lady to leave the lift first. 'My father's just had an operation,' Adam said.

'Don't expect too much sympathy from me, mate, my wife's just had twins. Are you married?'

'Yes, I am.'

'What a lot of bloody fools!' Alan said. 'A generation of bloody fools, that's what we were. Into bed and pull the sheets over our heads, quick as buggery and probably a lot less fun. Twins. Talk about getting a pair in your first test! Any kids?'

'Not yet,' Adam said.

'Keep it that way is my advice. The look on her face! Triumph. "I've got you now!" written all over it in letters of fire. Kid on each tit. Come and have a drink.'

'Well – why not? To celebrate your misfortune.'

'What else are friends for?' Alan said.

iii

'Cheers,' Adam said.

'And jeers to you,' Alan said. 'You know the biggest disaster to hit this country in the present century?'

'How many guesses?' Adam said. 'Neville Chamberlain? Ramsay MacDonald? *Not* Cyril Stapleton and the Squadronnaires?'

'Winston Churchill.'

'Winston Churchill,' Adam said. 'Of course! What the hell are you talking about?'

'The biggest disaster to hit this country in the present century.'

'Are we thinking of the same man – shortish bloke, a trifle on the stout side, smoked a cigar, inclined to make a certain gesture with the right hand – ?'

124

'Quit the Cambridge crap,' Alan said. 'Winston Spencer Churchill. He persuaded the British they were still the tops, they still knew how to do things, they still stood for everything that was good and right and decent. Freedom, democracy, humanity. You liked Cambridge, didn't you?'

'Yes. Didn't you?'

'It's all a con, sonny. This whole country is a con. The best thing that could have happened to it is if we'd lost the war. I'm going to do a new series at the BBC.'

'On what a good thing it would have been if we'd lost the war?'

'Fleet Street's finished. There are still some pickings, but I've got all there is to get out of newspapers. The box is the thing. They're putting me in as editor of this new current affairs set-up. You ought to do something for us.'

'I thought you'd never ask,' Adam said.

'I want to go in with a few ideas. Anything you like.'

'A thousand words on anything you like – I can never think of a thing. I'll tell you one person I am interested in. They'll never do it though.'

'I *am* them,' Alan said. 'As of next month anyway.'

'That's Stephen Taylor,' Adam said.

'Christ Almighty! Why Stephen Taylor?'

'Why?' Adam said. 'Because I really want to tear him to pieces. Why else? You wouldn't allow that though, would you?'

'Not allow it?' Alan said. 'You're making my mouth water. If I can have someone torn to pieces once a week in front of ten million mindless moggies, my friend, I shall have the world at my feet and I can't think of a better place for it.'

'Did you know the BBC still rehearse in one of the buildings Stephen Taylor designed?'

'We'll make them pull the bugger down,' Alan said. 'Before our very cameras. There isn't going to be a lot of money in it, old son, I ought to warn you.'

'I don't care about money; if you'll only do it.'

'We'll do it,' Alan said. 'It's done.'

'Your wife was Barbara Ransome, wasn't she?' Adam said, tapping his tankard for the barmaid.

'Held to Ransome, that's me all right.'

'Only mine's called Barbara too,' Adam said. 'Same again, please.'

'Next time they meet they can say snap,' Alan said.

'I thought she was going to be an actress, your Barbara.'

'So did I. And make our fortunes. But she did one lousy film with Mike Clode and suddenly found she had a great and immediate craving for motherhood. She intends to have four before she's thirty and then go back to the boards. They'll probably give way under her by that time. The theatre's finished anyway.'

'Do you think anything's got a future at all?'

'Three things,' Alan said. 'Television. You. And me. Jeers.'

iv

'If you'll lay the table,' Barbara said, 'I can do the apple amber.'

'I can think of things I'd rather lay,' Adam said, 'but OK.'

'I'm not a thing, thanks all the same,' Barbara said. 'What time did you tell them to come?'

'Not before eight. You know Ken and Anna. I was very specific.'

'You know Ken and Anna,' Barbara said. 'I just know they're coming to dinner the same night I've got twenty-five essays on James the First to correct.'

'Sorry,' Adam said. 'Sorry. You're lucky I didn't ask Alan Parks to dinner as well.'

'I thought you didn't like him.'

'What's that got to do with it? I wanted him to like me, didn't I? Well, if not like, at least approve.'

'Did you tell your father I was preggers?'

'He guessed. Well, I set it up for him.' He caught her round the waist and held her firmly. 'I love you, Ba. You know that, don't you? All I want is you.'

'Well don't sound so bloody miserable about it. Here I am.'

'I know you are,' Adam said. 'But why are you?'

'Adam,' Barbara said, rebuttoning her shirt, 'they'll be here in no time, for God's sake, behave yourself. *Do* you love me? Really?'

'I love you,' he said, 'and I love all who sail in you. I'd really sooner take you to bed than have people to dinner.'

'I'd *much* sooner,' Barbara said.

'And sit up all night with your specs on correcting essays, I know. You don't really like them, do you? Ken and Anna? I don't know why we asked them. Apart from the fact that he runs a bookshop and she runs a book programme. Oh well, I like Anna. She's bright.'

'And Ken?'

'He's bright too.'

'There's obviously no need to light the candles,' Barbara said, going into the kitchen. 'What about wine? Have you done anything?'

'Hell. I'll buzz down to the corner. You look terrific. I really do wish they weren't coming. I love you, Ba.'

'You'd better,' she said.

'What would you do if I didn't?'

'Kill myself.'

'No, you wouldn't.'

'Kill you,' she said. 'Or more probably kill her.'

'You might give me her address first. Don't you ever imagine having someone else? Or having *had* someone else.'

'Would you like it if I'd had a lurid past?'

'Like Anna? I don't know. I might. I should never be short of material, would I? Happiness is a useless subject for a writer. Especially in English. Why do you think that is? English seems particularly suited to irony and sarcasm, to suggesting the emptiness of human hope and the futility of human illusions.'

'I'm sure she'll be very impressed,' Barbara said.

'Who?'

'Anna. Oh, sorry, weren't you rehearsing?'

'What kind of writer do you want me to be?'

'I want you to be the kind of writer who goes and gets the wine before the guests actually arrive and then gets back in time to draw the cork, put out the glasses and do the drinks.'

'That's not a writer,' Adam said, 'that's a butler.'

'In that case I don't want a writer,' she said. 'I want a butler.'

v

Adam was on his way back with eight and sixpence worth of Nuits Saint Georges when he heard yelling from a side street and saw that a street speaker had set up his soap box there. He joined the small crowd around the platform, which was hung with a Union Jack. A billboard advertised The Britannia League. A man in a bowler hat was trying to sell literature. The speaker was wearing a blue mackintosh and had rather long greasy hair combed across a shining scalp. He had neither charm nor humour, yet there was a grating force to his rhetoric which drew Adam down to join the audience.

'Who's letting them in here?' the man shouted. 'Who's letting them in? Who am I talking about? You know who I'm talking about. I don't have to tell you who I'm talking about, because you know who I'm talking about. You think I'm exaggerating. Go up to certain streets in Notting

Hill – not half a mile from here, go up there, my friends, and see if I'm exaggerating. Ask Jim Hanson here if I'm exaggerating. Jim Hanson and his family, wife, three sons and two daughters, they were thrown out onto the street two nights ago by a party of visitors armed with the somewhat un-British weapons of two hammers and a machete. Do you know what a machete is? Jim Hanson here will tell you. A machete is a sharp implement that our Commonwealth friends use to cut sugar cane. Only it wasn't sugar cane they had come to cut that night, my friends, it was Jim Hanson's throat. And tomorrow night it may be your throat. Tomorrow night it may be your children's throats.'

Adam consulted the faces of the crowd. It was convenient at times to see oneself as a camera, vigilant and uninvolved.

'What is the government going to do about it? What is the government going to do about it? The government is going to do nothing about it. Nothing. And what is the Labour Party going to do about it? What are our friends at Transport House going to do about it? I invited one of them to come here tonight and tell us what he was going to do about it. He didn't feel inclined, my friends. He did not feel inclined. I don't wonder, do you? So who's going to do something about it?'

'Who's paying you?' one of the crowd called out.

'You see, ladies and gentlemen, you see what this country has come to?'

Adam smiled at the heckler. The speaker's finger shot out. 'You smile,' he said. 'You smile. Well, some of us, my friend, don't think it's funny.'

Adam shrugged, smiled and looked at his watch and backed from the scene.

'Come back here,' the speaker called, 'I haven't finished with you.'

Adam waved his bottle. 'People coming to dinner,' he said. 'Sorry.'

'No reply,' Adam said, holding out the cawing telephone on which he had just dialled Ken and Anna's number. It was after nine o'clock and they had not yet arrived. 'They've obviously left anyway.'

'Possibly,' Barbara said, slapping another exercise book onto the pile at her feet, 'but where for? The Bahamas?'

'I told them tonight. I remember distinctly. Thursday.'

'You're sure you said this Thursday? You're not always that clear. You didn't say Thursday week or anything?'

'Not always that *clear*? I read philosophy, woman. And as Wittgenstein said, the philosopher never says Thursday next if he means Thursday week. God, it's a quarter past nine. They're really not coming, are they?'

'Tell me when you want to eat,' Barbara said. 'They probably got asked to something more important.'

'They wouldn't do that.'

'Anna? Wouldn't she?'

'Not deliberately,' Adam said. 'I didn't realize you disliked her that much.'

'I don't. But then of course there isn't that much of her to dislike.'

'Are you as hungry as I am?' Adam said. 'I know: that's not a question anyone can answer. How can we know the hunger of another? I'm still amazed sometimes when you want to make love as much as I do.'

'The food's probably ruined,' Barbara said, opening the next essay.

'Come on,' Adam said, 'chicken gets better. Like sex. I hope. Let's eat. Let's *something*. Anything to get those specs off the end of your nose.'

'I'm trying to correct these wretched children's work.'

'She's obviously not going to review my book. That's probably it, she hates my book and she's too embarrassed to come. Ba, I bet you I'm right.'

'What?' She didn't look up.

'Frankly, if they come now, I don't think I'm going to open the door. We'll let them ring. Ba, I'm going to get the food. OK? We're going to eat, OK? What you need is a touch of the old Marengo. *Ça rejouit le cœur.*' He got the casserole out of the oven and took it to the table. 'We won't bother with the candles. Would you care to come and see me do the famous roll dance from the *Gold Rush* at only a fraction of the price?' He did a rather neat imitation of Chaplin. They had been to see the film at the Everyman. Barbara did not look up. 'Look, I've said I'm sorry. Why do you have to be such a cow about it? *I'm* not late, *I* haven't failed to turn up, I'm here and I'm hungry. I want you to come and eat.'

'You're hungry,' she said, 'so you want *me* to come and eat. Typical!'

'Well, I am typical, I am. I'm sorry, maybe it's because I'm typical, maybe it's because I'm a Londoner, maybe I'm not a blue-eyed charmer, but I do my best to give you a good time –'

'Why do you always have to try and make people laugh?' she said. 'Especially when they don't want to.'

'Do you want the three-volume answer or the abbreviated paperback edition for use in choirs and places where they sing? I have to try and make them laugh because that, dearest wife, is the price of admission.'

'Admission to what?'

'England. Home. And beauty, my beauty.'

'It's just a kind of greed really, isn't it?' she said. 'Making other people want what you want.'

'Perhaps,' Adam said, 'you should ask yourself why I always have to beg you on my knees to do the things everyone else does quite normally?'

'If you don't want to live with me, don't.'

'Now she tells me,' he said.

She threw down the remaining exercise books and went

into the bedroom and slammed the door. Adam sat there trying to eat and then, of course, he had to go and try the bedroom door. 'My God,' he said, 'you haven't seriously locked the door? I thought this came later in our romantic story. After you discover the powder on my collar.'

'If you want to come in,' she called, 'push. I told you it needed fixing.'

She was sitting at the dressing table.

'Look, what the hell is this really all about? *Ba*, please. My God, one has to use all one's bloody ingenuity and everything else in order to repair something one didn't even know was broken. If it's this hard just living together, how the hell am I going to remake the whole damned world at the same time?'

'It's all right,' she said. 'It's nothing to do with you. It's to do with me.'

'That is to do with me.' The phone started to ring. 'Well, at least it's not the door,' he said.

'Yet,' Barbara said.

'Hullo,' Adam said, coldly. 'Oh, hullo, Mummy, it's you. Everything all right? Oh, he told you. I was going to phone you. Guests? No, we haven't, that's the point. We haven't and we should. We've been thrown on our own resources and they have surprisingly sharp points. It doesn't matter. We're fine. Well, I'm glad you're pleased. Yes, of course. She's fine. Tremendous. Well, not very tremendous but fine. Well, she's – she's – I know she'd like to talk to you some time, but – no, she's fine.' He whispered into the receiver. 'She's a bit upset, about the dinner, these people. I'll – yes, I'll tell her. Of course. I know. I know. Well, we're both very happy,' he said more loudly. 'I will. Yes, doesn't he? Yes. And I was to see him. It's all in the past. I'll talk to you soon.' He put down the phone. 'Oh boy,' Barbara had come out of the bedroom. 'My mother. Congratulations, she says. She wanted to talk to you, but –'

'I'm sorry,' Barbara said, 'I can be a cow.'

They sat down to the cold Marengo.

'You certainly can moo a bit, when you feel like it,' Adam said. 'I'll stick it though, till your hooves start coming through. Cold feet I can stand, but cold hooves . . .' He took her hand. 'No more jokes. I swear.'

'I like your jokes.'

'I don't like them,' Adam said. 'They're like a foreign language, only one that one's begun to think in. As an alternative to thought. That's what I feel like sometimes, someone who's forgotten his native tongue and's become so fluent in English that no one can ever guess he isn't a native, not even himself. But somehow one's feelings aren't in English at all. I sometimes dream that my mouth is full of some sort of goo. Did you ever chew gum when you were small and then add a sweet or something to it and it went all sort of mealy and you could never get it out? It stuck to your teeth and your gums and you kept tasting it. I dream I'm trying to get rid of all that muck out of my mouth, like hairs in a basin sometimes, and I seem to have endless lumps of it, I can never get it all out. Horrible. Sometimes it has pieces of glass stuck in it, like a college wall. Have you ever tried living in a country with only one citizen?'

'You've got me,' Barbara said. 'That makes two citizens.'

'That's what you think,' Adam said. 'Foreigner!'

'Last-word Morris,' Barbara said. 'And there's a third in the oven.'

'Keeping warm,' Adam said. 'Promise me something. When we've finished supper, you're not going to clear the table; you're not going to tidy the kitchen; you're not not not going to look at any more of those bloody kids' essays or whatever they are – '

'You've eliminated everything I like best,' Barbara said. 'What am I going to do?'

'I'm going to make love to you for several hours.'

'Yes, but what am I going to do?' she said.

'You can bloody well think of something,' he said.

They left the table with its two used and two unused places. From the distance, through the half-open window, came the sound of shouting and whistles, hardly louder than the traffic. It was none of their business. They went into the bedroom.

'I must say,' Adam said, 'you are a girl who can take her clothes off with remarkable speed when she wants to.' Barbara was lying on the low bed, naked, propped on one arm watching him. 'You know, if we never talked, we'd never quarrel. Whereof one cannot speak, thereof one should bloody well keep silent. Words aren't really to the point, are they?'

'Oh shut up,' she said, stretching out her hand to him.

He came over and kissed her belly, very gently, where it had begun, faintly, to dome. The doorbell rang. 'Well, they're here,' Barbara said.

'I am not going to answer the damned thing,' Adam said. 'I am not.'

'Not even for Anna?'

The bell rang again. This time the ring was accompanied by an urgent and violent banging. Adam scampered into his clothes while Barbara lay there and quaked with laughter. 'I'm glad you can see the joke,' he said, 'because what's the joke? Bugger Anna, frankly. Unless, of course, she's trying to knock the door down because she's in such a hurry to tell me how much she liked the book. Well, she can bloody well shout the good news through the letter box. It can't really be them,' he said. 'They wouldn't knock like that, would they?' He opened the door angrily. 'What the hell goes on?'

There was a couple on the doorstep, but they were not Ken and Anna. The girl was black, the man short and wearing a brown corduroy suit. 'It's only us,' he panted. 'Could we possibly come in?'

'Bill. For God's sake, what's going on?' Adam called to Barbara: 'It's Bill Bourne.'

'And this is Joann, he continued.'

'Hullo, Joann.' Adam turned on lights. 'We were in bed,' he said. 'Almost.'

'Sorry, he apologized, only we had a bit of trouble.'

'He added, with true British understatement.' In the light, Adam could see that Joann had an ugly wound on her forehead. Blood had run down into her eye. 'We'd better call a doctor.'

'Joann is a doctor,' Bill said.

'In that case we'll call her doctor,' Adam said. 'What the hell happened? Were you in a car or what?'

'Actually,' Bill said, 'we ran into a bit of a riot, I suppose it was. Not of our own choosing.'

'We got chased,' the girl said.

'And caught, by the look of it. Come in here, we'll get some water on it anyway.'

'They threw things,' Bill said. 'It looked rather ugly until we discovered how fast we could run.'

'Where was this?'

'Down the road, he indicated. Notting Hill. We'd been to a louche club – to hear a supposedly rather good tenor sax man, who was actually rather a sell, I thought – and we were suddenly assaulted by a person or persons unknown. And they certainly deserved to be. We ran as far as Holland Park Avenue and they sheered off. A friendly man in blue. Then I remembered you were here and – well, I hope you don't mind, he blathered.'

Barbara appeared in a cotton wrapper. 'You remember Bill,' Adam said, 'and this is Joann. *Doctor* Joann. I'm afraid –'

'Joann Case. I am sorry about this.'

'That looks horrible,' Barbara said. 'I'll get some cotton wool and some TCP.'

'It's not serious,' Joann said. She might have been talking about a third party. 'Luckily I've got a rubber face; it just bounced off.'

'You're being very brave, but I don't like the look of it.'

'How are things?' Adam said.

'Good,' Bill said. 'Not bad. Until just now anyway. I'm lecturing away.'

'Of course you are,' Adam said. 'Listen, what about some food?'

'We've got loads,' Barbara said.

'We've even got some wine.'

'Sounds very attractive, he confessed ruefully.'

Adam took Bill into the kitchen and set about reassembling the Marengo.

'She's working at a local hospital, he informed him. Pam and I have split up, you know.'

'Ah,' Adam said. 'What's she going to do?'

'She'll probably apply for a librarianship abroad somewhere. She's thinking of Africa.'

'There's going to be a divorce, then, is there?'

'We're all entitled to make one mistake, he averred.'

'If we get the chance,' Adam said.

vii

They ate the food. They drank the wine. They talked and talked and eventually, at one o'clock in the morning, they went to bed.

'Where were we?' Adam said, as he kissed Barbara. 'Can you remember?'

'You were about to take a vow of silence,' she said, 'since when you have not stopped talking.'

'Critic,' he said.

They began to make love. They did not have a spare room so Bill and Joann were camping in the sitting room. Soon there were unmistakable noises through the thin wall, whispers, mild cries of surprise soon turning into cries of surprising strength. 'At least,' Barbara said, 'Anna and Ken would've gone home eventually.'

'Other people's happiness is pretty hard to take, isn't it?' Adam said. 'If they'd come here to commit suicide, we'd've been dosing them with coffee and good advice and feeling as smug as bishops.'

'I should like to live in the country, I think,' Barbara said. 'In a small house in the middle of a large park, preferably surrounded with large barbed-wire dogs.'

'Oh lover, lover, lover . . .' Joann cried out.

'Done!' Adam said.

'It certainly sounds remarkably like it,' Barbara said.

'The house, I mean. One day.' He kissed her ruefully and rolled over to his side of the bed. 'What a night it was, it really was, such a night! Goodnight, wife. We shall doubtless meet again some sunny day.'

II

'"I am working",' Stephen Taylor said, peering at the letter he held in his hand, '"' on a series which will concern itself with major artistic and political figures and their contribution to the twentieth century. I look forward very much, if you are agreeable, to a chance to meet and discuss the possibility of your figuring in such a series. Yours sincerely . . ." I can't read it.'

'Adam Morris,' Adam said. 'I did write it underneath.'

'Yes, so you did. Morris.' Stephen was tall and gaunt-faced, with thick grey hair falling forward over his rumpled forehead, though cut short over large ears, in an almost military style. He wore flannels and an open-necked khaki shirt with a Harris tweed jacket. He had greeted Adam with a sort of surly shyness and hustled him through the house into the conservatory where they sat on sagging wickerwork chairs. Lawton Hall was an old rectory, approached through once-white gates up a pot-holed drive infested with squirrels who clearly did not expect visitors. The house was large, but without pretensions, with a terrace beyond the conservatory overlooking a long field that fell away from the house towards thick woods. It was warm in the conservatory, but Stephen Taylor wore a pair of khaki mittens. He took off his glasses and looked at Adam. 'You've visited all my buildings, you've read all my books! I'm flattered,' he said. '*Am* I flattered?'

'I don't think flattered,' Adam said.

'"Major artistic and political figure". My political career was a fiasco.'

'It didn't seem so at one time,' Adam said.

'Napoleon entered Moscow,' Taylor said. 'His invasion of Russia was still a fiasco.'

'Do you still believe in what you believed in then?'

'What did I believe in?'

'What did you?' Adam said.

'They wouldn't listen to me,' Taylor said, creaking in his chair. 'I warned them and they wouldn't listen to me. As soon as I was proved right, they wouldn't let me speak either.'

'Who are "they"?'

'The people in London,' Taylor said. 'Your people.'

'My people? Who do you mean by my people?'

'The BBC never reported my speeches; they slandered the movement; they distorted our intentions.'

'Which were?'

'I never went to Cambridge,' Stephen Taylor said. 'I never went to university. I worked. I worked with my hands. I was apprenticed to a stonemason, that's how I

138

learned about stone. Stones are different; they do different things; they have different strengths and different weaknesses; they're good for different things. No democracy among stones! They accuse me of being rich. They accuse me of making money out of the movement. That's nonsense. I never made a penny out of it. Are you interested in money?'

'Not as such,' Adam said.

'What are you?'

'Hard to say. I think I'm interested basically in getting things straight.'

'Things aren't straight,' Taylor said. 'They never will be. Lines are straight. Theories are straight. Cambridge thinks things can be straight; they can't. Things are never straight. Nothing is straight that's alive, that's natural, that's part of the earth. Are you afraid?'

'Afraid?'

'What do you fear?'

'Hard to say. The Irrational – '

'The Irrational! I'll tell you what you fear. You fear yourself. What you really are. What are you? Live as long as you can and as well as you can, is that what you want? Safe, is that what you want to be?'

'We were going to talk about you,' Adam said.

'For the BBC. The BeeeBeeeSeee. Why have you come here for the BeeeBeeeSeee? Because you didn't dare to come on your own? Without a warrant? You needed an excuse, am I right? A cover. What is this programme you want to do? What are your plans, eh, what's your – your scenario? A few words from our sponsor, a walk round the estate, a glimpse of the library, a few shots of some buildings I once built, now surrounded with concrete public conveniences in the international style, is that what the BBC is going to do, is that what Master Adam – ' he peered again at the letter on his knee '– Morris has in his straight-edged Cambridge mind? Well?'

'You supported Franco; you supported Mussolini; you as good as supported Hitler. You also wrote some of the best books about – '

'Supported? Supported? Where do you get that from?'

'I mean you believed they were right and you told the people so.'

'Ignoramus,' Stephen Taylor said.

'*Didn't* you?'

'You're an ignoramus. Were you in the war?'

'I was too young.'

'You're still too young. You'll always be too young. I built buildings; I wrote books; I worked and I worked and you come down here and tell me that I supported this man or that – '

'What about your Tottenham Town Hall speech, 1936?' Adam said.

'Were you there?'

'I didn't have to be there. I read the speech.'

'You read the speech! In some stuffy little office, and you thought "Now I've got him, now I've got him. Tottenham Town Hall, 1936; now I've got him!" I'm not a German. I'm not a Spaniard. I'm not an Italian. I'm a Briton, Mr Morris. Tell me, do you like this country?'

'Aspects of it, yes,' Adam said. 'I like it a lot better than Spain or Italy or Germany, at least as they were in 1936. But let's get down to cases, may we? You advocated time and again a "radical and final reckoning with the enemies of the British people". Everyone knew *exactly* what you meant.'

'I wanted to be a builder,' Stephen Taylor said. 'Not an architect, a builder. I never wanted to be a politician. I wanted to build, stone by stone. I wanted to be a writer who carved his words, who thought about every letter. I wanted to be a man who lived every day in simplicity and humility. I wanted to touch nothing I hadn't grown myself, live under no roof I had not hammered and tiled and caulked myself. I can hew stone and I can dress stone and I can live on a handful of grass if need be. I want to depend on no man and I want no man to depend on me. Now!'

'That is very eloquent,' Adam said.

'That is the truth.'

'There is no rule against the truth being eloquent.'

'Don't smile,' Stephen Taylor said. 'I don't want you to smile.'

'Only how do you reconcile all that with searchlights and bully boys?'

'Bully boys. You're the bully boy, my smiling friend. You've come here to crucify me. You're cruising for a crucifixion! Do you deny it?'

'I have neither nails nor cross,' Adam said. 'What would the world have been like, what would England have been like if things had gone your way?'

'Are you satisfied with England as it is then? Is this England something so immaculate that it must gag its critics – '

'Was freedom of speech a feature of your programme?' Adam said. 'I hadn't realized.'

'Do you know what frightens modern man most?' Stephen said. 'Silence. He can't bear it.'

Adam said: 'I – '

'You see?' cried Taylor. 'You break it at once. You can't bear it, can you? Silence.'

Adam sat there. Suddenly, out of the imposed silence, Stephen Taylor let out a great bellowing guffaw, and pointed at Adam. Adam shrugged, indulgent and uncomfortable.

Naomi Taylor came in, a large, blonde woman in a floral gardening smock. She looked keenly at Stephen and then around the conservatory, as if she feared something might have got broken. 'Will you stay and have lunch, Mr Morris?' she said. 'I'm sure you will.'

'He's from the BBC,' Stephen said. 'Of course he'll

stay to lunch. Have you seen Frank? Is everything all right?'

'Everything's been taken care of,' she said.

'We've had a really good old chin-wag, haven't we, Mr Morris?' He winked at Adam.

'That's good,' Naomi said.

'I was just about to show Mr Morris the wild flowers I collected this morning. He was going to identify them for me. Did you know, Naomi, Mr Morris is an expert on the subject of British wild flowers?'

'Really?' She looked at Adam with new eyes.

'He knows everything there is to know. This one, for instance, what did you say this one was, Mr Morris? I didn't quite catch.'

Adam said: 'I know nothing about flowers.'

'But there must be some mistake!' Stephen said. 'I could have sworn that you said that you knew this island as well as any man alive. You're toying with us, Mr Morris. You're pulling our legs!'

'Lunch will be ready in about ten minutes,' Naomi said.

'I thought you'd read all my books.'

'I have, but – '

'But, but, but, but, but. How can you have? Had you really read them, you would be an expert on the flora and fauna of East Anglia. You would know these flowers literally inside out.' He was tearing the flowers to shreds and showing the wrecked blooms to Adam in the palm of his hand.

'I'm not good on flowers, I'm afraid,' Adam said.

'But, but, but, but, but, Mr Morris. You came down here to crucify me, Mr Morris. To lay my ghost, isn't that right? You've nothing to learn from me, have you, because you know it all? You went to Cambridge. You've read my speeches. You have nothing to learn from any-one. Frank, Frank.' He dusted his hands together and stood up. 'We'll see him at lunch. Come on. You can cast your eye around the premises, work out your camera angles, how best to show me in the worst possible light, eh, Mr Morris?'

ii

When Stephen and Adam were already at the dining table, a thickset young man, of about twenty-eight, came into the room. He wore sooty brown corduroy trousers and a tartan shirt. He shucked his Wellington boots at the French windows and put on a pair of brown shoes which were waiting there for him.

'Well, Frank,' Stephen said, 'everything all right?' The young man sat down without reply. 'This is Mr Morris,' Stephen Taylor said, 'who has come from London to pay homage at the shrine. Mr Morris thinks of your father as someone worth a pilgrimage, Frank.' Frank looked at Stephen and then at Adam. He still said nothing. 'Well, I wonder what's for lunch? I wonder what the wizard has cooked up, don't you?'

Frank said: 'Roast chicken, I should think, wouldn't you?' He had a surprising accent: Liverpool? Belfast? Adam could not place it.

Stephen Taylor put both elbows on the table and leaned his face suddenly forward at Adam. 'Do you wrestle, Mr Morris?'

'*Wrestle?*'

Stephen turned away, indifferent to Adam's amazement, as Naomi brought in a large earthenware dish that smelled of stewed lamb. 'Of *course*,' Stephen said, 'I was forgetting. We're having stewed lion for lunch. In your honour, Mr Morris.' Adam smiled and looked at Naomi. She dished up. They began to eat. 'My wife looks after me very well, don't you agree, Mr Morris?'

Adam was caught with his mouth full. 'Yes,' he said. 'Yes, it's – it's – '

'There you are, Naomi, endorsement,' Stephen said. 'Endorsement from Mr Adam Morris of the BBC. "It's, it's," he says, and you can't say fairer than that, can you? It's, it's! We've been together now for forty years, Mr Morris, and I am able to say, without a trace of irony, that it doesn't seem a day too long, does it, my dear?' Naomi continued to eat with placid anguish. 'Mr Morris, you know, is a social critic. He's passing judgement on our society. He was educated at Cambridge and his mind is razor sharp. There is no hair he cannot split, he was telling me – '

'I don't think I ever said that,' Adam said.

'Your bearing says it, your style says it, my friend. Hairs split, ghosts laid, lies nailed, all for the price of a BBC commission. You have come down here with your critical faculties honed, there's no other word for it. Honed! You know what is what, and you know which is which and the sooner the world pulls its socks up and stands to attention the better for the world. Mr Morris has seen all my buildings, he has read all my books, Naomi, and he has conned all my speeches. Nothing I have done has escaped his eagle eye; it *is* an eagle eye, isn't it, Mr Morris? Have some more lion – '

Adam said: 'Thank you, it was – '

'It was, Naomi, did you hear that? It was. What greater praise can there be from a Cambridge man? Mr Morris is a cultural sanitary engineer, one of the new, scientific generation who never misses a target or a trick. He is a man who knows where the boll weevil skulks – eh Mr Morris? – and how to winkle him out with his nimble little winkling iron. He has come all this way with a winkling purpose and winkle he will, whether we like it or not.'

'I should hardly describe you as a winkle, I think.'

'Tell us, then, Mr Morris, how you would describe us? You speak excellent English; almost like a native. Explain

144

to us in your own words what your purpose is. When the green light shines, Mr Morris, pray fail us not.'

'OK,' Adam said, 'if you really want to know. How can a man who wrote a book like, let's say, *The Fenlanders*, or built a building like the Roper House – '

'You see, Naomi? You see? Chapter and verse! Chapter and verse! Impressive, Frank, impressive, eh? With foot-notes and appendix.'

' – a man of imagination and even vision – also – '

' – even vision! Not uneven vision, *even* vision! Also do what?'

'Also be the enemy of liberty and the condoner of mass murder?' Adam said.

'The enemy of liberty and the condoner of mass murder!' Stephen put his hands flat on the table in front of him. 'Well, Naomi, have you no answer for the gentleman? He's driven all the way from Portland Place in his motor, doesn't he deserve a snappy answer?' Frank wiped his mouth, stood up, and walked out through the French windows, taking his Wellingtons with him. 'That's Frank's answer. Rather a rough answer, rather a crude answer, I'm bound to own. But you, my dear – Frank, come back here – you, my dear, must have a more telling, more revealing, more humanly interesting answer for poor Mr Morris, who has come down here, at the risk of his skin, to pose the question – and question the pose – on behalf of poor suffering humanity.' Stephen spoke without rant, but he got up, agitated, and stumped into the conservatory. 'I shall have to teach that boy some manners.' Adam heard him shouting out through the door. 'Frank, Frank ... I want a word with you ...'

Naomi said: 'You should not have come.'

'Why not, Mrs Taylor?'

'You just shouldn't, that's all,' she said. 'I advise you to leave now.'

'Is he your only son?' Adam said.

'And chop it properly,' Stephen was yelling. 'Properly, do you hear?'

Adam was almost relieved when Stephen came back into the room; he had a reason no longer to return Naomi's blue-eyed stare.

'I've told him this time,' Stephen said. 'This time it's got to be chopped properly or else, or else. We have no nonsense here, you know, Mr Morris. When I ran this place during the war, do you know we outproduced every farm, every farm in the district?'

'Is that so?' Adam said. 'I –'

'– thought I was locked up in the war, did you, Mr Morris? Enemy of the people, did you?' Naomi had collected the plates and took them out to the kitchen. Stephen sat by the fire in a leather chair and rolled himself a cigarette. 'We had some friends of yours not ten miles from here,' he said. 'Pacifists, pansy-boys, moaning minnies, conscientious objectors, the whole do-gooding, bedwetting community, scratching the soil for Jesus and Marx and Freud and points south. The enemies of fascism – your friends, Mr Morris – couldn't speak English half of them, and we outproduced them, we outproduced them in every department. We weren't commissioned, Mr Morris, we weren't given grants or promised that the world owed us a living. We buckled to and we ran a damned tight ship and we outproduced every farm from here to Kingdom come. After the war I wanted to go on. I had plans for an enlarged community here, I was willing to make over every acre I had. No money. Everyone working for everyone else. No profits. No bosses; promotion through merit: merit meaning hard work. They owed me money, the people in London, they owed me plenty, but all I wanted was the right to develop my ideas. Then your friends got in. They took my men away. They sent my men all over the place. Forced labour. Mines, factories, I don't know what, and then they seized half my property. That was their idea of liberty, of a free country; that was their thanks, that was their idea of grateful thanks for services rendered. Mass murder!' There was a silence. Adam found himself wishing Stephen would go on. He did, with a smile. 'You know better, of course, you could run this place better than I ever could. You know the truth and the truth has made you free. You don't need experience; you don't need effort and energy and trial and error; you don't need anything but a cellophane packet of sterilized truth issued by the University of Cambridge and you can do anything, run anything, put anyone in their place.'

'You don't think the truth is very important then?' Adam said.

'Truth is work,' Stephen said, 'truth is apprenticeship, truth is pain and effort and dirt and sweat and blood as well. Wince if you will, object if you will, make a point or two if you will. Truth isn't an argument or a correct phrase, that's all words, that's lawyer's truth – and who knows a greater liar than a lawyer? There's city truth and there's country truth. There's lawyer's truth and there's human truth. Thought-up truth and lived truth. You're all thought-up, Mr Morris, dreamed-up, worked-up, souped-up and, of course, turned-up.' He had circled behind Adam's chair and now Adam felt Taylor's strong thumbs working on his shoulder blades, caressing and threatening. He shrugged round and saw Taylor grinning down at him. 'I know what you have in mind. I know what you have in mind: a show trial, am I right? Camera, lights, action – and the fearless D A as played by Adam Morris puts paid to the mass murderer, the nasty Caliban from the wood-shed and the world is made safe for democracy, positivism and the thirty-six-hour week for the thirty-six-inch man. You've come to beard me, am I not right, and if I have no beard, you'll draw one in with your miracle, make-it-yourself villain kit? How can *I* possibly have anything to teach *you*, anything to teach anyone? They won't even let me into my own buildings in this great free society you're so proud of, they won't print my articles, they won't sell my books, they won't allow me a voice at all, unless it's the voice of the defendant in this show trial of yours, butchered to make a pygmies' holiday.'

'Have you got any plans,' Adam said, 'for the future? I mean – '

'The future,' Taylor said. 'No, I've got plans for the past though. Thousands of them. Come with me, I'll show you what the present could have been and what the future never will be. Come on. What's the matter with you?'

'My foot's gone to sleep,' Adam said. 'Sorry.'

'My dear fellow,' said Stephen, 'allow me – '

'No, no,' Adam said. 'I can manage perfectly well on my own.'

'Are you *sure*?'

iii

Adam stood at the chart table while Stephen heaped drawings in front of him: schools, assembly halls, railway stations, accommodation for labourers, barns and pier-heads, pubs and shopping arcades and sports centres. Some of the drawings were at an advanced stage, with detailed elevations and even builder's specifications. Others were hardly more than sketches torn from some dream, part vision, part nightmare. It was impossible to say whether it was the work of a frantic crank or of a frustrated master. Adam lacked the knowledge; the work itself, devoid of all links with a recognizable context, gave no indication of human scale or practical worth. The sheer volume of it, and the challenging contempt with which it was heaped in front of him, served to silence Adam and amaze him. 'You thought I didn't work any more because I've had a fit of the sulks, I suppose?' Stephen said. 'Not one building of mine have they built since the war, not one book have they published, not one letter to the coterie press – and you thought it was because I hadn't the gumption, didn't you? They won't have me, Mr Morris, your friends, they won't listen to me, they won't look at my drawings – '

'Surely if you went in for a competition,' Adam said, 'they wouldn't – '

'Competitions are set by the people who win them,' Stephen said. 'Cathedrals to preach the gospel of a mixed economy; Festival Halls for those with nothing to celebrate; Colleges of Further Education to create a generation of further idiots; Art Galleries for the artless, restaurants for the overfed, aerodromes for those with nowhere to go. What use is anyone going to have for stone and wood and silence and idols that man should really have? Genius measured by the hour, cures for death and sentences for life, that's the society that wants to build a mausoleum to embalm the truth and slap a plastic condom on the spirit of man. That's the society you *condone*; not mass murder – mass misery, mass tedium, mass impotence, mass lifelessness. You're welcome to it. You are welcome to it. Now put your hands right up in the air.' Adam, with a half smile, turned and found himself looking into the barrels of a shotgun. 'It's loaded,' Stephen Taylor said, 'and I can use it. At ten feet it will make a hole in you the size of a soup plate. Now.'

'I suggest you put it down,' Adam said.

'I suggest I put you down. Now.'

'What exactly is the idea?'

'Exactly. We must have exactitude, mustn't we? The exact idea is that I want you to know that I am not a fool. Put your hands right up in the air.'

'Are we making a Western suddenly?' Adam said.

'Do as I say.' Adam put his hands in the air. 'Of course it may not be loaded,' Stephen said.

'I sincerely hope it isn't,' Adam said.

'On the other hand,' Stephen said, 'who lays down his life on behalf of the BBC? Not a long list of applicants for that particular job, I fancy. That particular post. No annual increments there, no pensioned pay-off. I am not one of those, Mr Morris, who goes meekly to his fate, who bows to judges he despises and makes his apology to a public gallery full of cretins and pansies and barrow-boys. Do you seriously suppose that I was ever going to consent to appear on your show trial, for the greater glory of Adam Morris, the great debunker, the great skeleton-hunter-out-of-cupboardser? You're trespassing here, Mr Morris. You've come from London with your roll of money and you're trespassing here. You're on private property, my friend with the bring-and-buy face. You're intruding on private property. *Frank.*' He pushed Adam at gun point back into the dining room. 'The dirt, that's what you came for, isn't it, the dirt, the low-down, the griff, that's what you're after, isn't it? Empty your pockets. There on the table. Empty your pockets. I want to see what you're carrying. Frank. Come here. *Frank*, I've got a job for you. A little commission. All of them, everything, on the table. No false moves. One false move and – ' Frank stepped in through the French windows. His Wellingtons made a noise Adam detested as he crossed the polished floor. 'Frisk him, Frank. Weapons, hidden messages, drugs, cash, on the nail or otherwise. Thoroughly, Frank. You know how clever they are.'

'I advise you to leave me alone,' Adam said. 'Weapons! I haven't any weapons.' He was appalled to see how dull and apparently empty was Frank's face.

'It's no use attempting to recruit Frank, my friend. Frank is incorruptible. The one and only. The last faithful follower I possess. Frank is true England, through and through. Your hands up, Mr Morris, until further notice.'

'Dictator for an unlimited period!' Adam said. 'I

imagined you doing a lot of things, but never making a fool of yourself.'

'Of whom do you seriously suppose I am making a fool?' Stephen said. 'Have you ever been thrashed? Have you ever been thoroughly thrashed?'

Naomi came in from the hall, carrying cut flowers, in the best traditions of drawing-room comedy. 'Oh Stephen, for God's sake,' she said, and lifted the gun from his hands as if it might have been an unwanted cup and saucer. Stephen stood there, looking at his empty hands, and he gave a terrible roar, half defiance, half despair. Frank had him by the arm, very firmly. 'Please go now, Mr Morris,' Naomi said.

'I want him to stay,' Stephen said. 'Don't leave me, Mr Morris. Don't leave me.'

'What *is* this?' Adam said.

'I told you, please to go,' Naomi said.

'We were having a joke, weren't we, Mr Morris? We were having a joke. We were thinking of something to amuse the viewers, weren't we, for the BBC, a bit of business, something to add spice to the suburban evening? Tell them, Mr Morris. She doesn't look like a gaoler, does she? The governor of Lawton Hall, the giver and the taker away. Well, that's what she is. You must inform a magistrate, Mr Morris. Inform a magistrate. Swear out an affidavit. Or do you condone this, Mr Morris, do you condone this, private prisons, confinement without trial? Am I a war criminal still in your eyes? A man to be kept out of sight, under lock and keeper? Do you know what they'll do to me when you've gone? The basement cell. Bread and water . . .'

'We shall give him some tea,' Naomi said. 'And a biscuit.'

Frank drew the old man towards the door. Stephen began to make sad noises.

'Is there anything I can do?' Adam said.

Stephen drew himself up and gave Adam a look of consummate derision. '*Do?*' he said. 'You? *Do?*'

'He talked so brilliantly,' Adam said. 'He really did.'

'Always,' Naomi said.

'Yes, but there was more to it than that. He wouldn't have shot me, I'm sure of it. I never seriously imagined –' Adam looked at Naomi. 'What he needs –'

'Oh, you know what he needs, do you?'

'Room, I suppose. Space. He seemed so frightened. It was fear, wasn't it?'

'He likes fear,' she said. 'In himself. In others. Go back to London now, Mr Morris. You've seen what you came to see.'

'He could have done great things. One really feels that.'

'Is greatness so important?' she said. 'I don't know and I don't care.'

'No,' Adam said. 'I can see that.'

'Can you?' she said. 'Can you? Yes, you damned well can.' She snatched his hand and pulled him out into the sunshine. 'Come with me, Mr Morris. Come with me.'

iv

She ran down the path, dragging Adam after her. Her heavy flesh jolted on the hard path. There was a cleared area under the shadow of the big trees at the side of the field. It was surrounded with wire. The air was gritty. Inside the wire were the burnt remains of chicken coops. And everywhere, against the wire, in the trees beyond it, were feathers, feathers and the half-burned corpses of chickens. In a pit, in the run itself, some fifty scorched birds were lying in an open grave which Frank had clearly been filling with earth. 'There,' Naomi said, 'there.' She gave Adam a look of accusing triumph. 'Now keep away from here,' she said, 'because that's what your great man did. Now stay away. You and everyone else.'

'Wrong can of beans,' Alan Parks said.

'I suppose. One funny thing incidentally,' Adam said. 'He hasn't got a son. This character Frank, he kept calling him his son. They never had any children. I checked.'

They were sitting in a small screening room where Alan was viewing some footage shot by a young director who sat in the row in front of them, chewing his fingers.

'We'd better try something else,' Alan said. 'How about a programme on T. S. Eliot and his contribution to the war effort?'

Adam said: 'I believe he did a wonderful job in the WAAF, didn't he? Little sung but much admired by all who came in contact with him. No, actually, in principle I'd like to do something very much – only – '

'Only? I know! You've sold your bloody novel to the movies.'

'This man Lazlo wants me to go and see him.'

'Bruno! Does he really?'

'Do you know everybody?' Adam said.

'He did Barbara's movie, the one Mike Clode directed. A wank at Cambridge, you know. Ugh!'

'He's got Mike for this one, mine – '

'He's done one or two damned good things actually, since,' Alan said. 'Mike. You can't knock what he's been doing in the theatre.'

'I can try,' Adam said. 'Actually I'm really looking forward to it.'

'A hundred thousand dollars?' Alan said. 'Who wouldn't?'

'Working with him. A hundred thousand dollars! Don't be silly. Nobody gets that. How are the twins by the way?'

Alan took out his wallet, turned on the console light in front of them and passed some photographs across to

Adam. 'Will you look at the balls on those two? They'll be opening for Australia, old son, you see if they don't. What a pair of little bastards, I'm telling you, Christ.'

'And Barbara?'

'Smashing. Terrific. In the pink. And back on the job. Marvellous.' The film ran out into white. Adam could hear the young director's teeth click on what was left of his thumbnail. 'There's some quite tasty footage there, Nigel,' Alan said, 'quite tasty. Especially early on. I liked the fire-eater. Reminded me of you, Adam. Tell you what, arrange with Denise for Norman to see it, because I think it's the sort of thing Pat might well want to show to David.' Alan opened the door of the screening room. 'Well, I'm sorry old Taylor isn't a goer, but for God's sake let's do something and meanwhile remember what I said: go for the dough and don't let them bullshit you. Take the cash and the art'll look after itself. I go this way. You go that. Jeers.'

III

Bruno Lazlo's office was in the basement of his Pimlico house; it was plumply furnished and badged with the symbols of mild success in the film business: a Silver Bear, some framed citations from festivals, posters from recent productions and, with pride of place, a framed letter from the head of the Rank Organization terminating Lazlo's contract forthwith. 'Since when, I must say, I haven't looked back.' Mike Clode was slumped in a long chair. He wore a black corduroy suit with a military-type tunic and black boots. 'All what I wanted to say,' Bruno said, 'is that in many ways we are tired, Michael and I, of films which are not about modern life. We want to make a film about modern life: the desperation, the playboy world, the fast cars, the emptiness of life, but at the same time – '

154

'We want to say something about England,' Mike said.

'The world of the jet-setters, the gambling, the search for the – the – '

'The shit at the end of the rainbow,' Adam said.

'Absolutely right,' Mike said. 'Absolutely right.'

'The shit at the end of the rainbow,' Bruno said. 'My God, what a title in many ways! But tragic, a girl tangled up in the world of the playboys, the Mick Hamishes – that girl he had that drowned herself in champagne, pathetic when you think about it – the Maggie Penroses – '

'Is this going to be for Jill?' Adam said.

'Ideally, yes,' Mike said.

'Pathetic. Tragic. Trapped. Drugs. Drink. Sex. Do you want a cigar?'

'Everybody's story,' Adam said. 'No thanks, I don't.'

'I can give you a lot of ideas from my own personal experience,' Bruno said. 'Take that other girl, what was her name?'

'Sandra?'

'Sandra. Marion in many ways.'

'Jean.'

'Jean. Deborah. Deborah, my God!'

'Ursula.'

'Was slightly different. I must say. Linda, though. Linda certainly. Of a loneliness beyond!'

'I thought she was married now,' Mike said.

'But my God, the man! Kenneth Jenks, he treats her, I must say, like a bastard. Beats her, I don't know what. Locks her in the cellar.'

'Ken does? *Ken?*' Mike measured a man four feet tall. 'She's a giant – '

'He is a sadist, I must say, and not a particularly nice one.'

'Look,' Adam said, 'forgive me, but I thought we were going to talk about my book. I thought – '

'Personally I thought it was very good. Mike gave it to

me, I read it; I must say I thought it was excellent, a little long perhaps, but excellent. The dialogue.'

'I'd like to talk to you about it some time, Adam, when you've got a minute, because I do honestly think it could make a bloody marvellous film. And one day we'll do it. I promise you.'

'I will tell you quite honestly,' Bruno said, 'make a film with us, a successful film with international appeal, and after that we can do anything we want. The three of us.'

'This time,' Mike said, 'we've really got to do something big. Not just parochial. Not just the UK.'

'I have this image,' Bruno said, 'I have one image, this girl in the flat, with everything, everything, the cocktail cabinets, the televisions, the – '

'The poodles.'

'The poodles, the white telephones, the African sculptures, everything and she's crying and crying, in a desperation beyond; she has everything, she has nothing. She walks to the window and she lights a cigarette in a certain way and we know everything. That is my image.'

'Haunting,' Adam said.

'But we need a peg,' Mike said.

'But we need a peg,' Bruno said.

'And that's where I come in,' Adam said, 'I'm big on pegs.'

'I want to do it for real, Adam. I want to do a film that says it all about the futility of London and ambition and success and money.'

'All the things we want,' Adam said. 'Well, I expect we could do that.'

'You must have plenty of time to think. I put an office at your disposal. I introduce you to some people. Tommy, for instance. And – '

'And Imogen,' Mike said. 'The world of the his and hers race horses and the casinos and the call girls – you must meet a lot of people, you must spend a lot of time with the

Bob Reids and the Mick Hamishes and the Sir Michael Mitchells – '

'I don't think I want to do that,' Adam said.

'What?' Bruno said. 'There is only one way to make a good film and that is to work and work for weeks and weeks, all in the same room, looking for the right image, the right idea. It must be witty, it must be sharp, it must have movement – it must be clever like hell, but clear, simple, understandable – before you can begin to create a scenario, there must be many conferences and research and interviews – and conferences.'

Adam said: 'Can Jill play English?'

'She can play anything,' Mike said. 'Did you see *Dime a Dozen*?'

'Good ideas,' Bruno said, 'don't grow on trees. They take weeks of work. With Fred and Jack, we sat for hours and hours to get one idea – sometimes we sat here all night – '

Adam said: 'What if the film was about a girl who was owned by five men – say a comedian and a banker and a politician and an aristocrat and, well, why not? – a film producer? I'm thinking of Jill, obviously, and it's all about these men who are her clients, she lives in a company-owned penthouse and she's literally their wholly owned subsidiary: she is a director and, of course, the house-keeper and bed maker, what else? That way, she's actually a tax loss, so the more she wants, the more they're glad to give; and that's basically your story, the relationship between her and the five directors and, of course, between them. But all done absolutely realistically – clear, simple, understandable.'

'For real,' Mike said. 'It must be for real.'

'Absolutely. Basically it's the story of the girl. Imagine the annual general meeting though. They have her cast in ice cream and literally sit and eat a portion of her each. Another spoonful of thigh, Sir Henry!'

Bruno said: 'What an image, I must say, in many ways! Not bad, Mike, what do you think?'

'Fabulous,' Mike said. 'Adam, as your agent, I advise you not to say another word.'

'One thing I do insist on,' Bruno said. 'He has to meet Julia, in many ways. That I insist on.'

ii

They filmed one of the scenes of *The Girl in Question* at a country house near Cambridge. Mike and Bruno liked to have 'the writer' on the set. Adam was bored and he was excited. He slipped away one afternoon (when things were going well on the set, neither Mike nor Bruno addressed a word to him) and flashed into Cambridge in his new secondhand Sunbeam Alpine to see his brother. Derek had gone up to Trinity the previous October.

'How's it all going?' Derek asked, producing Fitzbillies' Chelsea buns.

'Oh Christ,' Adam said, 'they're all so fucking stupid. "Yes, yes, yes, but will they understand it?" That's all they care about. It's going fine. I love it, God help me! I've written a fantastic script, I really have. Lots of brand new clichés. Terrific.'

'I believe you,' Derek said. 'Thousands would and so would I.'

'Clever! You know the biggest help? A classical education. You write Greek verses, you write Latin verses, Greek proses, Latin proses; this style, that style, they name it, you do it and they hand out the prizes. Well, films is just one more verse metre, one more style; get the hang of it and you can turn it out by the yard. Money for jam. I'll tell you something ridiculous that worries me more than anything. You know this baby we're having?'

'I did hear something about it,' Derek said. 'The result

of a misunderstanding between yourself and a young person, wasn't it? What about it?'

'If it's a boy, should we circumcise it or not? You can laugh,' Adam said, 'but it won't be Jewish, you know that?'

'Send it back,' Derek said.

'It seems a funny thing to do, snipping bits off new-born babies without their permission.'

'Perhaps it'll be a girl.'

'God, I hope so,' Adam said. 'Otherwise ... OK, it's ridiculous but on the other hand I'm not sure that I could stand a foreskin around the house.'

'House!' Derek said. 'Congratulations!'

'We're looking. We're looking,' Adam said. 'How's the golf?'

'I'm in the team so far,' Derek said. 'Under an assumed name, of course.'

'I suppose you'll be in the Hawks' Club next year. I always envied those bastards their ties. No trouble with women then!'

'I don't have any trouble with them now,' Derek said. 'Do you? Actually I quite probably won't be elected.'

'I thought it was automatic, if you got your Blue? ...'

'Not automatically,' Derek said.

'Since when?'

'Since an influential Old Blue,' Derek said, 'who doesn't approve of the wrong kind of nose in the club.'

'Nose? You're not serious? You don't mean –'

Derek nodded. 'There was a bloke this year, captain of some Half Blue sport, they're usually elected, but this time there was at least one black ball among the gold apparently. It just so happened he was one of us.'

'I don't believe it,' Adam said.

'What, in our house? Our beloved Cambridge? True, I'm afraid.'

'Six million Jews!' Adam said.

'As Sir Winston once said, what would we do with six

million Jews, all of them wanting to join the Hawks' Club?'

'We're bloody well going to do something about this,' Adam said.

'We're bloody well not,' Derek said.

'There's always the press. There's Alan Parks – the BBC – it's just the sort of story he'd like. Christ, Derek, we can't just stand by – '

'Look, Ad, why make waves? Put it in a film. That's the best thing. Make mock. Enjoy it. Try satire, son, try satire. Make a bob or two out of your limp, why don't you?'

'Satire leaves everything as it is. All you care about is getting your bloody Blue and never mind the principle of the thing – '

'The principle of the thing is that the world is a fucking unfair place. How else do you explain us both going to Cambridge, after all? Ad, if you could clean it all up, fine; but you can't. No one can. Do you know the story about the little Jewish fellow went into the travel agent's – '

'"Have you got another globe?" Dad told it to me. I hate those stories.'

'You don't want to be a Jew,' Derek said, 'you don't want to be a Gentile. What in hell do you want?'

'I don't know,' Adam said.

'You want to be a writer; be a writer. You want to be a rich writer; be a rich writer. But for God's sake, stop trying to put the world to shame already, will you?'

'Oh don't use that awful mock Jewish tone with me, Derek. I've heard enough of it. Who do we know who actually talks like that?'

'I'll tell you something'll keep you busy for a week or two: be a *great* writer.'

'About what?' Adam said. 'I want to show them – '

'Take down your pants and show them then,' Derek said. 'Everything's a gesture with you. Something to shake in people's faces. Prizes, scholarships, books, money, even – '

'Even what?' Adam said. 'You're thinking of Barbara, aren't you? You're including Barbara. You think – '

'Now you want a fight with me,' Derek said. 'Well, be careful. I'm bigger than I was. Ad, does it ever occur to you what a conformist you are? A conformist looking for something to conform to. You don't want the world to change any more than I do. You want it to take notice of Adam Morris, to pat him on the back and never threaten him, only tell him how well he's doing and how much he's wanted.'

'Have you got another globe?' Adam said.

The door of Derek's room opened and a blonde came in, wearing jeans and a white Mykonos top. 'Oh, sorry.'

'It's O K, Jess, this is my brother, Adam. Jessica Moxon.'

'Listen, I'll see you later,' the girl said. 'O K?'

'I was just going,' Adam said. 'I must. In case they need help with the two-syllable words.'

'Bye,' the girl said.

iii

It was a boy. Adam put his head round the bathroom door on his way to watch *The Alan Parks Interview* on the new television set. 'How goes it?'

'He loves it,' Barbara said. Tom was lying on his back in the water, kicking.

'Does he often have erections in the bath?'

'Doesn't everyone?' Barbara said.

'I'm glad we had him done,' Adam said.

'Reminds me of old times,' Barbara said.

'Old times! What's Oedipus got that I haven't got? And don't bother with Shmoedipus, because who needs an old hat in this weather?'

'You'll miss your programme,' Barbara said.

'Their programme,' Adam said.

'Well, there we are,' Alan Parks was saying to the camera, 'a clip from Mike Clode's *The Girl in Question* which has been nominated for this year's Oscars. Mike Clode and producer Bruno Lazlo are here in the studio with me literally on their way to the airport. Mr Lazlo, that now famous ice-cream scene, how did it come about?'

'Well,' Bruno said, 'an image of that kind doesn't just come in a flash of inspiration. It is the result of many hours of thought deep into the night in many ways; Mike and I sit and we talk and we think of ideas and then we throw them back and forth. I forget now which of us thought of that particular idea first, it may have been me, it may have not – I think – I don't know – probably possibly it was –'

'Mike, this film really does set out to say something about English society in the sixties, the Never-Had-It-So-Good world we live in, doesn't it?'

'Yes, absolutely,' Mike said. 'All this success the film has had has really been rather a surprise. Bruno and I set out to say something rather tough, uncompromising, and now . . .'

'You feel the applause has rather drowned the social criticism?'

'Yes, I do,' Mike said, 'and now the whole American bit; of course, the biggest thrill for me personally has been Jill's success –'

'Your wife, who unfortunately –'

'Is in America, at the moment; which is frankly a bigger incentive for me personally to go to LA than the Oscar ceremony. Dreadful gangbang, that is! Everyone knows the Oscar's a lottery and frankly I don't think I shall win. I hope you do, Bruno, but –'

'You win it, of course you win it, who else is there?'

'This is a film you've always wanted to make together, is it?'

'We were both fascinated by the character of the girl,' Mike said. 'As soon as she came to us, well, we were hooked!'

'And you've certainly made her very memorable,' Alan said. 'A great British picture, Mike, congratulations. Witty, true and, I must say, very alarming in its implications.'

'I'm glad you liked them,' Mike said.

Adam poked the set into darkness. Barbara came in, carrying Tom.

'You missed the two writers on the box,' Adam said. 'Off to collect their just rewards.'

'I hate them,' Barbara said. 'I hate them, I hate them, I hate them.'

'Oh come on,' Adam said. 'Just because they're shits? Your standards are ridiculous. Don't worry: I'm never a-gonna do another movie with those bastards.'

iv

'Telephone,' Barbara said.

'What time is it?'

'A quarter to seven,' Barbara said.

'Who the hell – ?' Adam scrambled out of bed and went into the other room. 'Hullo? Yes, yes, it is. What? Speaking. It's California,' he called. 'Bruno? How are you? What the hell's going on? You got me out of bed. Did you win the Oscar? Oh. Did Mike? Ah. Better luck next time. *What? I* did? Well, what do you know? Did you collect it for me? Oh, I thought as you wrote the script –' He put his hand over the receiver and called out. 'I won the Oscar. Sorry,' he said into the mouthpiece, 'I was just telling Barbara about it. My wife. They want us to do what? You and Mike and me? I see. Are they just? A hundred and fifty thousand dollars. What do I say? I say ask for two hundred. Well, you'd better talk to Geoffrey: most probably he'll want to ask for more. Well, that's nice news to go to work on. What? Oh only a book. B-o-o-k. Well, fine, terrific. OK, I'll see you then. Hey, what about doing *A Promised Land*? My novel. You may remember you read it. Next time. You promise? No, OK, what do you mean de swollen head? Anyone can win an Oscar.'

A
Country
Life

'You ought to give a ball occasionally, you know, Graham,'
Dan said. 'There were two people unmarked at the back of
the box.'

'I scored, didn't I?' the boy said.

'Another time,' Dan said, 'no one's going to bother
to run for you; not if you never give a ball.'

'Then I'll just have to score again on my own, won't I?'

'How much longer, sir?' said a smaller boy.

'About ten minutes,' Dan said. 'You want to get into
the game a bit. Keep warm. Run about.'

'And take your hands out of your pockets, Rex, please,'
said Tim March, one of Dan's colleagues, who was playing
against Dan's team. 'How many shirts have you got on,
boy?'

'Don't know, sir.'

'You don't *know*?'

'I was cold, sir.'

'Then you ought to run about,' Tim said.

'Graham never gives a ball, sir.'

'Never mind about that.'

'Mr Bradley said so.'

'Have we stopped playing, sir?'

'We'll stop playing when I say, Bruce,' Tim March said.

'Who's the ref around here?' Graham said. 'I thought
Mr Bradley was.'

'One shirt, Rex, that's the rule. And I heard that,
Graham. Get them off, lad, however many there are of
them.'

'His tits'll fall off.'

'What was that, Bruce?'

'I was saying something to Graham, sir.'

'We're all friends here,' Tim said. 'What was it?' Dan was doubling on the spot, a tactful hint to his colleague that perhaps they should get on. 'Well, Bruce?'

'I said his tits'd fall off, sir.'

'And that's funny, is it? Shall we go on with the game now?'

'Ready when you are, sir,' Graham said.

'And I want no more talking until the whistle goes,' Tim said. 'Ready when you are, Mr Bradley.'

Dan put the ball on the centre spot, blew his whistle and kicked off.

'Oh, we can talk now, can't we?' Bruce said.

'Don't be silly, lad,' Dan said, hurdling Bruce's tackle and heading for goal. Tim March moved to tackle. He took the ball from Dan and passed it to Graham, who raced towards goal. Dan turned and chased. He caught Graham on the edge of the area, tackled him once, was neatly side-stepped, and then tackled again, just as Graham was about to shoot. Graham fell flat on his face on the penalty spot.

'Penalty,' Rex said. 'That was a penalty!'

'I'm the referee, Rex,' Dan said, 'not you. And that wasn't a penalty. It was a fair tackle.'

'Fair tackle!' Graham sat there while Dan took the ball past Tim and shot into the net at the far end. 'Like hell it was – '

'Sir, how much longer?' Rex said.

'Off you go, lad,' Dan said. 'You heard what Mr March said. No talking until the whistle.'

'You just blew it, sir.'

'I said off. You wanted to know how much longer. Well, as far as you're concerned, no longer at all. Now, off when I say. Go on, early bath for you today, Rex.'

'All right, Graham?' Dan said, as they crossed for the kick-off.

'More or less,' Graham said.

'I went for the ball, not you,' Dan said.

'Sure,' Graham said.

Dan looked at his watch, blew two blasts on the whistle and picked up the ball. 'Full time. Well played, you colours. Thanks for the game, Tim. Not a bad game.'

'If only some of them would try,' Tim March said.

'And if only some of them wouldn't.'

'How *can* a boy put three shirts on, on an afternoon like this?'

'Incredible.'

'You heard about Rex finally owning up last night, I suppose?'

'Pissing in the linen cupboard?'

'Urinating is the Head's preferred term. How could he ever expect to get away with it? That's what beats me.'

'Did he necessarily want to get away with it?'

'Oh I know what you think, Dan. Father in prison . . .'

'It might have something to do with it, don't you think, sir?'

'He's not the only one with that particular problem. I suppose one day he'll end up there himself.'

'With the right assistance from the right people,' Dan said. 'What action did the Head take?'

'The usual,' Tim said. 'Six of the best.'

'You know,' Dan said, 'I sometimes think the Head can't have a particularly rich imaginative life. Well, I must go and see who's managing to get drowned in the communal tub.'

ii

Dan stood looking at Joyce for a moment from the low gate. She was hanging up the washing. Stepping round the motor bike and side car which was parked beside the vegetable patch, he went in and helped her with the sheets. 'Everything OK?'

'Fine,' Joyce said. 'You?'

'You looked so beautiful just now. I was watching you. There's something about the way you do the simplest things – '

'With a bad grace, you mean,' Joyce said.

'Pegging the things. It's very – lovely,' he said. 'Did you manage to get into town?'

'Couldn't in the end,' she said. 'They've messed the buses about. They're not doing the one from the Cross any more.'

'I'll take you in the morning. Kids OK?'

'They're OK.'

'Is something wrong?' Dan said. 'I get the impression – '

'We're going to have a visitor,' Joyce said. '*Visitors.*'

Joyce looked down at her red hands. Dan took them, almost roughly, and kissed them. 'Well, come on,' he said. 'Who?'

She went into the cottage. Dan followed, frowning.

'Is that you, Mummy?'

'Hannah, when was it ever anyone else?'

The place was simply furnished: there was an old oleograph on the wall and a map of the district pinned above a desk covered with Dan's work books. There was a shotgun on a high bracket. The two girls, Hannah and Carol, were on the floor of the back room, playing with bricks and some ragged dolls. Joyce took a telegram off the table and handed it to Dan.

'Well, what do you know?' Dan said.

'How the hell did he know where to find us?'

'Oh God,' Dan said, 'people like that! They can find anything.'

'Do you want to see them?' she said.

'Ten years,' Dan said.

'Because I don't.'

'He doesn't exactly give us much option, does he? "We shall be in your area." Sounds like a royal progress!'

'A royal progress or a free offer. Have your packet tops ready when Mr Big Shot calls.'

Dan put his arm round her. 'We'll tell him to go away. It's perfectly simple. We'll just tell him to go away. What can they do to us? We'll just say, no thank you, and that'll be it.'

'Just like we did to the world,' Joyce said. 'I shall have to get some food in. They say lunchtime.'

'Perhaps they'll bring a hamper,' Dan said. 'I wouldn't bother.'

'I do have *some* pride,' Joyce said.

'I love you,' Dan said. 'I love you.'

Joyce said: 'I can do Irish stew, OK?'

'Fine by me,' Dan said. 'Where's the lad, by the way?'

'Peter? Playing,' Joyce said. 'He went to play at Damian's house after school.'

iii

'We can't be far,' Alan Parks said. 'I think I'll just stop and shout.'

'You'll frighten the birds,' Barbara said.

'Story of my life,' Alan said. 'I'm really looking forward to seeing Dan, you know that? Are you?'

'Let's hope he's looking forward to seeing you.'

'I liked Dan. You never knew him really, did you?' He changed down and the red Alfa moved slowly down the lane. Barbara was wearing a suede coat with fur lining and a fur hat. Alan was in a tartan lumber jacket with a pom-pom hat and a mile of red scarf. 'See if you can find this Lockhart Hall place, will you, on the map in the whatsit? I don't suppose it'll be marked.'

'Not unless it's in Southern Spain,' Barbara said, taking the map out of the flap in the door.

'Oh sod; there's another map, somewhere. I bought a whole raft of the bloody things a couple of days ago. Look on the floor.'

'Nothing but thick wool carpet,' Barbara said, 'as far as the eye can envy. We'll have to ask.'

'I hope we're doing the right thing. But, Christ, Barb, one has to try. Don't you agree? With people?'

iv

'Tell me something, Graham, what do *you* think of this essay? Are you satisfied? Is this really the way you want it?'

'I was a bit pushed, sir,' Graham said.

'Never mind what's happening in the other room.' The boy had turned at the rattle of dishes. Joyce was laying the table, helped by Hannah and Carol. 'In other words, you left it till the last minute, right?'

'Not the *last* minute, sir.'

'The hell of it is, this could be a really outstanding piece of work. The ideas are all there, but you haven't worked them out, have you? And how do you spell "business"?'

'B-u-s-i-'

'And is that how you've spelt it?'

'No, sir.'

'Twit,' Dan said. 'Aren't you? What are you going to do about it?'

'Don't know, sir,' Graham said. 'Do it out again, I suppose.'

'Do it out again. And right this time. Joyce, doesn't that sound like somebody? Peter?' Dan called out of the window. '*Peter*! Is that a car coming? Because go and give them a wave, if it is – '

'I don't know them,' Peter said. He was practising high jumps in the garden.

'*Peter.*'

'Well, I'll be off, sir, then,' Graham said.

Alan leaned out of his car. 'Hullo.'

'Hullo,' Peter said.

'I've got a feeling we've come to see you,' Alan said, 'am I right?'

'I think so.'

'I think so too. Don't you, Barb?'

'He's got your hair,' Barbara said.

'Yes, well, we won't talk about that, O K?' Alan opened the door and indicated the back of the car. 'Hop in, why don't you?'

'What sort of car do you have?' Barbara said.

'We don't,' Peter said. 'We have feet.'

'That sounds like Dan's kid all right,' Alan said.

v

'Out of the blue,' Dan said.

Alan shook hands. 'And what better place to be out of, eh?'

'Was it a frightful nerve on our part?' Barbara said.

'I like nerve,' Dan said.

Alan held out the end of his red scarf to Peter. 'Catch hold. And now pull. Not *too* hard.' Peter pulled and Alan swung round and round, like a top, and started to lurch about the room, as if completely dizzy.

'I think this cottage is *bliss*,' Barbara said. Joyce came out of the kitchen, wiping her hands. 'Joyce!' Barbara said. 'What a long time!'

'Yes,' Joyce said. 'Isn't it?'

'But nobody,' Alan said, 'but *nobody*, would think so. You don't look a day over. She doesn't look a day over, 'does she? Honestly. Here, you haven't bloody well gone and cooked, have you? For us?'

'Not *gone* and cooked, *stayed* and cooked!' Joyce said. 'The natives often have a meal at lunchtime.'

'Often have a meal at lunchtime! Didn't you get my wire?'

'We'd look a bit more surprised than this if we hadn't,' Dan said.

'I did try to call you, but – '

'We haven't got a phone,' Dan said.

'No wonder there was no reply. Only we were taking you out to lunch, that was the whole idea.'

'It's all ready,' Joyce said.

'Christ, you must think we're the absolute prize spongers of all time! Joyce, you shouldn't have.'

'I know,' Joyce said. 'But I did.'

'God, you look marvellous! Marvellous. Ten years. A lifetime! And you look absolutely marvellous.' He grinned at Joyce and ruffled Peter's hair. 'It's been too bloody long, it really has.'

Joyce said: 'This is Hannah and this is Carol.'

'Hullo, this is Hannah and this is Carol. This is Alan. And this is Barbara. I expect you know your father. What a terrific cottage!'

'Isn't it? Barbara said. 'It's the prettiest one we've seen, easily.'

'Come on through,' Dan said. Barbara followed him into the back room. French windows looked out over the marshes, glistening in the autumn sunshine.

'You look exactly the same,' Barbara said.

'You don't,' Dan said. 'You look better than ever.'

'Ten years and three children later!' Barbara said. 'Don't make me laugh.'

'I never make people laugh,' Dan said. 'Ask anyone. They'll laugh.'

'Just the air is worth the journey. Honestly, the country! What wouldn't I give for it?'

'Not what they're asking,' Alan said. 'The prices, you wouldn't believe it. You must be sitting on a bloody goldmine.'

'It isn't ours,' Dan said. 'It's rented.'

'Tremendous to see you both,' Alan said. 'To see all of you. You won't believe how often we've talked about you. How often everyone's talked about you. I feel really bad about this lunch business though. I thought you'd realize –'

'Don't worry. You're only getting what we're having anyway.'

'OK,' Alan said, 'you've broken my last stubborn resistance. What're we having anyway?'

'We don't lead the grand life, I'm afraid,' Dan said.

'That's absolutely grand as far as we're concerned,' Alan said.

Barbara said: 'I do envy you this. London's impossible.'

'Only one place worse than London,' Alan said. 'New York.'

'What about New Delhi?' Dan said.

Joyce said: 'Do you spend a lot of time in New York?'

'As little as possible,' Alan said. 'I've been having to go a lot lately in the way of trade, but if it's anything to do with me, it's quickly in and quickly out, if you know what I mean. Thank God.'

'Who wants sherry,' Dan said, 'and who wants Scotch? Barbara?'

'Sherry for me. Dry if you've got one.'

'We've only got one, but I think it's dryish. What will Alan have? Whisky?'

Barbara held up two fingers half an inch apart. 'No more.'

'What are you actually doing these days, Alan, on the television?' Joyce asked. 'Because we hardly ever see it. We don't have it.'

173

'I *thought* there was something missing in this idyllic set-up. That's exactly what makes it so idyllic, of course. No box. Do you really not have a box?'

'I'm afraid not.'

'This is Mutiny, Mr Christian – Mrs Christian, and all the little Christians. Don't you *like* it?'

'We can't afford it.'

'*And* we don't like it,' Dan said.

'We all have to swallow a peck of dirt in our lives,' Alan said. 'Or, in my case, once a week.'

'He loves it,' Barbara said. 'Every time he sees himself – '

'It's frying tonight. The mercury shoots straight up to the top. It's perfectly true.'

'Oh, you actually *appear*?' Joyce said.

'Do I actually *appear*? You're still wearing woad, you bloody spud-bashers, aren't you? I'm only the scourge of the nation, the hammer of the Scots, the chisel of the English and the block and tackle of two continents. Or soon will be. If my American programme gets off the ground and into the ratings. Do I *appear*?!'

'You said America was all set.'

'Friend David has given me his solemn word that there is "absolutely no question in the network's mind" – so obviously nothing's certain yet, but – '

Barbara said: 'Have you really never seen him doing his stuff?'

'We did once, didn't we? At your mother's.'

'Grilling some trade-unionist. My parents thought you were the voice of righteousness itself.'

'And they were absolutely right,' Alan said. 'Actually I'm getting a bit brassed off with the front man bit. I'm thinking of hanging up my sincerity at the end of next season.' He rehearsed it for them. '"Thank you and – g'night."'

Barbara said: 'What I call his "think-about-it-till-I-tell-you-to-think-about-something-else" face.'

'I think we could eat actually,' Joyce said.

'How dare you,' Alan said, 'live in a bloody paradise?
I'm going to have to do a big exposé of shady characters
who maintain their integrity and live in places like this. I
reckon I could work the whole country up into a fury of
indignation against undemanding, unspoiled people like
you. What if everyone decided to lead a simple, decent life
without giving an envious thought to wall-to-wall carpet-
ing and the second car? Anti-social opters-out! I'll give
you hell, you see if I don't. Christ, I'm hungry.'

vi

'Do you never see television at all then?' Alan said.

'Sometimes,' Peter said.

'Don't you have it at school?'

'At school!' Joyce said. 'Mrs Hedingham would die,
wouldn't she, Peter?'

'Then let's get it!' Peter said.

'Do you like games at all? Soccer, cricket . . .?'

'A bit.'

'A bit! Come on, Peter. He's in the football team.'

'That's terrific,' Alan said. 'Do you support anyone?
Arsenal, Chelsea . . .'

'Ipswich,' Peter said.

'Ipswich?' Alan said. 'What's Ipswich?'

'If you don't know who Ipswich are,' Peter said, 'you
don't know who anyone is.'

'My favourite soup,' Alan said. 'Delicious. You know
why we came down this way, don't you? Did Ba tell you?'

Joyce said: 'Presumably you're in the market for something.'

'In the market for anything,' Alan said. 'You know me.'

Dan said: 'How many children have you got these
days?'

'Three,' Barbara said. 'The twins and now Donald.'

Alan said: 'The last kid's a bit of a problem. Kept Ba pretty busy one way and another, hasn't he?'

'Both,' Barbara said.

'He's spastic, Donald, the poor little bugger.'

'Is it bad?' Dan said.

'In spades, hearts, diamonds and clubs, poor little sod. Can't do anything for himself except all the things you don't want him to do.'

'And is there any – you know – hope?' Joyce asked.

'None,' Barbara said, as if it were the best news in the world.

'Don't let it cast a blight on the day,' Alan said. 'It may be news to you, but it's not news to us. So – '

'Where have you left him?' Joyce said.

'I've got a wonderful girl luckily,' Barbara said.

'When you let her do anything. Ba's so ridiculously devoted to that kid, I can't tell you.' Joyce came back with the main course: mashed potato, stew, carrots, red cabbage. 'Red cabbage!' Alan said. 'The one thing I like! You must be psychic, Joyce.'

'No, she isn't,' Dan said. 'It also happens to be the one thing I like.'

'Brother!' Alan offered his hand across the table.

'You still haven't told us what you're here for,' Dan said.

'I have in a way,' Alan said. 'I wanted Ba to myself for a couple of days. And nights. Apart from that, we're looking for somewhere we can get away to. With the kids, and without, sometimes, I hope, and I mean that very sincerely. Country air, no telephone, no television. How much do you want for the place?'

Hannah said: 'They can't have this house.'

'Don't fret yourself, Hannah. I'm not about to chuck you out of your house,' Alan said. 'Only your mummy and daddy.'

'The man isn't serious,' Dan said.

'Not serious? We've looked at every decrepit, clapped-out pigsty over three thousand quid between here and there and you know where. And you'd better watch out: because the whole of middle-class London's on the march in this direction. If you listen carefully you can hear the tramp of their cheque books even now.'

'London today,' Barbara said, '– murder.'

'We wouldn't mind a decent theatre sometimes, would we, Dan? Maybe not permanently, but – '

'Why don't we do a swap occasionally?' Barbara said. 'You could have Clarendon Road and we'll have this – '

'Clarendon Road. That's Notting Hill, isn't it?'

'London A to Z, aren't you, Joycey, even after all these years in the sticks?'

'I wouldn't exactly call it Notting Hill.'

'No. More like Willesden Green, the end we live. Which is why there are going to be changes.'

'Have you got a big house?' Joyce said.

'Average gigantic,' Alan said. 'Well, it's the cheapest way, isn't it? We got it before the district started going up. Couple of years ago, when it was all open fields and unspoiled gasometers. Look, I'll tell you what, though I shouldn't even be mentioning the subject after a blow-out like this, but you're going to bloody promise me something. Tonight we're bloody well going to take you out to dinner.'

'*He* says bloody all the time, doesn't he?' Peter said.

'He's allowed to,' Dan said. 'He's famous. Famous people can say what they like.'

'Famous!' Alan said. 'Listen, I don't have any illusions. We take the good times when they're here, but how long it'll last – ? Well, till dinner time anyway, and you know who's opened a place near here, don't you? Denis Porson. You remember Denis, don't you? Junior Treasurer of the Theatre Club at Cambridge.' He flapped his wrist. '*Denis!*'

'Oh, *Denis*,' Dan said. 'Of course.'

'Anyway, he's become quite a force in the fancy nosh

business. The man who put the scoff in Escoffier kind of thing. These days, you know, people have got more money than they know how to eat.'

'Some people,' Joyce said. 'It sounds dreadfully smart.'

'It's just a simple country pub, served slightly under-done, with a tossed green salad and just a tincture of whoops-dearie.'

'Sounds just our thing,' Dan said.

'Mummy, can we go?' Hannah said. 'We've got our hospital.'

'Off you go then,' Joyce said. 'It's not long dresses, I hope, this place – ?'

'No long dresses, no long faces. The food's terrific, apparently. I was reading about it in Harper's Disaster. He's called it Bumpkins, which is rather poppety of him, don't you think so, Anthea? Not that I fancy doing much more eating today. Intended as a compliment. And taken as a condiment, I trust. I only insult people for money, isn't that right, missus?'

'Right, squire.'

'God, this is nice though,' Alan said. 'Seriously. Being here. Seeing you.' Dan took the vegetable dishes off the table, while Joyce went to get the pudding plates. Alan, Barbara and Peter were alone at the table. 'Here we really are, Ba, after all this time, eh?'

'Yes,' Barbara said, 'aren't you? Both of you!'

II

Bumpkins was delightful. It had been a blacksmith's shop and the old forge was still there; they grilled steaks on it. Denis Porson had renovated the place with ingenuity and wit. Horse brasses hung against black pillars and old cart wheels hung from the ceiling, studded with candles. They had on-the-house glasses of cold Chambéry before the meal, and Alan insisted on a couple of bottles of 'The Widow' when they got down to the serious eating. 'It's all perfectly simple really,' he told them, 'if I hadn't been a vulgar, crude, overbearing Australian peasant, I'd probably still be playing Buttons at the Oldham Rep. No, it's true . . .'

'I didn't hear anyone deny it,' Barbara said.

'We live, my friends, in the age of the shameless bastard. There's only one thing the Great British Public won't stand for – and that's the still small voice of reason, moderation and common decency. Try writing that sort of prescription for the national health and you'll have them bunging up the gutters with the stuff.'

'I still believe in those things.'

'I should bloody well hope so, Daniel. I still believe in them too. We all believe in them. But try peddling them to Mr and Mrs Gore-Blimey and their friends, Mr and Mrs Plastic-Bucket. They don't want to know.' They had reached the pudding stage. The Spanish waiter wheeled up the trolley. 'Christ, that looks disgusting! Joycey? It's all yours. No, what they want to hear is that everyone who stands for anything which takes a little time or a little effort is nothing but a sodding great hypocrite with a big head who actually spends most of his time with one hand up a chorus girl's skirt and the other one in the till.'

'I'm not quite clear whether you're talking about yourself doing all this or other people doing it.'

'In America, they're planning to call me The Man Who Dares to Speak the Truth. Who wouldn't, at five thousand bucks a throw? You know, sometimes you really think you've got the world by the scruff of the neck – the full double Nelson – and then the world turns round and says, "That was wonderful, darling, can I have the same again next week? You'll find my purse in my handbag."' He took a cigar from his inside pocket and offered one to Dan.

'I don't smoke,' Dan said.

'Don't smoke? Watch out, Daniel. If there's one thing I hate, it's people who're incorruptible.'

'I must go and phone,' Barbara said, 'just to make sure –'

'Sweetheart,' Alan said, 'for one night –' But she had gone. 'You know what I wish? I wish they'd put a pillow over his face by mistake on purpose. They must've known.'

'One can't do things like that.'

'Look,' Alan said, 'I don't mind for myself, all I have to do is shell out, which is the least of my present worries, frankly. It's Barbara. She's not really here even now. And what sort of life is he going to have in the end? I'd rather she was shagging somebody on the quiet. It'd be a lot more healthy for her – and me too, probably. I'll tell you something funny, shall I? I called him Donald as in Brad-man. You wouldn't think it of me, would you? Well, I did. Now I guess people'll think it was Donald as in Duck. Quack-quack-quack! I can't exactly see him opening the batting for anyone.'

'Did Bradman?' Dan said.

'She won't give up with him, that's what gets me,' Alan said. 'She was going to go back to the acting, but she won't. I could get her some interviewing and stuff to do, no trouble at all, but she won't hear of it.'

'I think that's very honourable,' Dan said.

'Of course it's honourable. It's also bloody maddening and the next best thing to downright disloyal – not allow-ing me to exert improper influence on her behalf.'

Dan said: 'We ought to be going soon. Tim March's daughter's only fifteen and – '

'All she's doing is *sitting*,' Joyce said.

'I wonder if Denis has got a box on the premises,' Alan said. 'Because I'm on in a bit.'

Barbara came back with Denis Porson, who wore a plum velvet smoking jacket, with elaborate frogging on the front and the cuffs. 'Well? Everything all right?'

'Denis,' Alan said, 'I absolutely loathe having to say this to an old friend, and you know I wouldn't do it if I could possibly help it, but it was absolutely bloody marvellous. You remember Dan, don't you? The King of the Cambridge Kong?'

'Best Mercutio I ever saw,' Denis said.

'And a plague on both your houses!' Dan said. 'Do you remember Joyce, my wife?'

'Of course. I hear you've acquired a cottage down this way.'

'No. We just live here,' Dan said.

'Ah. Oh. Super! You know who's just bought a little place down the road, and that's Ted Paris.'

'Ted Paris?'

Denis did the old number.

'"I'm a little starlet from J. Arthur Rank,
Brixton-born and a voice like a Yank –
I'm all set to make it,
I'm all set to shake it.
I'm a starlet from J. Arthur Rank.

'Next verse – "I'm a starlet from J. Arthur Rank,
And my – eyes are as big as a bank,
For success I've a lust –
California *and* bust –
I'm a starlet, I said a starlet, I'm a starlet from J. Arthur
Rank!"'

Everyone clapped. He did it so well!

'Ted Paris,' Denis said. 'Footlights '55. He's nursing the constituency.'

'He's certainly got the tits for it,' Alan said. 'Denis, you haven't got a box on the premises by any chance, have you?'

'Box? Oh *box*! I think the boys've got one upstairs somewhere.'

'One quick ogle, Daniel? Just to see how the other half lives; then we'll drive you home.' Alan took his wife's arm and they started out of the room. 'Don all right?'

'He asked where we were, apparently. Maria told him, and he hasn't murmured since.'

'*Asked?*' Alan said. 'He must've come on a bit in eight hours!'

As Joyce and Dan followed the Parkses from the restaurant, one of the diners at the next table touched her arm. 'Excuse me, but isn't that Alan Parks?'

'Yes,' Joyce said, 'that's right.'

'Do forgive me for asking. It's ridiculous really, isn't it, but one feels one knows him so well.'

Joyce said: 'He really is famous.'

'Yes,' Dan said, 'isn't he just?'

ii

The guest on *The Alan Parks Interview* was Ronald Braithwaite M.P., Under-Secretary for Defence. He was of the same generation as Dan and the others, but responsibility had thinned his hair and thickened his waist. He wore that look of wary candour which Alan often provoked in his 'guests'.

'I take it,' Alan was saying, 'that you don't deny that these weapons are being made?'

'I think we should stick to the point – '

'I understood you'd agreed to come here and talk about Defence. Is that right?'

'Yes,' Ronnie said.

'Now I want to get this quite clear. Is that yes-yes or yes-no?'

The studio audience laughed and clapped. 'Fifteen-love,' Alan said to Joyce. He did not take his eyes from the box. Joyce watched the unmatching mirror, Alan looking at Alan, with disdainful fascination.

'Minister,' Alan said, 'we have these cases of dead cattle, blind and haemorrhaging and showing obvious signs of extreme physical suffering – and the trail, if I may put it that way, leads right up to your back door.'

'Compensation has been fully paid,' Braithwaite said.

'And I'm sure the cattle's next of kin have been informed, but is that quite the point?'

'The electorate was not directly consulted on the development of the Spitfire,' Ronald Braithwaite said. 'If it had been, this country probably wouldn't have had the plane when the time came.'

'And what time is it that's coming, Minister, when we shall need to introduce agonizing chemicals into the drinking water of a potential enemy? I mean, what enemy deserves that sort of treatment, would you say?' As Ronnie started to answer, Alan poured himself a glass of water from the carafe on the low glass table in front of him, and raised it thirstily to his lips. At the last moment, he checked and looked into the glass with appalled suspicion. He shrugged, toasted the audience and drank bravely. Ronnie's reply was drowned in the applause.

'No wonder they hate me,' Alan said.

'No wonder they do,' Barbara said. 'Alan, I'm just going – '

'Oh for fuck sake,' Alan said.

'I have seen this before, you know, darling. I only want to know how he is.'

'Well, I'll promise you one thing,' Alan said. 'He isn't sitting up in bed reading Proust.' He leaned over to switch off the television. 'It gets a bit draggy from here on in.'

'Please leave it,' Joyce said.

'Sometimes,' Ronnie Braithwaite was now saying, 'this kind of research can lead to a medical breakthrough – '

'That's rather like defending the use of the rack on the grounds that it might help to find a cure for rheumatism, isn't it?'

After the laughter, Ronnie said: 'Mr Parks, your job is to amuse the public, ours is to protect them in a world where, I'm sorry to say, they face bigger enemies than their own elected representatives and bigger dangers than getting less than a hundred laughs to the gallon.'

'We don't amuse,' Alan said. 'We inform, but Ronald Braithwaite, thank you very much. That's all we have time for tonight, and so until the same time next week, thank you for being with us, and – g'night.'

Alan winked at Joyce. 'Hold look of warm-hearted, tough-minded, thick-skinned, level-headed, keen-witted, straight-talking Aussie news-hawk,' he said, 'until the studio manager gives us the old wind-up, and then you can all piss off home, thank you very much.'

Dan had left the room after Barbara. She was on the 'boys'' telephone at the end of the landing.

'All right?' Dan said.

She nodded and nodded and then put down the receiver. 'He's asleep,' she said. There was an odd brilliance in her eyes as she looked at Dan. She walked back along the corridor towards him, lips rigid in a red smile. Only when she seemed about to pass him without another word did she fling herself into his arms and sob against his chest. It lasted only a long second. By the time Joyce and Alan had come out of the telly room, she was quite composed.

'Last bus for paradise,' Alan said. 'All aboard.'

'Do you mind terribly if I don't come with?' Barbara said. 'Only – '

'We'll see you tomorrow, won't we?' Dan said. 'Come over in the morning. Try my home-made beer.'

iii

'What the fuck's going on?' Alan said, rubbing at the condensation on the windscreen. Up ahead, in the darkness round the cottage, wild lights were weaving about. The

Alfa spat pebbles as Alan changed gear and charged up the lane. It was boys, on bicycles. They were whooping and riding round and round Mill Cottage. When the car lights caught them, they swerved and dodged and rode up the verge to get past and away. Dan jumped out and raced towards the back door. He tried to grab one of the boys as he went past, but his real fear was for Jenny March, and the children.

'I'm all right,' the girl said. She was sitting in the back room, school books in front of her, knees under her chin, huddled yet comfortingly calm.

'They didn't come in, did they?' Dan said.

Joyce ran in. 'What happened?'

'Nothing,' Jenny said.

'Damned village louts,' Dan said. 'And they call our boys delinquent. Some of those village kids are twice as bad.'

'Nothing really happened,' Jenny said.

'They just seemed to be riding round and round,' Alan said. 'They don't seem to have done anything, do they?'

'I'll take you home, Jenny.'

'There's no need, Mr Bradley. Mr Bradley, please don't tell Dad, will you?'

Dan took the torch and they went out.

Alan said: 'I had no idea the natives were so restless in this part of the country. God Almighty, look at this.' He picked something up from under the kitchen window and brought it to Joyce. 'You've got some continental post,' he said. 'French letters!'

'I *hate* this village sometimes,' Joyce said. 'I hate it.'

'Well,' Alan said, 'you can say one thing for 'em, they're better organized than we managed to be.' He grinned and Joyce smiled ruefully. 'Christ, I was a selfish so-and-so, wasn't I? Just think – if – '

'I don't think I will,' Joyce said.

'He's a hell of a nice kid, Peter.'

'Yes,' Joyce said. 'He is.'

'I hope I didn't ruin your life, Joycey. You seem pretty happy, I must say. He's a terrific character, Dan, my God! Next time I wear a hat, I'll take it off to him. What about schools around here, Joyce? For Peter.'

'He's at the local primary,' Joyce said. 'It's not too bad. Shall I make some tea or something?'

'No, for God's sake, I always go on a diet between midnight and eight the following morning. That's how I keep my double chin. I was thinking about when he's older.'

'There's always the Grammar School,' she said, 'if he gets in.'

'And if he doesn't? Tell me something: how much does Daniel make a year?'

'I shall start work myself when Carol goes to school,' Joyce said.

Alan said: 'I'm so loaded with cash, I've got two men digging holes and another two looking for new places, you know the story. Branches everywhere. Joyce, I want you to have some of the money. I want Peter to have some of it.'

'No.'

'Dan doesn't have to know.'

'What do you want to do to us?' Joyce said. 'Of course he'd know.'

'Do I have to find a selfish reason to want to help my own kid?'

'He's not yours,' Joyce said. 'I think you should go. Dan'll be back in a minute.'

'Then I'll go in a minute. The trouble with people like you is you take money so bloody seriously. Why the fuss? What's a thousand a year to me? I spill more than that.'

'Congratulations,' Joyce said.

'Dammit, Joyce, quit that; you're a pigheaded cow, aren't you? Haven't changed a bit! Suppose a distant uncle left you five thousand quid, would you take it?'

'That's different.'

'Meet your distant uncle! Christ, I don't get it from immoral earnings, you know. Or if I do, I'm the one who does the whoring, so what's the problem?'

'I don't care what you sell,' Joyce said. 'I just don't happen to want to be bought.'

'Well, I'll tell you something, shall I? That's a bloody selfish attitude. Look, I'll set up a Trust Fund for your kids, the whole lot of them – I don't intend to start discriminating between Dan's genes and mine, for Christ's sake – and you needn't speak to me or see me again. I'm not trying to buy an interest in your bloody family. I've got one of my own. With a discretionary trust most of the money won't even be mine, it'll be the Chancellor's, and he's not likely to buzz down and see how Peter's doing in the nets, is he? Or ask for a kiss at an awkward moment.'

Dan stopped outside the back door to tie his shoelace. It broke as he pulled it and he had to repair it. He listened, with a curious contentment, to the voices coming through the window.

'Is that why you came down here?' Joyce said.

'Not entirely,' Alan said. 'I didn't know how I was going to feel, did I?'

'And as we've made a favourable impression, you've decided to make us a grant, is that it?'

'I thought we were all old enough – ' Alan said.

'Oh we're old enough,' Joyce said.

'What am I supposed to do with my money, for God's sake? Waste it?'

'You can't have him,' she said. 'You can't have him.'

'He's my kid,' Alan said, 'that's one thing you can't change. Are you ever going to tell him?'

'I hadn't thought about it.'

187

'Well, think about it,' Alan said, 'because I should have thought that if there was one thing we'd had enough of from our parents' generation, it was the domestic lie.'

'I don't like being called a liar,' Joyce said.

'No one does, do they?' Alan said. 'But what happened, happened. Remember?' He grabbed her roughly by the shoulders and, grinning at the same time, kissed her violently on the mouth.

Dan stepped into the cottage. Alan had tactful time to turn away from Joyce. 'All quiet on the Western front?' he said. 'No ravening hordes of teen-age dolly-birds lurking in the shrubbery?'

'Shouldn't be.'

'Oh well,' Alan said, 'I'll go anyway.'

'Stop over for coffee in the morning,' Dan said, 'and I'll show you round the penal colony. I usually have a kick around with the boys Sunday morning, if you felt like it.'

Alan patted his paunch. 'Wouldn't do me any harm,' he said. 'Well, thank-you and – g'night!'

iv

'He talks a bit,' Dan said.

'He certainly does that. I don't think this place has ever been quite so flooded with words.'

'No,' Dan said. 'One feels that his victims probably have to be rescued by helicopter.'

'What do you think of Barbara?' Joyce asked. She was sitting at her dressing table in her nightie, brushing her hair.

'You haven't got any reason to be jealous,' Dan said.

'And is that a good thing?' Joyce said.

'Did he upset you, Alan?'

'You know what he wants, don't you?'

'Well, he can't have him, can he?'

188

'No,' Joyce said. 'Do you ever think he's not really yours? Peter. Be honest. Do you?'

'Never,' Dan said. 'Never.'

'No wonder you're so difficult to live with,' she said. 'Tell me something. Why did you marry me?'

'What's he been saying to you?' Dan said.

'That's no answer,' Joyce said.

'Why do people marry people?' Dan said. 'Because I loved you.'

'Too quick. Too easy. Too everything you're usually not.'

'I wish they hadn't bloody well come.'

'Are you happy?' Joyce said.

'Happy? What's happy? I don't necessarily believe in being happy. Happy's what people like Barbara and Alan are, until he fancies some woman in New York or she – gets tired of him or it or whatever she gets tired of. Then suddenly they aren't *happy* any longer. I'm happy because I've got you, I've got the children, I've got – what I want.'

'And it's nothing to do with me at all, is it?' Joyce said.

'Joyce, it's nearly half past one,' Dan said. 'Are you trying to have a quarrel? Because if you want to have a quarrel, let's have a quarrel. Only – '

'It would make a *change*,' Joyce said.

'I don't believe in quarrels,' Dan said. 'Why should we have quarrels?'

'Dan, do you love me?' Joyce said. 'Do you really know who I am?'

'Oh, love, love, love,' Dan said.

'Thank you,' she said. 'Thank you.'

'For what?'

'For sounding just a little bit impatient. I can't tell you what a relief it is.'

'Joyce, what is this *about*?'

'What's it about? It's about us. Us. Us. Us. Us,' she said. 'Us. It's about us.'

'Are you still in love with him?' Dan said.

'You were being kind when you married me, weren't you?'

'Kind?'

'Protecting me, weren't you?'

'I wanted you,' Dan said.

'And protecting yourself,' Joyce said. 'From women like her.'

'Was I?'

'Women like Barbara. Women who wanted things, *demanded* things. So you decided to be kind to me instead. Poor, lost, impregnated-by-a-shit Joyce Hadleigh. Which rhymed with Bradley, which was as good a reason for marrying me as any other.'

Dan said: 'I am what I am.'

'As God once said.'

'Joyce, I'm tired. I'm tired and I've got kids to cope with in the morning.'

'You didn't want a wife at all, did you?'

'This is what I didn't want, Joyce. This. Precisely this. What I've got at this very moment. Satisfied?'

'I might be if we went on all night.'

'I don't know what you're talking about,' Dan said.

'Well, try,' Joyce said. 'You didn't love me *despite* my being pregnant. You didn't love me *despite* my having made a silly mess of my silly life. You loved me *because* I had. Because that meant you could play God with me and lift me up. Just like you play God with those boys, those horrible, ugly, beastly boys who're all of them going to end up in the clink and you know it. Oh you bring them to the house and you talk to them and you understand them and you hold out that helping hand of yours, the great and gentle Dan, who isn't part of the big ugly system and who really understands individual human beings, no matter how helpless and delinquent they may be. After all, he married a woman no one else wanted, didn't he, a woman despised and rejected of the people, big with another man's child? Oh the man is a saint, a saint, and nothing short of a saint. He saith unto one go, and he goeth – '

Dan slapped her hard across the face. She grinned blood at him. He tore her nightie down from her shoulders and flung her down on the bed. Afterwards she just lay there, smiling at him, with her legs apart until he thrust her under the bedclothes and turned out the light.

III

The presence of a stranger, and a famous one, made Graham display all his skills. He teased Alan, who elected to go in goal, with dazzling ruthlessness.

'Have you ever thought of becoming a professional?' Alan asked, as they came off the field. 'Only it so happens that a London club which I am not at liberty to disclose, at this moment in time, has asked me to become a director and I was thinking – '

'London?' Graham said. 'I don't suppose they'd want me – '

'I'll have a word with Billy Thomas, who's by way of being a mate of mine – '

'You'd appreciate that, wouldn't you, Graham?' Dan said.

'Might,' Graham said.

'I won't forget,' Alan said. 'I never forget people who make a fool of me.' Graham nodded and ambled away. 'He might make it. He's certainly got a shot.'

'He's quite a bright lad, actually,' Dan said. 'I'd be glad if you didn't – '

'Didn't what?'

'Push things too fast. He's coming up to O-levels and I'd hate to see him – you know – sidetracked.'

'Sidetracked? I'd swap all the O-levels in the world for a hat trick against Newport County reserves.'

'I've spent a lot of time working with this lad,' Dan said, 'giving him confidence in himself, persuading him there's more to life than – '

'The roar of the crowd, eh?'

'Yes. If you like.'

'And is there?' Alan said.

'Show him the bright lights now,' Dan said, 'and – '

'Oh Jesus Christ, Daniel, I want him to be a footballer, not a chorus girl – '

'He's mine, that boy,' Dan said. 'I've done the work day by day, week by week, with that boy, trying to keep him from – from – '

'From what? Mucky books and dirty talk and village girls with pliable knees – ? Dan, it may surprise you, but I'd like to do some good in the world too, you know. Help a kid who needs help.'

They were walking along under the elms towards the gate of the school. Some boys went past on their bicycles. 'Morning, sir,' they said.

'It's always easy to help the ones who need it least,' Dan said.

'Like you with this Graham?' Alan said.

Dan said: 'I want the lad to have something stable to rely on first; after that the rest can follow.'

'You mean you want him to rely on you,' Alan said.

'Why did you have to come down here?'

'I didn't. Have to. I just did. And I'll tell you. Because I'm a stirrer. Isn't that what you want to hear? I like making trouble.'

'Well, why don't you try doing the hard thing for once?' Dan said. 'Finding out how things really are. What the real consequences are of a place like this. Instead of – '

'Forgive me for trying to help,' Alan said. 'Forgive me for trespassing in the sacred grove. I didn't realize the kid meant so much to you.'

Dan went for him with sudden savagery. He grabbed Alan round the waist and flung him onto the gravel. They rolled over and over, cuffing rather than punching, yet punching all the same, though not at each other's faces, as if they were observing some schoolboy convention. They rolled in under the trees, among some laurels. And from behind the bushes, with a sort of sheepish indignation, emerged Jenny March and a boy. Dan and Alan stood up, grinning furiously, and brushed themselves off.

'Hullo, Jenny,' Dan said. 'All right?'

'Hullo, Mr Bradley.' She touched her mouth. The lipstick was smudged. She turned and walked away, followed by the boy.

'One of yours?' said Alan.

'Wasn't he one of those boys last night?' Dan said. 'I'm damned sure he was.'

'Making up for lost time, weren't they?' Alan said. 'But then don't we all?'

ii

The weather had broken. For two weeks following the Parkses' visit, it rained steadily from a low, depressing sky. The cottage never seemed smaller than during such unrelenting days. Hannah and Carol squabbled, were pacified, and squabbled again. Dan worked, came out to play peacemaker and went back to work again. After a few minutes, Hannah was again saying, 'It's mine, it belongs to me . . .'

'What's the matter now?' Dan called.

'One doll,' Joyce said, 'two mothers. I've made some tea, if you're interested.'

'If only people could learn to share,' Dan said. 'Of

course I'm interested.' He came in and picked up a publicity leaflet with 'PRIZES! PRIZES! PRIZES!' printed at the bottom. '"I'm so happy with my Satin Finish because" – '

'Don't mock me, Dan, please,' Joyce said, pouring tea into the blue-hooped mugs.

'I'm not mocking you, I'm mocking this damned stupid competition of yours – '

'What other hope have I got,' she said, 'of ever having anything?'

The front door bell rang.

'Probably one of your wretched pupils,' Joyce said.

'Or Peter. He went over Damian's. I'll get it.'

A man in overalls was standing there with a television set. 'Name of Bradley?' he said.

'I never ordered a television,' Dan said. Joyce had come into the hall. 'Did you order a television?'

'No,' Joyce said.

'Perhaps you've won one!' Dan said.

'It's all written down here,' the man said. 'Name of Bradley.'

'I don't care what's written down where,' Dan said, 'we don't want it.'

'Of course we want it,' Joyce said. An envelope was sellotaped to the side of the box. She opened it and took out the delivery note. 'It's a present. "In the kingdom of the blind, the one eyed-monster is King. Love to all, Alan."'

iii

The doll lay neglected in its hospital bed. A great peace descended on the cottage. The children watched television. They watched as soon as they got home from school and they were carried up to bed with eyes that strained to catch the last delicious commercial before enforced oblivion. Dan no longer had to come out of his little den in order to impose a truce. The children shut his door, so that his voice, when he had Rex or someone in for personal tuition, did not compete with *Crackerjack*.

Rex was reading one of his compositions: 'The news that the monster was in the district made everybody very excited. The police drove up and down the streets and they asked everybody if they had seen the monster. The monster was very fierce, they said, and anyone who saw it was to tell them right away. The monster was dangerous and it was dangerous to have it in your house or let it hide anywhere in the garden. They showed pictures of the monster to all the people and they also showed them what its tracks looked like in case they found tracks in the garden or anywhere like that. It was forbidden to feed the monster or to leave milk out for the cat. It was even forbidden to leave scraps out for the birds in case the monster came and ate them. The monster was laying low.'

'Lying low,' Dan said.

'Lying low. They looked on the common and they sent frog men down in the lake. It was fun to hunt the monster. Everyone volunteered to join in. The ladies made pots of tea and buttered buns. Then one day the monster was found in one of the houses. The house was surrounded with tanks and policemen with dogs. A policeman with a loudspeaker shouted to the monster to come out or they would go in and get him. He did not come out, so they stormed the house and broke down the door and filled the house with tear gas and then they dragged the monster out of the armchair where he was sitting and put a blanket over him so that he shouldn't frighten the people and then they took him off to a prison and locked him in and then they threw away the key. And that's all I had time for, sir.'

'You never describe the monster,' Dan said. 'Was that on purpose?'

'I always thought of him as just like an ordinary man, sir,' Rex said, 'really, to look at from the outside.'

'That's funny. That's rather how I saw him. Just an ordinary man.'

'Yes, sir,' Rex said.

'It was the rest of the people who made him a monster really, wasn't it?'

'I suppose so, sir,' Rex said. 'Can I go now? Because – '

'Off you go, lad,' Dan said. 'And good work. Good work, Rex.'

'Only I've got Mr March, sir,' Rex said.

Dan took his shotgun from the rack and had to cross between the children and the television on his way out. 'Oy, Dad,' they said, and motioned him aside.

He went onto the marshes. He revelled in the flat danger of the mud, through which he moved with the expert twist of the heel which was the secret of progress over the treacherous surface. The tide was out. The remaining pools gleamed like quicksilver in the late light. The rain had eased, but the sky was heavy with it still. He went down to an old hide, a favourite haunt of his, and squatted on the sodden boards. He took an old balaclava from the pocket of his donkey jacket and crouched down. There was not much game about, but he loved the sensation of being invisible in the landscape. He merged with the succulent richness of the marshes and lay there, mute and patient, listening to the slow return of the tide.

iv

'You came,' Alan said. He was lying on a suede-covered sofa in a room gleaming with tax-deductible clobber. He wore a pair of earphones which were plugged into a tape-recorder. The Italian maid shut the door. 'I'll just finish listening to this,' he said, 'and I'll be right there.' Joyce was wearing a slim black skirt, white turtle-necked sweater and her best black shoes. She sat down, knees together, on the second sofa. 'And here I am,' Alan said, taking off the earphones. 'Narcissus never had the fun we have, I'm telling you. If he'd had the sound of his own voice as well as his pool we should *never* have heard the last of him.'

'Nice place you've got.'

'Half this lot's due to go down to the cottage, soon as the painters've finished,' Alan said. 'If they ever do.' He shook his head. 'Can't believe it! Even when you said you were coming, I never thought you would. How are you? How's everyone?'

'Everyone's fine,' Joyce said. 'You're positively God in our house.'

'I have to be God in *everybody*'s house. Otherwise I'm slipping. The box, I assume. I thought Dan might be displeased.'

'He was. It's his favourite occupation. If his hair shirt didn't scratch, he'd change his tailor.'

Alan said: 'Barbara's down at the cottage with the white woman's burden. She'll be sorry she missed you. She loves it down there.'

'And the children?'

'Absolutely. It's a smashing place, I must say. And once we've got the Olympic pool and the squash court and the two-pony garage, I must get Dan to come over and beat the shit out of me. It's not that far. Or that difficult.'

'I see the American deal went through,' Joyce said.

'The networks' darling, that's me. Long as I don't shave and tell jokes so old they haven't heard them before. It's going well, it's going well. You look better than ever. How do you do it?'

'I save the coupons,' Joyce said.

'Good. I like it. I like it. So anyway here we are, you and me, who'd a thunk it, eh? What did you tell the folks in the village?'

'That I was having a day in London.'

'Going back tonight?'

'Unless the fog thickens,' Joyce said.

Alan looked out of the window. It was a clear London day. 'Getting thicker every minute,' he said. 'Cheap day return?'

'What else?' she said. 'Alan, I'll tell you why I've come. I'm a bit desperate, though I may not look it.'

'If this is what desperation looks like, we must have more of it.'

'That's why I wrote to you.'

'You don't have to be desperate before you write to me, you know,' Alan said. 'Why do you think I put this whole incredible operation together? To put your eye out. Why else?'

'I'm sorry?'

'So I could make you see what you'd missed. Conspicuous presumption, that's me. I wanted to make my name half so you'd be sorry for walking away.'

'That's silly.'

'Of course it's silly. The whole thing's silly. It even applies to Barbara.'

'Alan – I haven't come here – '

'Prettiest girl in the WRENS, that's Barbara. The one they all want. Best references.' He made breasts with his hands. 'Corr! You thought I wasn't good enough.'

'That wasn't it at all.'

'Every time I go to bed with a girl I think of you somewhere along the line.'

'You're – '

'– only saying that? Am I? You know the nicest thing about success? It makes you so damned attractive. Look at me. I'm attractive.'

'I always thought you were,' she said.

'Did you, Joycey? Well, anyway, here you are at last and don't think I'm not chuffed, because I'm chuffed.

Look at me. Chuffed. You don't have to be desperate any longer. I swear.' He came and lifted her by the elbows so that she stood in front of him. 'And it's big moment time in the life of overweight telly-idol, Aussie-born, Atlantic-hopping Alan "Welcome-to-the-Show" Parks.'

'Alan,' Joyce said, 'there's something I want – something I don't like to ask – '

'We pride ourselves on giving a prompt, clean and efficient service,' Alan said. 'What?'

'You're the only person I – '

'Don't apologize. It interrupts lubrication. Tell Uncle. What can I do for you you can't do for yourself?'

'I – I want – a job,' Joyce said.

'A job.'

'Yes.'

'A *job*! Joyce – ' He kissed her passionately. 'I love you. I *love* you. Suddenly it's love. You're corrupt! I *love* you. You're corrupt. You're beautiful. Nothing easier. Nothing in the world. She's corrupt! Joyce Hadleigh is corrupt. I love her. I love her.'

'Can you do anything?' Joyce said.

'I can do everything,' Alan said, 'with knobs on.'

ii

Graham was having an exceptionally good game. He played intelligently and with fierce commitment. Having scored an early goal, he made another one for a black lad who was soon doing one-twos with him and with whom he struck up the quick, arrogant understanding of those who recognize each other's talent. Dan could not see how he could fail to impress the youth team trainer who was squatting, in a blue tracksuit, on the cinder track surrounding the practice ground. Graham was beating his full-back as and when he pleased. The full-back retaliated by tripping him. The referee took no notice. Graham banged the ground angrily and got up slowly, glowering. Dan looked at his watch. The next thing that happened the black lad had crossed a good ball, fifty-fifty between the keeper and Graham. They went up together. The ball went into the net, Graham's fist shot up in triumph and caught the keeper in the face. He went down in the mud. The referee ran up and caught Graham by the shoulder. 'It was an accident,' the boy said. 'I – '

'You do that again . . .' the referee said.

'He put his face there,' Graham said, 'honest. It was already in the net.'

The trainer stood up, glanced at Dan and ambled onto the field. 'All right,' he said, 'we'll change things around a bit now, shall we?'

Some other hopefuls were standing on the touchline. Graham shrugged and walked off towards Dan. The trainer caught him up and put his arm through the boy's. Graham shrugged him off.

After the boy had changed, Dan took him to a steak house.

'What did he say about me, sir?'

'He wants me to keep him posted,' Dan said. 'You shouldn't have done the keeper, though. That was silly.'

'I was tripped, wasn't I? Ref didn't do nothing so – '

'Didn't do anything,' Dan said. 'You know it was silly.'

'I didn't play bad.'

'Badly. You played well. Except for that.'

'This is the life then.'

'As seen on television!'

'Right.' Graham helped himself to more fried onions. 'I was talking to that blackie after, fifteen he is, like me, know what he's making? Eighteen quid a week. On a building site. Eighteen quid.'

'Fifteen?' Dan said. 'Why isn't he at school?'

Graham grinned. 'Did the keeper, didn't he?'

'It's not so bad, is it? School?'

'English Social History? It's not exactly a life, is it? Eighteen quid a week, no trouble. Problem is, you need a few bob to get you started. A grant really, that's what I need. From the government or someone. I mean to say, there's better things to do in life than go pissing in linen cupboards, aren't there? Sir? He's in digs, that blackie, got a girl living with him and all. Beats O-levels, you must admit.'

Graham cleaned his plate with a piece of French bread. Dan was moved by the beauty of the boy's candid greed. It was as if he had undergone a spiritual transformation. He took out his wallet and put ten pound notes on the table in front of Graham.

'What's this?' Graham said.

'English Social History,' Dan said, and left him there.

iii

The children hardly seemed to notice Joyce's absences. She left food ready. They watched television. Occasionally, very occasionally, Dan allowed them to stay up to see their mother doing her stuff. Joyce was a success. Her neat, quick-witted manner soon made her a mild celebrity. She was no Alan Parks, but one of him was enough, perhaps. Sometimes she did her programme live and if it was unusually late, she would stay in town overnight. Dan did not reproach her. He did not even cleave to her company when she was at home. He often took the opportunity to go onto the marshes and spent hours in the hide, watching the changing water and the passing birds, at which, though he had cartridges in his pocket, he rarely fired. When he was alone at night, he read Shakespeare and Milton. And of course there was always school work to correct. He seldom invited any of the pupils to the cottage any more. He worked in his den. They had the telephone now. Joyce's work made it essential. Someone in the BBC spoke to someone in the Post Office and there was no difficulty. Joyce could call him from London when she was going to be late. It happened more frequently now that she was able to inform him about it.

'You're sure you don't mind?' she said.

'I never mind,' he said.

'You might tune in tonight,' she said, 'if you haven't got anything better to do.'

'How could I have anything better to do?'

'Because I'm interviewing that writer, Adam Morris.'

As it got dark, Dan neglected to turn on the lights. The cottage grew slowly crepuscular. He told the children a story and went downstairs and sat near the French windows and watched the dying sky. The tide filled the marshes and the striped water lapped against the tussocky foreshore. Dan sat, with his gun broken on his lap, polishing the stock with a darkening rag.

He went at last and turned on the television. The blue light from the screen stabbed his eyes like boxed lightning. He sat placidly and watched. The sound jarred, so he went and turned it down. Joyce appeared, mouthing intelligently, her head cocked on one side, in the manner sharp satirists were already imitating. Dan watched her with his head back against the wall behind him. After a time, he closed the gun with a practised snap of the wrist, took aim and, without any change of expression, shot his wife.

An
Academic
Life

'Anyone sitting here?' Bill Bourne opened the door of the compartment and came in, a plastic cup of coffee in his hand. 'Room for a white man in here, baby?'

'In where?' The black girl turned a page of her magazine.

'Cuppacoffee?'

'No thanks.'

'They say black women is great in the hay,' Bill said. 'Is that true?'

'Ab-so-lute-ly!'

Bill opened a copy of *Plato, Education and Society* by Austin Denny. He closed it again and put it face down on the seat beside him. 'Still about twenty minutes 'fore we get into the big city,' he said. 'Feel like getting laid? I'd sure appreciate a piece of black ass at this moment in time.'

'You is the mos' charmin' thing I met all day, Charlie. I just cain't unnerstand why I ain' in the mood right now.'

'Well, shee-it, that's all.' He picked up the book again. 'I heard tell you black chicks was always in the mood.'

The girl held up the *New Statesman*. 'Want the Funnies?'

'I read it fifteen years ago.' Bill looked out of the smeared window. 'So here we are in little old England.'

'Anything's better than the Land of the Free, baby, A.D. 1970.'

'No waffles in Staunton, Lincs., darlin'.'

'I'se going straight home on the next boat!' Joann said. 'Homesick for Dullsville, Ohio, already, Professor?'

'Know the trouble with England?' Bill said.

'You can't get a cup of honest-to-God American coffee, not like in Vietnam.'

'And the black chicks won't lay.'

'You is one uppety white man, Professor.'

'I'm a lucky sod,' Bill said. He leaned forward and kissed her. 'Aren't I?'

'You're lucky as long as I don't catch you at it,' Joann said.

'Dark lady.'

'Tickets, please.'

Bill stopped kissing Joann and reached into his top pocket. He took out a single ticket and handed it to the collector. The collector clipped it and handed it back. He then turned to Joann. 'Ticket, please.'

'*Vous avez votre billet, Mademoiselle?*' Bill said.

'Bill,' Joann said, 'please show the man my ticket.'

Bill grinned and reached into his top pocket and pulled out a second ticket. The ticket-collector clipped it and handed it back.

'Don't do that again,' Joann said.

'My old man was on the railways,' Bill said.

'Ever.'

'Please accept my prominently displayed apology,' Bill said.

'Forget it,' Joann said. 'Only remember.'

'Lo, the spires of Academe!' Bill said. The train was going past a factory: DENT'S OF STAUNTON. Black smoke rose from a tall chimney and was snatched away by the wind. 'It's been very nice meeting you,' Bill said. 'You wouldn't care to get married, I suppose?'

'I'se married already,' Joann said.

'Well shee-it,' Bill said.

'He sure is,' Joann said, 'but I love him. Yes-suh!'

ii

'It's not America,' Austin Denny said. 'But – '

'But it's doing its best – ' Bill said.

'I wouldn't put it quite like that – '

'The blue light indicates that a joke was intended,' Bill said.

Austin was walking Bill round the 'factory' as he put it. Everything was new and had about it the strict elegance of the architect's drawings, except that there was none of the Italian sunshine which had lent the fountains in the broad *piazza* a charm their driven spray did not possess on a raw East Anglian afternoon. Austin opened the glass doors of the Sociology Department and took Bill into the main lecture room. 'Does it seem to you rather cold in here?' he said. 'They're supposed to have this underfloor heating – '

'Which is fine,' Bill said, 'if you're under the floor – '

'Details, details!' Austin said. 'And my God, aren't they important? They do have things I envy, of course, your friends the Yanks – '

'Money, for instance.'

'Money doesn't bother me too much. Classlessness. The heating *ought* to be working – '

'*Classlessness?*' said Bill, the traveller.

'One language,' Austin said. 'One society. All right, tell me I've got it all wrong. Some ass has switched the whole thing off.'

'That might account for it. What's the town like, Staunton itself?'

'It's not Cambridge,' Austin said, clicking the control switch to ON. 'And just as well. None of the old town and gown dichotomy. Not so far anyway. And people've been incredibly enthusiastic – try it now, will you, Bill?'

'Enthusiasm in negotiable form, I trust?'

'And a lot more promised.'

'I think it's a bit warmer,' Bill said.

'You'd be amazed how much real contact there is between us and them already – '

'And does that mean there's already us and them?' Bill said.

'What the hell are you doing?' A Pakistani in a white coat had come through the door at the far end of the lecture room.

'*Il est en colère*,' Bill said.

'You very nearly killed me, you see.'

'I beg your pardon?' Austin said.

'I'm the Maintenance Man. Who are you?'

'I'm Mr Denny.'

'Well, Mr Denny, you very nearly killed me, you see. When I switch something off, I switch it off for a purpose, you see. I was repairing a faulty junction, you see, in the gentlemen's cloakroom and I could easily have received considerable injuries – '

'I'm really terribly sorry. It never occurred to me – '

'Which is why it very nearly occurred to me, you see. These boxes should have locks on them. That's a considerable fault in my opinion. They should have locks on them.'

'So fools can't rush in,' Austin said. 'I agree with you entirely. Some people can't be trusted.'

'Now you go out of here, please.'

Austin nodded contritely and opened the door for Bill. They went out into the *piazza*. Dodging the cold pebbles of water from the fountain, they headed towards the Lodge.

The University had been built in the grounds of a handsome Jacobean country house. Most of it had been burned down in a wartime accident (an American fighter had crashed on it) but there was enough left to make a handsome house for the Vice-Chancellor. Austin and Bill walked across the lawn towards it, putting the brave towers of the new buildings behind them.

'And of course,' Austin was saying, 'blast him, he's

absolutely right. Arts people who've never heard of Thermodynamics – let alone what the second law is –'

'And what is it, anyway?' Bill said.

'– scientists who've never heard of Propertius – he's the only man who's had the nerve to spell it out – give him that –'

'Two cultures with but a single vulture!'

'I'm with him, part of the way,' Austin said. 'Culture today simply cannot go on being the province of the leisured and the treasured –'

'The leisured and the treasured. I like that. That's very good.'

'My dear fellow,' Austin said, 'I do say as good things every day were they but taken down and recorded!'

'Nice pad,' Bill said.

'Pad? Oh! The Lodge. Yes. The architect refused to pull it down, so –'

'You refused to let him.'

'Exactly.' The Vice-Chancellor frowned at a Rover with a House of Commons badge on the front. 'His nibs,' he said. 'March at attention!'

Ronald Braithwaite was the new Minister of State at the Ministry of Education. He was waiting in the drawing room.

'I'd like you to meet Bill Bourne,' Austin said. 'Ronald Braithwaite, our guardian angel.'

'He always calls me that,' Ronnie said, 'when he wants me to sell the Minister some particularly expensive idea.'

'I thought you were the Minister,' Bill said.

'I'm *a* Minister. There is an upper and a nether millstone. I'm the nether.'

'There's usually some tea somewhere,' Austin said.

'I did see your wife,' Ronnie said. 'She was on her way out with a visitor. I told her please not to wait. A black lady.'

'My wife,' Bill said.

'Ah, oh – well, there we are then – they were going to see a house they said – '

'Bill's just come from America,' Austin said. 'We've given him a Chair here, rightly or wrongly – Interdisciplinary Studies.'

'Ah! Austin, I had no business popping in like this without a visa,' Ronnie said, 'but I thought you'd like to know I've had a word from their nibs about the Media Complex.'

'Depends which word it is,' Austin said.

'Largely yes.'

'Splendid.'

'And the merest suspicion of no. The word being that if your local people are willing and able to find forty per cent of the money, we'll try and find the other sixty, even in these 'ard times.'

'I've got Tim Dent coming to dine tonight,' Austin said. 'Local industrialist,' he explained to Bill. 'I'm sure he can rally the moneybags. Why don't you stay, Ronnie?'

'I must go and vote, sadly.'

'Bill's coming, and his wife, aren't you, Bill?'

'If asked,' Bill said, 'never refuse.'

'There's just this small question mark about the second cinema,' Ronnie said. 'Do you really need two cinemas?'

'We're not asking for Odeons,' Austin said, 'but a Media Complex with only one cinema, it's like, well – '

'Kitty with only one titty,' Bill said.

'So to speak,' Austin said. 'It means only one group of students using the film library at a time.'

'We had six in Ohio.'

'I'm afraid,' Ronnie said, 'that our days of keeping up with Ohio have yet to come or, alas, have already been.'

Mrs Thorpe, the housekeeper, knocked and came in. 'Excuse me, Vice-Chancellor, but the Reverend is here.'

'Oh yes – we did say five o'clock.'

Ronald Braithwaite stood up. 'I must be on my way

back to the Boys' Club, as Michael always calls the House. And rightly.'

'Bill – if you wouldn't mind hanging on . . .'

'Can I take Professor Bourne somewhere?'

'Oh Ronnie, could you possibly? It's on your way as you leave the Campus, Battle Road.'

'I know Battle Road,' Ronnie said.

'It's number eight. Medlar Cottage. My dear Minister, do forgive me, but – '

'My dear Vice-Chancellor!' Ronnie allowed Bill to precede him to the door. 'I expect you're still suffering somewhat from the jetties, aren't you, Professor?'

'Sorry?'

'The jetties. Jet-lag.' As they got into the car, Ronnie said: 'Austin's doing a tremendous job down here. I don't know anyone else in the world who could have done it.'

'But what?' Bill said.

'Nothing,' Ronnie said. 'Nothing at all. He's put a lot of thought into it. A lot of thought. Have you read his book?'

'Yes,' Bill said.

'First-class,' Ronnie said.

'Thank you.'

'The book, I meant,' Ronnie said. 'The book.'

iii

'We'll expect you for dinner, about eight,' Ursula Denny said. 'Oh, you haven't got a car, have you?'

'We can walk,' Joann said.

'No need. I'll ask Gavin Pope to call in for you. You're practically neighbours. He won't mind.' She turned to Bill. 'Did you know each other? At Cambridge?'

'Not really,' Bill said, 'so it should be all right.'

'If there's anything you need – ' Ursula said.

'The place is called a shop, right?' He saw her out of the

front door and came back to find Joann opening packing cases with a claw hammer. 'That was Ursula,' he said.

'She's a lot older than Austin, isn't she?'

'Not really. It's just that he's a lot younger. She's all right. How about you?' He put his arms round her waist. 'Tell me something, Doctor, does the pad run to a bedroom?'

'Upstairs. Why?'

'The reason,' he said, 'sticks out a mile.'

'You flatter yourself, Professor.'

iv

Joann had the American woman's skill in arranging furniture. She cut flowers from the garden, she re-hung pictures (and added some they had brought with them) so that by the time the front door bell rang, the place looked, as she put it, 'a little less like a Customs' shed'. She fetched glasses for the Scotch and the Bourbon and ran upstairs as Bill led Gavin into the sitting room. 'My wife's just getting dressed,' he said.

'Mine's in the car,' Gavin said.

'I'll go and call her – we can have a drink – '

'She's all right,' Gavin said. 'She's knitting, I think. We can still have a drink.' Gavin wore a pair of old twill trousers and a jacket with leather patches. Bill had changed into a blue suit. 'So here you are,' Gavin said, 'back in the sinking ship.'

'Sinking? Is it? Do you know something I don't?' He handed Gavin some Scotch in a cloudy tumbler.

'Almost everything, I should think,' Gavin said. 'Isn't that why we're going to work together? What do you think of the place?'

'Very nice for the time of year,' Bill said.

'Massachusetts Institute of Technology with a few roses round the edges. You, me and Piers Cobbett, the Lord protect us. The kept boys of industry, that's what we are really.'

'You really like it that much?'

'Oh look,' Gavin said, 'it'll suit you down to the bargain basement. After all, your first professorship's a bit like your first shag, isn't it? With a bit of luck you move on smartly to better things. Personally, mine's out knitting in the car. Lionel Parker moved off smartly enough when the horizon turned light blue.'

'I don't want to go back to Cambridge.'

'Cambridge Fame-bridge, that's what they all say till it happens.'

'Then that's what I'll say until it happens. Didn't you used to *beagle* and things at Cambridge?'

'That was in another country,' Gavin said, 'and besides –' Joann came into the room. She wore a dark-blue dress spangled with white dots, high-heeled patent leather shoes and dark crimson earrings. 'Bloody hell,' Gavin said, 'you don't need a lift.'

'I'm sorry?' she said.

'How many wives have you got, you swine?'

'This is my wife,' Bill said. 'Gavin Pope.'

'Joann.'

'It shouldn't bloody well be allowed,' Gavin said.

'What's that?' Joann said.

'I don't know though,' Gavin said. 'Maybe there is something to be said for new universities after all. If they bring stuff like this to the sticks. I heard you were married to a doctor.'

'He is,' Joann said.

'God Almighty, we're going to have the longest sick-list in the country.'

'Is that your wife waiting outside in the car?'

'She's used to it,' Gavin said, holding out his empty glass. 'One more slug of traveller's joy and then we'll be off to Kafka's Castle. The last time I met Bill, his wife was a dull little white lady with crocheted spectacles and a tendency to acne. What the hell's the secret?'

'Just a little make-up,' Joann said.

'If you're going to turn out to be witty as well, I don't know how I'm going to keep my hands off you, Mrs Bourne.'

'Doctor Bourne to you, Pope,' Bill said.

'Everybody's got second wives except me. What am I going to do?'

'Don't worry about it and keep on taking the pills.'

'I'm R C,' Gavin said. 'We're not allowed to. Never mind, Doctor Mrs B., as soon as you're lonely and dissatisfied, come and tell your favourite sociologist.'

'We'd better make tracks,' Bill said.

'Doctor Mrs B., you remember now. When all else fails, or indeed at any other time . . .'

'I feel better already,' Joann said. Bill patted her on the behind and they went towards the door. Gavin took another measure of the whisky Bill had pushed to the back of the table, drained it and followed them out of the cottage.

II

They dined at a long narrow Jacobean oak table by the light of three sets of Paul de Lamerie candelabra. ('They're not quite in period, of course,' Austin said, 'but somehow I couldn't be purist enough to refuse them.') Apart from the Popes and the Bournes, Austin and Ursula had invited the managing director of Dent's, the local plastics people, and his wife, Jeanne, a Parisienne whose London hair-do and Rive Gauche dress announced her class. John Cadman, whose production of *Romeo and Juliet* Bill Bourne was able to remember having seen at Cambridge, sat next to Ursula, opposite Bill. Austin did not bring in a casual mention of the big news until they reached the Stilton.

'They've given the go-ahead for the Media Complex, by the way, Tim,' he said. 'Ronnie Braithwaite was here this afternoon.'

'Was he really,' Gavin said, 'on his way up to what?'

'What is a Media Complex exactly?' Jeanne said.

'A Media Complex,' Gavin said, 'is when you can't resist rushing up to London and trying to get your face on the television, your voice on the radio and your fingers in the gravy. Isn't that right, Doctor Bourne?'

Joann said: 'I'm not going to say no to anybody, not on my first night.'

'In that case,' Gavin said, 'you're likely to have a very busy night indeed.'

Austin said: 'It means you finding forty per cent, Tim, but – '

'Can do,' Tim said. 'I told you.'

'And it's also agreed we should call it the Richard Dent Memorial Building.'

'Who is Richard Dent exactly?' Gavin said.

'Tim's father,' Jeanne said. 'He was killed in the war.'

'You were also an actor, weren't you, in Cambridge?' Bill said to Cadman.

'Part time!' Cadman said. 'I suppose I still am in a sense. Part time! I just turned my collar round and decided to play a different sort of fool.'

'When did this happen then?' Bill said. 'The dog-collar?'

'I was in the Foreign Service,' Cadman said, 'and they sent me to Peru.'

'Where else?' Bill said.

'I was very happy.'

'Did you see the erotic sculpture?'

'The Toltec stuff? I did. I did. Among other things. Wonderful colours. And then Suez came along.'

'To Peru?' Bill said. 'I had no idea.'

'It happened to coincide with one of their earthquakes.'

'Those damned Titans,' Bill said. 'They will go on groaning.'

'They had more than three thousand dead,' Cadman said. 'It wasn't an easy time to be suave and diplomatic.'

'John,' Gavin called down the table, 'you underestimate yourself.'

Bill winked secretly at Gavin, at once siding with him and hoping to silence him. Gavin winked shamelessly and openly back. Bill said: 'Anyway, you saw the Light?'

'You're not a Christian, I take it?' Cadman said.

'Er, no. I allowed my subscription to lapse.'

'But you're married, I see.'

'We had a Jewish wedding.'

'Oh, is your wife . . . ?'

'The blue light,' Bill said, 'indicates that a joke is intended. Tell me, what did Suez have to do with the earthquake exactly?'

'Exactly nothing. But it seemed to me to underline the absurdity of our priorities. You'll probably find this mildly pretentious, but seeing what was happening out there, in the shanty towns and so on, well, I began to think of myself as Pontius Pilate.'

'Quite a sound man, old Pontius, I always thought,' Gavin said. He pushed a dish towards his wife. 'Have some more of this delicious pud, my love. It'll help you put on a little more weight.'

Jeanne said: 'You are a very rude man.'

'And you,' Gavin said, 'are a very beautiful woman. What do you say? Monday afternoon in the Kardomah? And we'll take it from there?' He looked up to see Tim Dent looking sternly at him. 'How's business?'

'Rather booming actually,' Tim said.

'I'm very glad to hear it.'

'I'm very glad you're very glad.'

'More power to your elbow, say I, or whatever part of yourself it is that booms.'

'They laughed,' Cadman said, 'when I told them what I wanted to do. I haven't regretted it for a moment.'

'How about the Peruvians?' Bill said. 'Are they feeling any better?'

'They're not noticeably any the worse.' Cadman balanced some Stilton on a digestive biscuit and put it in his mouth. 'I regard becoming a priest as a revolutionary act. Does that sound pretentious?'

'Did you say priest, Cadman, you old fellow-traveller, you?' Gavin said. 'There's only one priest that deserves the name and that, as my name is Pope, is one that recognizes the Bishop of Rome, not Canterbury. Or Cantuar as you call him, and rightly, since Cant he largely is.'

'Gavin,' Austin said, 'I'm going to be very upset with you in a minute. I'm the only person you haven't insulted yet tonight. I'm beginning to feel left out.'

'I always leave the best till last,' Gavin said.

'I rather favour the old rule,' Austin said. 'No religion or politics at the table.'

'Save it for the bedroom, Austin, you're absolutely right.' He turned abruptly to Jeanne. 'Tell me about sex, Mrs Dent. After all, you're supposed to be French. How do they order these things in France? By the gross?'

'I think you probably know more about sex than is good for you already.'

'I've heard a lot about it, of course, but tell me, where can I actually *get* some?'

'Is he being insulting darling?' Tim Dent said, 'because –'

'He is being so charming,' Jeanne said, 'I can't believe it.'

'I'm a sort of spiritual Z-car, you might say,' John Cadman explained to Bill Bourne. 'As the University has no chapel, I'm a sort of one-man priest-without-a-church –'

'Like San Paolo without the Walls!' Francesca Pope said.

She seemed as startled by her own wit as were the others. Gavin broke the silence. 'Your husband,' he said to Jeanne, 'is an unredeemed capitalist, don't bother to deny it.'

'So am I.'

'You must allow me to be your redeemer. Your husband'll have to find his own way home. Say eleven p.m. in the Media Complex? I always lecture best to a reclining audience of one.'

'I can hardly wait,' she said.

'Your husband's putting up the money,' Gavin said. 'I'll put up the rest.'

'I'm also running study groups in factories and hospitals,' Cadman was saying. 'I'm very much a believer in One Society. I visit prisons – '

'The universities of crime.'

'What a lot of ears you've got, Mr Pope!' Jeanne said.

'The devil has two penises, did you know that? His forked tail is simply a piece of late Victorian furniture.'

'And Gavin has two mouths. One considerably less charming than the other,' Austin said. He had seen Tim Dent looking severely at Gavin. Gavin saw the same thing. 'How's business?' he said.

'Have you always had a problem with drink, Mr Pope?'

'No problem at all,' Gavin said. 'I just pour it down.'

'Do you have children?' Joann said.

'Four,' Francesca replied. 'Twelve, eleven, seven and three.'

'No trouble getting sitters, I suppose?'

'Why?' Francesca said. 'Do you – ?'

'I meant being at a university – '

'Oh,' Francesca said. 'No. I'm sorry, I thought – '

'Are you planning to practise while you're here, Dr Bourne?' Ursula Denny said.

'I can't sit around all day waiting for Bill to show up, can I?'

'Don't you,' Francesca said, with startling force.

'I've got the modified plans for the Media Library in the other room,' Austin said.

'Oh terrific,' Tim said.

'I hope the academic company present is going to see eye to eye on this,' Austin said, 'because it's basically going to be their pigeon, after all.'

'We won't start fighting till it's grown a feather or two,' Bill said.

'And I hope not then.'

'We shall exercise our Reason,' Gavin said, 'and if that doesn't lead to a fight, I don't know what will.'

'It's going to be a beautiful building, Tim,' Austin said.

'What sort of stuff are we actually going to put in the library?' Bill said.

'Summaries of summaries,' Gavin said, 'epitomes of epitomes, the Modern Masters series of Modern Masters, the Modern Mistresses series of Modern Mistresses and large quantities of the number you first thought of. In a word, baby-tins. And – '

John Cadman said: 'Austin, tell me – '

'And, I was about to say, before I was so *diplomatically* interrupted – the problem with baby-tins, *experto crede*, is what to do with the empty ones.'

Cadman pointed to a prayer staff which was decorating the table between the nuts and the after-dinner mints. 'Is that Yoruba – ?'

'It is, yes – '

'And the trouble,' Gavin said, 'with sociology students is, of course, exactly the same.'

'What to do with the empty ones.'

'You've been paying attention, Professor,' Gavin said.

'I've been very impressed with some of the students,' Tim said.

'No one denies,' Gavin said, 'that some of them have eminently reputable knockers. You should try having some of them work for you. Then you'd find out.'

'I shall be very happy to have some of your people at Dent's. Industry today can always use a first-class graduate –'

'Of course it can,' Gavin said. 'I could use some myself. But what about the third-class ones?'

'I was a third-class student myself.'

'Well, of course,' Gavin said, 'Daddy did happen to own this little business, didn't he?'

'My father,' Tim said, 'was killed in the North Atlantic.'

'*Mutatis mutandis*,' Gavin said.

'We're always going to need educated people,' Tim said.

'Endless expansion?' Gavin said. 'Can it really last indefinitely?'

'I'm an optimist,' Tim said.

'I'm an optimist too,' Gavin said. 'And I think the whole system is going to collapse under its own weight. Just like the human anatomy if we all grew to be twelve feet tall. Its bones are going to snap like tinder. You'll see. Capitalism'll collapse like Moloch, from indigestion following immoderate consumption of its own children.'

'Is that accurate? he inquired of a neighbouring religious authority.'

'Blast accuracy, Professor Bill, I'm making a party political broadcast on behalf of the People of this Country. And it's not often you get a chance to hear them say a few words. The whole system's going to fall apart.'

'My wife's called our new cat Chairman Miaow,' Tim Dent said. 'I suppose you regard that as sacrilege?'

'Sacrilege,' Gavin said, 'is pissing on the altar and refuse all substitutes, isn't that right, your reverence?'

'Speaking as a mere heathen, I'd say you'd defined it with all your usual charm, Mr Chairman.'

Gavin leaned down the table towards Cadman. 'Forgive me, Father,' he said, 'I know *exactly* what I'm doing.'

'It seems to be an open question which collapses first,' Tim Dent said. 'You or capitalism.'

'That's easy.' Gavin refilled his glass. 'Me.'

Bill said: 'School's out, Gavin. More next week, eh?'

Gavin said: 'You once had a pale, pimpled wife to whom you swore vows – what happened to her?'

Bill said: 'She got tired of me.'

'Gavin,' Austin said, 'you need some fresh air.'

'The whole of England needs some fresh air. And we daren't give it to her. We daren't give it to her. Why? What is this fear of the new? It's bitten us all. We talk about the new and prepare for the old.' He turned to Jeanne. 'Think about that, *ma belle*. There are more things in heaven and earth than are dreamed of in the Richard Dent Memorial Complex. Think about that.' He looked across at Tim. 'Your father died in the war,' he said. 'I salute him.' And he did, stiffly. 'Up, two, three – down, two, three! And what are we going to die in?'

As Austin Denny stood up to lead them into the other room, Gavin seemed to rise too, before collapsing, face down, among the spent silver and glass.

'Half past ten,' Austin said, glancing at his watch. 'He's done rather well for him, Gavin.'

John Cadman frowned at his grandfather's half-hunter. 'I make it twenty-five to eleven,' he said.

ii

'Not much different from one of those evenings on the rocks with Bob and Lois,' Bill said.

'But different,' Joann said.

Gavin had driven them home in the VW minibus with an unexpectedly steady hand. 'Always drive carefully when I'm drunk,' he quoted.

'You must be tired,' Bill said.

'Must I?' Joann said. 'Why?'

'I meant – you know – the jetties – jet-lag.'

'I'm all right,' she said.

Bill was in a sagging armchair, fishing books from a packing case. Joann looked out of the window. The minibus was still parked at the gate. In the front, Gavin Pope was passionately embracing his wife.

Joann said: 'You coming to bed, big boy?'

'I'll be right there,' Bill said, checking a reference he was worried about. 'You go on up.'

She smiled and turned away. Bill put down his book, looked at himself searchingly and not unadmiringly in the mirror above the mantelpiece. There was a low coffee table between him and the door. He stood behind it, solemn, for a second and then, with abrupt agility, did a standing jump over it and tap danced his way to the door, where he stopped, appraised the room and then turned out the light.

iii

The next morning, Mrs Thorpe came into the drawing room, where Ursula Denny was doing her correspondence, with a large bowl of fresh flowers. 'Gavin,' Ursula said, before she even opened the note.

At the same time, a similar bunch was being delivered to Jeanne Dent. And at more or less the same time again, Gavin arrived in person at Medlar Cottage, carrying a third bunch.

'He's not here,' Joann said when she opened the door.

'He's in a Faculty Meeting,' Gavin said.

'Right.'

'Never mind, it was you I wanted to see.'

'I'm here,' Joann said.

Gavin held out the flowers. 'Ritual grovel time. I'm doing the sorry-about-last-night-can-we-ever-be-friends bit. *Bit*! I didn't behave all that well. And I don't want you to get the right idea about me. At least not right away.'

'Forget it,' Joann said. 'I never even noticed.'

'That's no basis for a relationship.'

'I'll never be able to forgive you,' she said. 'How's that?'

'Now you're talking,' Gavin said. 'Suddenly this thing has possibilities.'

'We'll have to leave it like that, I'm afraid, right now. I'm trying to get the place straight.'

'If you've come here to put us to shame, you're wasting your time. The English academic is beyond it.' He sat down in an armchair she was about to move. 'Look, we live just round the corner more or less. Grange Road. Inevitably! Francesca's there most of the time. If you feel lonely or you need anything – '

'That's nice of you,' Joann said.

'She asked me to say.'

'That's nice of her.'

'Don't let 'em crush you,' Gavin said.

'It takes quite a lot to crush me,' Joann said, 'but thanks.'

'It doesn't take much to crush anybody.'

'And who's going to crush me exactly?'

'You should work,' Gavin said. 'A doctor.'

'I'll remember,' Joann said.

'If necessary I'll find you a job in the sociology department. So be warned.'

'I'm warned,' she said.

He stood up, glanced at Bill's book open on the table, read a few lines and then smiled at Joann who smiled back.

He went towards the door and then, when he was all but past her, turned back and kissed her on the lips. It was the kiss not of a seducer but of a serious lover. 'Remember,' he said.

'I have to get a job,' she said.

'Like the parable says. The talents have to work.' He went out, unsmiling, a man who had accomplished a dutiful mission.

III

Bill bought a second-hand Triumph Herald in Staunton, from a fellow Brummie as it turned out, who promised him he was getting a bargain. On the way back through the Campus (the turn-off was signalled by a nice new sign, THE UNIVERSITY, which had been spray-painted LIVERPOOL FC) he was humming softly to himself when suddenly the windscreen shattered. He steered in to the side of the road and jumped out. There was a bridge over the road ahead, where lorries went straight to the canteen wing, and a copse to the left. He saw no one. The windscreen had been struck at a central point. The glass had fractured in a chain of cheap diamonds from that single notch. 'Omoi, omoi, omoi,' Bill said. He lowered the roof of the car and drove half-standing, like a cut-price Head of State.

He was late for a game of squash with Piers Cobbett when he was stopped by a delegation of students carrying banners protesting against the Vietnam war. He recognized some of Gavin's pupils, especially a very pretty, freckled red-head called Denise. 'Are you going to sign for us?' she said.

'I think I've already made my position clear,' Bill said. '*À plusieurs reprises.*'

'It's quite important,' Bryan Davies said. He was a very bright and exceptionally unsmiling third-year Marxist. 'So one more time won't hurt, will it?'

'Hurt whom?' Bill said. 'We're rather a long way from the decision-making process, don't you think?'

'Every little bit helps, Professor, doesn't it?' Sid Chase said. He was one of Bill's pupils, a quiet Public School boy.

'If it stops the bombing of Hanoi, I mean, sir.'

'I'll drink to that,' Bill said, 'if it does.'

'It's important that we take a stand,' Bryan said. 'Morally.'

'Ah. Tell me, have any other members of the Faculty signed yet?'

The students burst into whoops of laughter. 'You're the fifth one in a row to ask the same question,' Denise said.

'I believe you.'

'Why worry about the others?' Bryan said. 'It's simple. You sign or you don't.'

'He said threateningly.'

'You're the one who'll be threatening, Bill, quite honestly, if you refuse to sign.'

'Am I?' Bill said. 'How so?'

'Because you'll be saying you're in favour of the American position in that case, won't you? And you're part of the power structure. Hence – '

'*Illae lacrimae*,' Bill said. 'There are a lot of American positions, he attempted to explain.'

'There's only one Pentagon position, sir – ' Sid said.

'I have taught in America actually,' Bill said, 'and – '

'And I daresay you're quite keen to go back one day,' Denise said.

'Quite,' Bill said. 'I liked the waffles.'

'Oh that's where you learned to do it, is it?'

'Do what?' Bill said.

'Waffle,' Denise said.

'I did march on Washington,' Bill said.

'We know what you did,' Denise said. 'You and all the other celebrities. The cocktail marchers.'

'Unfortunately the Martinis never reached me,' Bill said. 'Look, I'm supposed to be playing squash. How about discussing this a bit later over a jar?'

'Just put your name on the bottom,' Bryan said, 'and it'll save you buying a round.'

Bill looked at his watch, shrugged, picked up the biro-on-a-string and signed his name.

'OK?'

'As long as you don't say we twisted your arm,' Bryan said.

'I shan't say that, he promised.' Bill walked off briskly. Sid Chase hurried after him.

'Professor Bourne, you said something this morning – '

'I said several things,' Bill said. 'I *hope* – '

'You said that ethical theories had, er, something in common with theories of *perception* – I wonder – '

'Judging and seeing are somehow linked, aren't they? And He saw that it was good, isn't that what the Bible says?'

'If you're going to play squash, sir, it's the other way,' Sid said.

'Rational design,' Bill said. 'And don't I hate it? Where the hell *do* I go?'

ii

'My overall impression of working conditions at Dent and Son was rather favourable, I'm afraid,' Michael Deakin said.

'There's no absolute necessity,' Gavin said, 'for every capitalist in the country to be grinding the faces of the toilers, you know – '

'Objectively, surely, though, Gavin, one's likely to find a pattern?' Bryan Davies said.

'Objectively one's likely to find the skull beneath the skin, is that what you're saying?'

'I don't think so.'

Gavin said: 'Michael, to what extent would you be inclined to say the – the fringe benefits are a sort of cushion against wage claims? A conscious or unconscious attempt to provide a – a – ?'

'Opiate,' Bryan supplied. 'Things like the OK Sauce on every table – you did mention that, didn't you, Mike?'

'Among other things.'

'That cost them practically nothing, right? They're all an attempt on the part of a paternalistic management –'

'Facts first,' Gavin said, 'speeches later –'

'Hark at the paternalist!' Denise said.

'Denise?'

'I said hark at the paternalist.'

Gavin said: 'Thank you, Denise.'

'It's a pleasure.' She looked down and started to doodle.

Gavin said: 'How do the wage levels at Dent's compare with wage levels locally and nationally?'

'Locally,' Michael said, 'they're better than everyone with a comparable work force, better than larger companies like Staunton Engineering –'

'Well, Christ –' Bryan began, and caught a look from Gavin.

'In fact,' Michael said, 'better than everyone except one small firm of specialist cabinet-makers – incidentally another family firm –'

'He's beginning to sound like someone from Central Office,' Bryan said.

Gavin said: 'How dare you come in here and tell us the truth as you found it, Michael?'

'If you can't recognize white-wash when you see it, I'm sorry for you,' Bryan said.

'How many weeks have you been mixing this white-wash, Michael?'

'Three months off and on –'

'And you dare to come in here,' Gavin said, 'on the basis of a mere three months' research and tell us that Dent and Son is a fairly decent business that pays its workers above the national average and doesn't put bromide in their tea? You bloody fascist swine!'

'It certainly doesn't do that,' Michael said. 'They have quite a sex problem, as a matter of fact –'

'Don't we all?'

'Speak for yourself, Gavin,' Denise said.

'I'm glad to know that you're getting enough, Denise. That relieves us all of a responsibility – '

'Don't worry about that,' she said.

'We have enough on our hands keeping Alice happy,' Gavin said. Alice Rivers lodged with the Popes and it was no secret that she was in love with Gavin. She was a pretty, shy girl whom Gavin treated with a sort of ribald tenderness.

'Sex problem,' Bryan said. 'What's that exactly?'

'Well,' Michael said, 'first of all you've got the growing numbers of women employed. Ten years ago they constituted twenty-two per cent of the work force, now it's forty-seven. And forty years ago – when the plant was producing components for the shipbuilding industry – they had only eight per cent, and they were mostly in cleaning and catering – '

'O K,' Bryan said, 'but what's the problem exactly?'

'Simple example. Toilet facilities – '

'The word is lavatories,' Gavin said.

'Very U!' Bryan said.

'U and non-U, are they skulking in the provincial shrubbery?' Gavin said. 'How nice it is to meet old friends again! Go on, Michael – ' He looked out of the window. Joann Bourne turned away and walked towards the bookshop. How long had she been standing there?

'Men get into the women's facilities,' Michael said, 'and write things. And then someone has to clean it off. It sounds silly – '

'It sounds hysterical,' Denise said.

'– but the cleaning force is mostly female or was – '

Bryan released a sudden honk of laughter.

'Bryan's sense of humour has made a break from cover,' Gavin said. '*Sauve qui peut*. Right, Michael. On we go: they can't ask the lady cleaners to clean the modern words off the walls of the jakes – '

'Unless,' Alice said, 'they got them to do it with their eyes shut, I suppose.'

'In the same way in which their mothers reproduced their species,' Gavin said. 'Alice has a thought there. Michael, did that occur to them?'

'Actually not. They decided to recruit some coloureds.'

'They decided to recruit some coloureds. Why? Why did they decide – because that's an interesting word – and why coloureds?'

'They were under a bit of pressure, I think.'

'Good old private industry!' Bryan said.

'We'll have the singsong later,' Gavin said. 'What pressure?'

'From the local Ministry of Labour people. There was an influx of coloured people from two urban centres as a result of overspill housing – '

Denise uttered a loud yawn.

'Isn't it tedious,' Gavin said, 'when you get down to actual cases of flesh and blood and bricks and mortar? I do apologize on behalf of dull facts everywhere.'

'Sorry,' Denise said.

'Well, that was the beginning,' Michael said. 'Because then, of course, they had coloureds as well as women on the premises and pretty soon – '

'They had the coloureds on the women,' Gavin said.

'As a matter of fact, that's more or less – well, that's more or less right.'

'You know, I get the feeling I've seen this picture before – '

Bryan said: 'You talked about *deciding* to take on coloureds, Mike.' Gavin nodded: Bryan had spotted the key point. 'Does this mean, did you discover, that the company had a policy of not taking coloured workers prior to these permissive slogans appearing in the female bog?'

'Cyril Easton – the Personnel Manager – simply said they hadn't felt any need to take on coloured workers – '

'Democracy,' Bryan said. 'Capitalist style.'

'Bryan,' Gavin said, 'that essay you were going to do me, I suggest you write it on the autonomy of the Soviet Republics between 1919 and 1924.'

'It's absolutely disgusting.'

'Do you know, Denise,' Gavin said, 'that the foolish folk of Staunton might well, and in a deeply depressing majority, find it more disgusting that your delightful nipples are visible through your charming jersey?' He turned to Michael again. 'You started by talking about a sex problem. I realize that that was largely a – saving your blushes, gentlemen – a way in, but is the problem still seen in those terms?'

'They still do have a policy, you see,' Michael said. 'No coloureds except as cleaners and maintenance people.'

'*Still?*' Bryan said.

'Right.'

'Apartheid.'

'Well, that's pitching it a bit strong – '

'It's apartheid. They employ blacks – because, I mean, that's what we're talking about – in segregated, limited capacities – '

'Let's call a spade a spade, what?'

'I don't know how you feel about this, Jim?' Bryan turned to Jim Shore, the Jamaican who sat next to Denise.

'As a member of an oppressed *class*,' Gavin said, 'or an oppressed *race* are you asking him that?'

'As a human being.'

'Me?' Jim said. 'Human? Thanks.'

'After all,' Bryan said, 'you are here. You are allowed to contribute *something*.'

'Bryan – ' Gavin said.

'Don't protect him.'

'I'm trying to protect you.'

'I don't need that stuff,' Bryan said. 'Tim Dent wants to be the local MP, doesn't he? He's politically ambitious, we

all know that. Obviously he has to pretend to run an en-
lightened business – '

'But Michael's already told us,' Gavin said, 'it *is* en-
lightened. Eighty-two per cent of the work force satisfied
with the management – rates of pay higher than the
national average – fringe benefits shared and excellent –
sports facilities – '

'Look, Gavin, I know what this is all about. This is the
firm which the University establishment – and that includes you, I'm sorry to say – needs and wants. For
financial reasons. I daresay it's unconscious, but you've
been deliberately protecting Tim Dent and the others,
you've been deliberately – '

'Deliberately unconsciously?' Gavin said. 'I don't know
my own strength, do I?'

'We're taking their money for this bleeding Media
Complex – '

'Where you will be able to make left-wing films with
the latest equipment – '

'And show them to no one outside the University
owing to the cartel system obtaining in the cinema and
television business. We're taking money from a firm that
practises apartheid, Gavin. Laugh it off, if you will – '

Gavin said: 'I think we should look into this as calmly
and scientifically as we can, doing some further research
if necessary – and I think it is necessary – and then –
we'll – see!' He stood up. The hour was over.

'See what?'

'Bryan,' Gavin said, 'you're dealing with reality here.
Be gentle. And patient. And right. Then act.' Gavin stuffed
papers in his music case and went to the door. 'I'll see you
tomorrow, if we live. Same time, same spots on your dials.'

Denise said: 'Gavin – '

'Miss Scott?'

'You haven't signed our Vietnam thing.'

'I've done it for the last five years, Denise dear. I think

I'll take a sabbatical. Maybe the Pentagon are waiting for a petition that doesn't have my name on it and *then* they'll stop the bombing. I'm late for lunch. Start the party without me for a change. I'm usually sick on the buffet. *Hasta mañana, compañeros*.' He showed them a clenched fist and departed.

'I tell you what I think we should do, Michael,' Bryan said, 'if you agree, and that's form an *ad hoc* committee – '

'Oh I can't wait,' Denise said, 'an *ad hoc* committee! It's got me all excited, hasn't it you, Jim?'

'I'm always excited, baby.'

'Some people make me sick,' Bryan said.

Sid said: 'I do think – '

'When?' Bryan said. 'When do you?'

'I *agree* with you, Bryan,' Sid said. 'I *agree*.'

'I think we need to take a responsible, serious attitude,' Bryan said. 'Denise, seriously – '

'Oh seriously, Bryan, I'm sure you're absolutely right.'

Bryan stood aside to let Jim Shore go out first. Jim stopped in the doorway and grinned at him. 'Who makes you sick, exactly, Bryan?' he said.

iii

'The flowers were beautiful,' Jeanne Dent said.

'Beautiful flowers,' Gavin said, 'beautiful woman – '

Jeanne said: 'Tim should be here but I think he must have gone by the sports ground. The team's got a semi-final in some cup. I forgot all about it until after I spoke to you – '

'Will he be long?'

Jeanne opened the door into the drawing room. The house was a Regency rectory, pink washed in the local style, with a rounded bay window overlooking a long lawn and, in the middle distance, a reservoir which Tim had stocked with fish. Gavin's flowers were in a Limoges vase.

'Not too long, I don't think,' Jeanne said. 'We can have a drink. What will you have?'

'I'll have a drop of whisky, if you've got one. I can always call Tim, if – '

'No, no,' Jeanne said. She came and sat opposite him. 'Do you send a lot of flowers to people, Mr Pope?'

'I find it quite remarkable, don't you, how people always take offence when a conversation ceases to be personal?'

'I took no offence at all,' she said.

'And when I'd tried so hard!'

'Now you're contradicting yourself.'

'I never go to women for lessons in logic,' Gavin said.

'What do you go to them for?'

'To see their husbands,' Gavin said. 'What else?'

'I really did forget about the game,' Jeanne said. 'I'm so sorry – '

'You can always send me some flowers.'

'You're a curious man, Mr Pope. I wonder what you're really after?'

'How extremely thoughtful of you!'

'Are you a Communist?' she said.

'Are you faithful to your husband?'

'I fail to see the connection.'

'I'm a curious man.'

'Yes, I am,' she said, 'faithful. I happen to love my husband.'

'I don't know whether you're going to believe me, Mrs Dent – '

'I wish you'd call me Jeanne,' she said.

'I know you do,' Gavin said. 'Isn't this dangerous and teasing, this conversation? I do like this sort of thing. What was I saying? Oh yes, the reason I'm here, what do think it is?'

'You want to see Tim, don't you?'

'Then why isn't he here?' Gavin said.

'I told you. He's at this wretched football game.'

'Then why am I here?'

'If you prefer,' Jeanne said, 'you can always leave a message and go.'

'I prefer to leave a message and stay.' He took Jeanne's hand as she reached for his glass. 'Do you know,' he said, 'that your husband's factory operates a colour bar?'

'My husband's factory?'

He turned her hand over in his. 'I assume you know that he has a factory? I also assume he's your husband. I'm taking a lot of liberties. A colour bar.'

'I don't know what you're talking about,' she said.

'They don't employ blacks at Dent's,' Gavin said. 'Did you seriously not know?'

Jeanne took her hand away abruptly, as if she had been looking for it everywhere. 'I think perhaps you had better go, Mr Pope,' she said.

'I thought we were beyond that,' Gavin said.

'This nonsense has gone far enough, don't you think?'

'As nonsense goes,' Gavin said, 'it hardly seems to have gone anywhere at all. I had the impression a few moments ago you were hoping for something with a considerably longer stride.'

'I don't think my husband would be very glad to find you here when he gets back.'

'Oh? This is an odd change of front, Mrs Dent, when you asked me to come.'

'I made a mistake, I told you.'

'Is he a very jealous man, your husband?'

'Very,' she said. 'He's also very strong.'

'Then you'd better be very careful, hadn't you?' Gavin said.

She slapped his face, hard. 'Get out, please.'

'You carry quite a poke yourself, if I may so put it,' Gavin said.

'I thought you were stupid and childish the other night, but I was prepared to give you another chance – '

'People are always giving me another chance to be stupid and childish,' Gavin said. 'It's when I want to be anything else that they tend to turn nasty. Tell Tim I called, would you?'

'You can tell him yourself, Mr Pope. I'm sure you'll be able to explain yourself more clearly than I could ever hope to do.'

'Oh, you want me to keep all this a secret then, do you?' Gavin said.

'All what?' she said.

He broke off a flower from the spray he had sent her and put it in his buttonhole. At the door, he gave her a charming smile and a wave of the fingers. '*Au revoir,*' he said. 'Jeanne.'

IV

The *ad hoc* committee came to call at Medlar Cottage. It was two weeks later and the bulldozers were due to begin work on the Media Complex on the Monday.

'You are the head of one of the principal departments concerned,' Bryan told Bill. 'If we don't act soon, it's going to be too late. We've done our side, it's up to you to do yours.'

Bill patted himself for cigarettes. Sid leant forward with his packet open. He had a lighter too. 'It is a scandal, isn't it, sir?' he said.

'I can see it's a problem,' Bill said.

'Cambridge,' Bryan said, 'pure Cambridge! A colour bar is not a problem, it's a fact.'

'Forgive me,' Bill said, 'but isn't there legislation to cover this kind of thing? If there's really a case – '

'How do you prove a negative fact?' Bryan said. 'The

University shouldn't accept tainted money. It's as simple as that. Legislation! There's only one way to bring this sort of thing to an end and that's direct action. Bring it into the open. Put it in the pillory.'

Bill said: 'I think I should talk to the Vice-Chancellor – '

The Committee burst out laughing, with the exception of Sid, who polished his glasses, and Jim Shore, who was reading *Plato, Education and Society*.

Bill said: 'Should I *not* talk to the Vice-Chancellor?'

'He wants his building, doesn't he?' Bryan said.

'And you don't want it?'

'We want it – ' Sid said, 'but, um, not unless it's um, clean.'

'We think it ought to be blacked,' Bryan said, 'the whole project.'

'*Blacked*?' Bill said. 'An interesting phrase in the circumstances, suggesting a long-rooted dichotomy in our society – '

'Furthermore,' Bryan said, 'we feel that arising from this there should be a general investigation, in the open, of all the sources of the University's revenue and its investments.'

'I've been here one term,' Bill said. 'I – '

Joann came in with mugs of coffee and a plate of Jaffa cakes.

'I would have thought you'd be behind us if anyone was,' Bryan said.

'Thank you,' Bill said, 'but why?'

'Obvious reasons. You've been in America. You've got a black wife.'

'So I have and so I have,' Bill said. 'But is that the point?'

'Mrs Bourne,' Bryan said, 'how do you feel about this? Because – '

'I'm not a member of the Faculty,' Joann said. 'And I'm not a student.'

'You are a human being,' Bryan said.

'Well *thank* you.'

'We would like to know, Dr Bourne,' Sid said, 'how you feel about it.'

'No comment,' Joann said. 'I just serve the coffee round here.'

'On balance,' Bill said, 'won't it be a very good thing, this Complex?'

'For you, you mean?' Bryan said.

'For us,' Bill said. 'For the place.'

Sid said: 'Do you think we shouldn't do anything then sir?'

'He wants us to wait till the right moment,' Bryan said. 'They always do. In England it's always either the wrong time or the wrong place.'

The door bell rang. 'It's Gav.' Alice said. The minibus was parked at the gate. Its windscreen was shattered and there was a large hole in the middle of it. Joann opened the door.

'Dr Freud?' Gavin said. 'My name is Pope. Not *the* Pope, just *a* Pope.'

'What have you been doing?' Joann said. 'That looks nasty.'

'It is. It's representative of the general state of bourgeois fists when driven through mass-produced windscreens.' Joann took him and the wounded hand into the bathroom. 'I gathered you needed the work,' Gavin said. 'Hullo! Do I hear the murmur of vigilantes by night?'

'They're waiting for you,' Joann said. 'They've got Bill painted into a corner.'

'Let 'em wait,' Gavin said. 'Bloody trouble makers.'

'Austin'll run rings round you,' Bryan was saying. 'That's what he was hired for. To run rings round people for the sake of the Establishment.'

'Did you know that Dent's also work on, on, um, defence contracts, sir, some of them integrally associated with um American companies?'

'No, I didn't,' Bill said.

'The Media Complex should be totally embargoed,' Bryan said. 'If work begins, it should be picketed. If the pickets are violated, strike action throughout the Campus – '

'Look – ' Bill said.

Bryan said: 'Let me finish, will you?'

'Is there a chance?' Bill said.

Bryan said: 'I think you're a bit out of touch, Professor, if you think – '

'If I think at all?' Bill said. 'Or only if I don't think what you think – '

'All right then,' Bryan said, 'if it's going to be like that. I sensed a hostility the moment we arrived here. The way we were welcomed – '

'Coffee instead of whisky? I apologize. No red carpet? All my excuses!'

Denise said: '*Bryan –*'

'No, look I'm sorry – '

'No, look, you're *not*,' Bill said.

'You, Professor, have taken the position from the beginning that we have no real business to question the running of the University. The old, old game. You took the position we had no business to have come here tonight at all – '

Bill said: 'I simply need to be convinced – '

'Yes,' Bryan said, 'and the more proof we bring you the more you need to be convinced. You live in an eternal regress – '

'All bought and paid for out of my own salary, I assure you,' Bill said.

'And you were originally working class!'

'Forgive me,' Bill said. 'I seem to have mislaid my Burke's Peerage during my travels.'

'Perhaps that accounts for your general position,' Bryan said.

'I don't *have* a general position,' Bill said.

'That *is* your general position,' Bryan said.

The door opened and Gavin came in, with a bottle of whisky in his unbandaged hand. Joann followed with glasses. 'Gentlemen,' he said, 'and others. Mafeking has been relieved.'

'Gavin,' Alice said, 'what have you done?'

'I attacked a lackey of the police state,' Gavin said, 'and received extensive lacerations. Everybody out, Trafalgar Square 2.30. Bill, you look angry. Has Bryan been catching you with his left jab?'

'You attacked *who*?'

'Forget it, Ally,' Gavin said. 'I had a punch-up with my windscreen – and lost. What I want to know here and now is the name of the premature revolutionary nut who goes around blowing out people's windscreens with an air gun. Bryan? Care to shop a mate or two?'

'Nothing to do with me.'

'No,' Gavin said, 'suppose not. After you'd finished rallying the troops, you wouldn't have enough air left in your gun to propel the pellet to the end of the barrel, would you?'

'I've really had about enough of this sort of thing from you, Gavin,' Bryan said.

'Tell me, O Comrade Freedom Fighter on a grant-assisted basis – '

'Always the same old joke. Ha ha ha.'

'Who is this character with the air gun? Does *anyone* know?'

'Probably some nihilist, sir,' Sid said.

'Because it's got to stop.'

'Or what?' Bryan said.

'There's going to be trouble, that's what.'

'What do you propose, *sir*?' Bryan said. 'Group fines? Forcible confinement in strategic hamlets? Free fire zones in the vicinity of the lacrosse pitch?'

Gavin said: 'I'm not yet ready to sacrifice my eyes to the cause of student self-expression. It's a bloody menace.' He raised his glass. 'Cheers and mingled boos,' he said.

'It's not a menace if you don't have a car,' Bryan said.

'Bryan, *is* this some stupid little lackey of yours doing this, because – ?'

'I don't know anything about it,' Bryan said. 'I don't know about it, I don't care about it. It's a complete irrelevance.'

'Bryan, when all else fails,' Gavin said, 'for God's sake don't ever try to rely on your charm.'

Bryan said: 'We wanted to put a simple question to you and then we can go – will the Faculty concerned with the Media Complex form a common front with the students in demanding an inquiry into and, if necessary, a reconsideration of the financing arrangements for the Complex in view of the entirely unsatisfactory employment policy instituted and followed by Richard Dent and Sons at their Staunton site?'

Gavin said: 'What was the first part of that simple question again?'

'Christ, Gavin – '

'Don't call me Christ yet, sonny,' Gavin said. 'Wait till I come again in glory – that'll be the moment.'

Bryan said: 'Has anyone ever told you how utterly *boring* you were?'

Jim Shore laughed. He cackled. He roared. He howled. And suddenly the whole room was in hysterics. Only Joann failed to laugh, Joann and Bryan. The others rolled in their seats, hugged their sides and gasped for air. Bryan sat very white in his place. Then he stood up, gave Joann a strange, insolent look and walked out of the house.

'We'll be sorry,' Gavin said, as he wiped the tears from his eyes.

Denise said: 'Funny book, Jim?'

'A laugh in every line,' Jim said.

'He wants to make trouble,' Bill said. 'We shall now have to see what trouble he makes.'

'Yes, well, we all have our own ways of advertising our virility.'

'*Do* we, Gavin?' Denise said. 'What's yours?'

'Knockers to you, Denise, my pretty.'

'In other words, chat,' Denise said.

'My Achilles tongue,' Gavin said, 'you're quite right.'

'Well,' Alice said, 'I think – '

'My little lodger is making polite noises about going home,' Gavin said. 'May I give you a lift, little lady, in my aerated Krautmobile?'

'Is he always like that,' Bill said, 'your friend Bryan?'

'Right, you mean?' Denise said. 'Bryan's got a point and I'm not about to betray him as soon as his back's turned.'

Bill lit a new cigarette. 'Gavin, he summed up, I've proposed that you and I go and see the Vice-Chancellor and present the whole situation to him – '

'The whole situation includes *us*,' Denise said. 'I don't intend to be paraphrased by anyone.'

Gavin said: 'Allow us our simple pleasures, Denise.'

'I'm solid with Bryan on this. We're not going to be diplomatically smothered.'

'If I did everything you wanted,' Bill said, 'what would I actually do? You still haven't told me.'

'Join us,' Denise said. 'Wholeheartedly. If that isn't asking more than you've got to give.'

'Thanks,' Bill said, 'but I still think on balance I'm better where I am.'

'Where's that?' Denise said, looking round the room. 'I can't see you anywhere.'

Gavin said: 'I can't see this ending in all power to the Soviets tonight exactly. I think I shall toddle up the wooden stairs to Bedfordshire, hum a few bars of the Red Flag and drop off for a few hours well-earned rest and recreation in the People's Republic of Nod.'

'Now you're above the battle too, are you, Gavin? A pair of clapped-out Olympians, look at you.'

Gavin raked the room with mock machine-gun fire. 'Aahahaha! I wondered when I was going to get mine.'

'Stir it up,' Denise said, 'and then turn it all into a game. Cambridge. Cambridge, Cambridge. Both of you.'

'Sorry we can't all go to t'best places, luv,' Bill said.

'You mean that,' Denise said. 'You fucking *mean* that.'

'It's true,' Gavin said.

'Come on, Cambridge . . .' Denise chanted.

Jim Shore stood up and put an arm round Denise. 'Come on, baby, time to go now.'

'*Cambridge*,' Denise said. 'They never grow up.'

Sid said: 'Um, well, thanks for the hospitality. Goodnight.'

'Goodnight, Sidney,' Gavin said. He put his hand on Alice's shoulder. 'Well, Alice the lodger, *kommst du?*'

Alice's poncho was hanging in the hall. As she put it on, Gavin said: 'He's a nice lad, Sidney.'

'I know,' Alice said.

'And quite bright.'

'I know,' she said.

'And you're a nice girl,' Gavin said.

She turned her face up to his. 'Thank you.'

'And that's all you get,' Gavin said. 'Sorry.'

ii

Bill had not moved from his chair. *Plato, Education and Society* lay on the sofa where Jim had left it. Joann cleared the glasses and picked up crumbs. 'Quite like old times in Ohio,' she said. 'Kids dropping by the house to tell you go fuck yourself.'

'Go fuck yourself, *Professor*,' Bill said.

'I applied for a job today,' Joann said.

'Oh? Where?'

'Didn't get it.'

'What was it?'

'A locum. They weren't sure I'd be happy – and all that. Just like old times! Staunton, Alabama.'

'I don't believe it. They seriously wouldn't have you?'

'They seriously said I could come in and sweep out any time.'

'They didn't.'

'How do you say? I was given to understand? I was given to understand.'

'We're going to do something about this,' Bill said.

'Forget it, Professor.'

'Are you kidding?' He caught her by the arm. 'Did this really happen?'

'Guess,' she said.

'God, I'm tired,' Bill said. 'I'm bushed.'

'Then I'd better go to bed,' Joann said.

'Those damned kids! You didn't have any trouble really, did you, today?'

'Me? Trouble? *Never.*'

'Did you?'

Joann said: 'It doesn't matter. I can't stay here, Bill.'

'Here?' Bill said. 'Where?'

'Staunton. I can't,' she said, 'I'm sorry.'

'Who was this damned doctor? Who – ?'

'It's how I feel; it's not what anybody did.'

'Since when?'

'I can't explain,' she said. 'I've got to go. I don't want to argue.'

'I'm not arguing,' Bill said. 'But why?'

'It's how I feel.'

'I was bad here tonight.'

'You were fine.'

'We're married,' he said.

'Do you love me?'

Bill said: 'Yes. *Yes.*' He wanted a cigarette. She had one. He said: 'What's wrong exactly?'

'It's just one day after another, Billiam,' she said. 'It's not what I want.'

'You don't love me,' he said.

'I want to go home,' she said.

'*Home?*'

'Right,' she said. 'Stateside.'

'Home!'

'We had a good time. And a long time. And I'm sorry.'

Bill said: 'Is there – someone else?'

'Yes,' she said. 'Me.'

'It's *really* not my night,' he said.

'I have to, Bill. I'll die here. I know I will.'

'Then do,' Bill said.

She kissed him. 'No offence. Professor.'

'Of course not,' he said. 'Doctor.'

She picked up the full ashtray. Bill took it from her, gently. And then, with a sudden passionate movement, he whipped it up and back and up through the air. The stubs flew; the ash filled the little room with grey freckles. He handed the empty ashtray back to Joann.

V

The banner said: 'NO TO TAINTED MONEY'. Denise and Bryan were holding the poles at either end. Other radical students were camped on the Vice-Chancellor's lawn, with a variety of slogans nailed to broom handles and stakes uprooted from the building site. A press photographer spotted Denise, the pretty student. She made faces. The photographer grinned and mimed for her to undo the top button of her blouse. She glared at him and undid all the buttons and took off her shirt. 'OK? What you want, are they?'

'Great,' he said.

'I don't give a fuck,' she said. 'Fleet street pimp.'

Austin Denny came out onto the front step of the Lodge. 'Won't you all come in?'

'And do what?' Bryan said.

'Talk,' Austin said.

'We don't want talk, we want action.'

'Talk is action.'

'Cambridge again,' Denise said.

Gavin was in the Vice-Chancellor's drawing room, together with Tim Dent and John Cadman.

Bryan said: 'This is a fix. We thought we were going to see Austin, not you. Alone.'

'I think you should hear Mr Dent's side of this.'

'And he'd better listen to ours,' Bryan said, 'because we're going to be picketing his factory unless he's very careful – '

'I'm always very careful,' Tim said. 'Mr – ?'

'Davies. Bryan Davies.'

'Our money isn't good enough for you, is that it?'

'Oh don't start *that*,' Denise said.

'Could we just listen?' Austin said. 'Why don't you come a bit nearer the fire?'

'Why do you say that?'

'I don't want you to get cold.'

'Why me particularly?' Denise said.

'Isn't it rather obvious?'

'What is?'

'You're wearing less than most of us,' Austin said.

Denise glared at Tim Dent. 'Well,' she said, 'do you like them?'

'Like what?' Tim said.

'My *tits*,' Denise said.

'Is this really relevant?'

'Phoney little man. Both of you.'

'Thank you,' Tim said.

'You operate a colour bar, yes or no?'

Tim smiled. 'Do I?'

'You bloody well know you do,' Bryan said.

'Mr Davies – '

'Bryan.'

'Never mind the label,' Tim said, 'it's what's in the tin that counts, isn't it?'

'You would think of people like bloody groceries, wouldn't you? This is a trick. We agreed to see the Vice-Chancellor, no one else.'

'I invited you,' Austin said. 'You came. I don't think any agreement was involved, was it?'

'Let's get this straight as quick as we can, shall we?' Tim said. 'Because I don't know about you, I've got work to do.'

'Look – ' Bryan said.

'*Listen*,' Tim said. 'Now listen.'

'Captain of fucking industry,' Bryan said.

'*Listen*,' the Vice-Chancellor said.

'We do employ coloured workers at Dent's.'

'To clean out the bogs, right?'

'We'd like to have more.'

'Very white of you.'

'Unfortunately – '

'They're not intelligent enough, are they?'

'It's not that,' Tim Dent said. 'We have tried employing immigrants on the shop floor.'

'Look, you want to be the next Conservative candidate, don't you, for Staunton – ?'

'I do. Yes. Is that a crime?'

'No,' Bryan said. 'Congratulations.'

'I don't see the relevance – '

'You don't! Talk about cant. You don't see the relevance? Can you see Nelson's Column?'

'Not from here,' Tim said, 'no. I'm trying to explain something to you, Bryan – '

'You don't want to be blamed for providing incentives

for blacks to come into the area, right? So a nice little policy of the closed door and anyone who can get through the letter box has got a job cleaning mucky words off the jakes wall, isn't that how it is, Mr Dent? *Tim?*'

'Not quite. You should have done your homework, Bryan.'

'I'm not a schoolboy.'

'Homework doesn't stop –'

'Oh for pity's sake.'

'The Reverend has something I'd like you to hear. Reverend . . .'

'I really do interfere in this matter with the greatest reluctance.'

'He said, kissing the arses of the firing squad. If you're so reluctant, why do it?'

Cadman said: 'This is a tape recording I made a couple of months ago.'

'How convenient!' Bryan said.

'With one of the senior shop stewards at Dent and Son's.'

'Put the fucking thing on, if you're so proud of it.'

'Bring 'em in here and you're going to have problems,' said a voice, with the sounds of machinery behind it. 'I'm not threatening now, but I am warning. The lads've got nothing against blacks as such, I'm not saying that, I'm not having anyone say it, but we don't want 'em in here, taking jobs from local people. You start bringing 'em in here and I won't answer for the consequences. If that's your plan, I say think again, but only because that's going to make trouble for everyone.'

Cadman pressed off the switch and wound forward. 'There is another passage,' he said, 'in which –'

'There is another passage,' Bryan mimicked.

'You see, Bryan,' Tim Dent said, 'it isn't just the wicked capitalists who are standing in the way of the brotherhood of man.'

'And aren't you pleased?' Bryan said. 'Aren't you triumphant? The workers are human, the workers don't love their fellow men as much as they should, or they could, or they would, if it weren't for your filthy newspapers and your beastly imperialist religion – '

'That's rather childish,' Cadman said. 'I hoped for something better, I must say.'

'Oh yes, you must, mustn't you? Self-satisfied upper-class puffter, pretending to love your fellow man and not wanting to touch him with a barge-pole, slaving your life away for Jesus and the hope of a bishopric. Oh you really caught me out, didn't you? Well, let me tell you something – '

'The day will come, won't it, Bryan?' Gavin said.

'It damned well will, Gavin, when we won't need any of you, not any of you, when we won't have to be right all the time in order to prove that we're right most of the time – when you won't be the judge and the jury and the goddam examining board – when we'll do the condescending and the patronizing and the superior-smiling and you can all mark each other out of ten till you're blue in the face for all the difference it'll make to the way things really are. You live in a bloody backwater, the lot of you, and how much longer are you going to be able to persuade yourselves that it's the open sea and you're all Admirals of the Fleet? You're Admirals of the creek, all of you, and you're further up it than you can possibly imagine.'

Tim Dent said: 'If there's any question of picketing or disruption of any kind, I shall, with the Reverend's permission, release these tapes to the press, radio and television.'

'Don't think I'm unsympathetic, please,' Cadman said, 'but life is a little more complicated than you think, young man. At your age one quite recognizes – '

'Try keeping your motto in your cracker, Reverend. I

suppose one's lucky in a way, having a chance to observe the last of the Dodos before they finally become extinct.'

Gavin grinned at Bryan as he came past him and raised his clenched fist.

'You think everything's funny, don't you, Gavin?' Bryan said, and thumped him, hard, in the eye. 'Laugh that off then.'

'That hurt,' Gavin said. 'That hurt.'

'The man's got a bad hand,' Tim Dent said, 'you big ape.'

'Big ape? Big *ape*?'

Austin Denny stepped between Tim and Bryan. 'Go to your quarters,' he said.

'*Quarters*?'

'Go,' Austin said. 'Now.'

Jim said: 'You OK?'

'I'm OK,' Gavin said.

Austin went to where Gavin was huddled in a corner of the settee. 'He *hit* you? Did that boy hit you?'

'It's nothing.'

'He hit you.'

'He didn't agree with the way I run my course,' Gavin said. 'Not everyone does.'

'Didn't *agree*? He hit you.'

'Did he?' Gavin said, covering his eye. 'I didn't see.'

'He's finished,' Austin said. 'He's finished.'

'Oh no, Austin, oh no!' Gavin looked at his bloody fingers. 'He's just beginning . . .'

'You're hurt,' Austin said.

'I shall survive to play Mr Chips yet,' Gavin said. 'Never fear.'

ii

Tim Dent's Triumph Stag was just passing the little copse on the way out of the Campus when his windscreen was shattered. He was out of the car and across the grass before the culprit even knew he was coming. There was a chase, but Tim had played some good-class rugger in his day. He was still fit and faster than the man with the gun. He brought him down comprehensively just short of his motorbike.

iii

'It turned out he was some chap who worked at Dent's. Some process worker,' Gavin said. 'He told the magistrate he was conducting a one-man war against the new privileged classes. You can imagine what kind of ice that cut.' He and the Vice-Chancellor were playing an often adjourned game of after-lunch chess in the Lodge.

'What did they fine him?' Austin said.

'A hundred quid and fifty quid costs. I need hardly tell you that I made a small anonymous contribution towards payment.'

'You would,' Ursula Denny said, from where she was doing her correspondence.

'I also think he should have been put in the stocks and horse-whipped.'

'Which you also would.'

'Well,' Gavin said, 'thanks for the coffee. I'll leave you to think about that one, Austin, because, as the modern wives say, I must loathe you and leave you. I have to catch the 3.18.'

'Going to London?' Austin said.

'I have to go and see someone. There's a full professorship going in Zambia – '

'Gavin!'

'Don't worry,' Gavin said. 'I'm not applying. Like Socrates, I prefer to stay and face the music, even if it is the Led Zeppelin. No, I have business of, as they say, a private character. My rich aunt is in town and I must go and hold my hand out. Integrity was ever preserved by generous patronage. No sane man relies on public funds.'

'Don't you *dare* go to Zambia.'

'Don't worry, Austin, I won't.'

iv

'Hullo.'

'Hullo,' Joann said.

'Been here long?'

'Long enough.'

It was a gallery in Bond Street. The paintings were mostly of English gardens with a surrealistic air, complete with roses, fat ladies, naked girls and tea on the lawn.

'The train had a puncture. Well, it had something. What do you think of them?'

'I like them.'

'Tell me, what's the place like?'

'Place?'

'You're living,' Gavin said.

'Habitable. I like your friend.'

'Tom? Don't like him too much, will you? Has he found you something to do? Because that's the main thing.'

'Yes, he has. And very interesting too. Is it really the main thing?'

'No,' Gavin said, 'of course not. I'm glad to see you. Very.'

'I began to wonder if you were coming.'

'I'm not that late.'

'Because I so wanted you to.'

'Thank you.'

'I must be mad,' Joann said.

'Thank you.'

'Loving you.'

'I took the point,' Gavin said.

'Do you think we could go?'

'Up to your place?' he said.

'Unless you've got a better idea.'

'Is there one? Before we go though – '

'What?'

'I think I owe it to you to make you a small declaration – '

'No need,' she said.

'Don't sign away your rights before you've seen the small print,' he said.

'Read it to me,' Joann said. 'I've forgotten my glasses.'

Gavin said: 'I never go to bed with my women. Shall you mind?'

Joann said: 'There's always the floor, I presume.'

'I do my best in all other regards,' Gavin said, 'but that one particular thing I never do. Shall you mind?'

'Mother Church?'

'I suppose that must have been it originally.'

'Surely it's still a sin – '

'One trusts so,' Gavin said. 'But there it is. Loyalty to Francesca, perhaps.'

'Loyalty of a kind.'

'I'm quite good at other things,' Gavin said.

'You'll have to be, won't you?' Joann said. 'I suppose it won't matter.'

'It won't,' Gavin said. 'I promise you it's purely academic.'

A
Double
Life

'Arabs,' Adam said, 'it would be marvellous if they'd all just disappear. Well, wouldn't it? Imagine: we wake up tomorrow morning, have a nice cup of tea and – what do you know? – over to the newsroom, they've all disappeared. Wiped off the face of the earth. All one hundred million of them. Gone. No blood. No mess. Nothing but empty camels, full oil wells and a very faint odour of the Angel of the Lord with Ealing in his wings. This time the Lord's really done things properly. No messing about with just the firstborn this time. This time it's the whole bloody lot, one-two. Jehovah's the one, we'd say, wouldn't we? He's the lad all right. Just the striker we were looking for to give us some much needed punch in the six-yard box. A deadly finisher old Jehovah wouldn't you say, Bryan? When it comes to Final Solutions, there are no final solutions like the Lord's. Bang, that's it. Frankly Bryan, I'm not the man to gloat, but where's your much-fancied Allah now? The old Maestro's silenced his critics, his team has won three big ones in a row and I'd say Zion was definitely theirs to keep after a performance like this, wouldn't you?'

Adam might have been addressing the nation, so careful with the consonants was his delivery. He now paused and considered his actual audience. There were not more than a dozen of them, in a small upstairs room in Belsize Park. It was a meeting of the Hampstead Jewish Historical Society. 'I once read an essay by Bertrand Russell,' Adam went on, 'in which he said this: he said that if we could be certain – *certain* – that eternal bliss could be obtained for

251

all mankind by exterminating the Jews, then there would be no reason for not exterminating them. Forget the Race Relations Act. If we had solid guarantees, signed by the Father, the Son and the Holy Ghost, then what objection could there possibly be to a spot of paradise-producing genocide? Well, I'll tell you something. Russell was wrong. Suppose the Lord, robed in majesty, with Seraphim and Cherubim continually crying on either side, were to address the world in person, simultaneously on BBC 1, BBC 2 *and* ITV, and solemnly swear that all would be forever well – that the lion would lie down with the lamb, the black with the white, the Jew with the Arab, in fact that everybody would lie down with everybody – provided – because there always has to be a provided, doesn't there? – provided all left-handed midgets – nobody else, no Jews, nobody of Our Persuasion – only a few left-handed midgets were consigned to quick-acting, all-consuming, they-won't-feel-a-thing North-Sea gas ovens – well, what would you think? Fair enough? Good bargain? Done? What do you say? Let's be realistic. Let's be hard-nosed. Who needs left-handed midgets? And it's not much of a life being two foot six, is it? Well, ladies and gentlemen, let me give you the bad news. Nobody's made us the offer? No. The bad news is that even if the Lord, and we know that He is still a figure that commands widespread respect, even if He promised us all of that, and a fourth channel of nothing but good news, there would not only be no need, there would not be the smallest justification for handing over the ugliest, dreariest, most untelegenic left-handed midget in the world. Man is more moral than God. More moral than any God I've yet to read about in the brochures anyway. Allah, Jehovah, the Trinity: I wouldn't trust them an inch, not any of them. Would you?' Adam turned away, almost angrily. There was a silence, followed by a patter of elderly applause. The chairman, Dr Seligmann, stood up.

'Before I disagree with our speaker,' he said, 'I should

like to apologize to him there are so few people here tonight. Unfortunately, there was a mix-up at the printers' – the announcement of tonight's meeting failed to appear in the last number of the Society's journal and in consequence – '

'It's always happening,' Adam said. 'For me, seven's a crowd.'

'Young man,' said one of the audience, 'I want to tell you something. Can I tell you something?'

'What else am I here for?'

'Because if you'll forgive me saying so, I think you're pretty typical of young people today going around telling people what they ought to think.'

'Not what they ought to think,' Adam said. '*That* they ought to think.'

'Because I tell you what *I* think. I think we ought to make it clear to the Arabs – I think we ought to make it clear to them – '

'We? You and me?'

'Israel is there for good. It's a fact of life. They'll have to get used to it. Because let me ask you one simple question.'

'Those are always the difficult ones.'

'Do you seriously think it couldn't happen again? The holocaust. Do you seriously think it couldn't happen again? Without Israel – '

'Or with it,' Adam said.

'You talked about Auschwitz. My name is Gustav Wexler. I *know* about Auschwitz.'

'Mr Morris, my name is Mrs Hersh. May I say something? Israel was bought and paid for with the blood of six million martyrs.'

'Maybe,' Adam said, 'that wasn't what the Arabs wanted for it.'

'Why do you think the Jews should be the only people without a homeland?'

'Do I think that? On the other hand, Mrs Hersh, where

is the homeland of the gypsies? What did their blood buy and pay for?'

'Gypsies?' Wexler said. 'What's gypsies got to do with it?'

'Half a million gypsies also died in the concentration camps,' Adam said. 'Doesn't that even earn them a couple of fields? One caravan site with running water? A day trip to a Stately Home? *Nothing?*'

'The gypsies,' Wexler said, 'have no historic homeland.'

'Ah, that must be where they made their big mistake.'

'The gypsies,' Mrs Hersh said, 'what culture have the gypsies got?'

'No culture?' Adam said. 'To hell with them.'

'Mr Speaker,' Wexler said, 'may I ask you something? Because can you give me the names of ten famous gypsies?'

Adam thought. 'OK,' he said, 'so they don't have people play the violin so good.'

'I agree with you about religion,' Mrs Hersh said. 'Up to a point.'

'Well,' Adam said.

'We should have shorter services,' Mrs Hersh said, '*that* far.'

'I see. Well, it's a start, isn't it?'

'Don't they make you proud, Mr Morris?' Wexler said. 'The Israelis? Because they make me proud.'

'If only Hitler could see us now, what?'

'I wish he could. I wish he could.'

'Yep,' Adam said.

'Before I thank the speaker – ' Dr Seligmann said.

'There's no need – '

'I'd like to tell you about next month's meeting. The subject will be Memories of the Warsaw Ghetto.'

'I took a chance you'd be in,' Adam said.

'And was I?'

'Busy?'

'No, I'm working,' Derek said.

'In that case I'll go.'

'In that case, come in. How's brother?' Derek was wearing flared jeans and a multi-coloured T-shirt with Hang Ten across the chest. He had a black moustache and horn-rimmed spectacles and a very slim waist.

'Christ!' Adam said. 'Jews!'

'Oh of course,' Derek said. 'The meeting. How did it go?'

'You know that Hitler?'

'Hitler, Hitler . . . don't tell me, don't tell me – who'd he play for?'

'They say he never met any. What would he have thought if he had?' Adam looked round the chromium and black-leather sitting room. 'Hullo, been to Heal's sale?'

'Sorry I couldn't come,' Derek said, 'only I had a meeting myself – '

Adam sniffed the air. 'Are you alone?'

'You were here just now,' Derek said.

'You wearing perfume these days?'

'I sometimes indulge myself. A little olfactory masturbation. It leaves the hands free for work of national importance. How's Barbara?'

'She's O K. She's fine. How's Julie?'

'Julie?' Derek said. 'She's O K. She's fine.' He tapped on the bedroom door. 'Hey, Carol,' he called.

'Fuck you,' Adam mouthed.

'I'm asleep.'

'You know that brother of mine you always wanted to meet? He's here.'

'Coming.'

'She's a fan. Reads your books and everything. That's how I got her up here.'

'I've got another one for you.' Adam opened his brief-case. 'Hence my call at this late hour. Number eight in the collected works.'

'*A Double Life*.' Derek turned the book over. 'Who's this handsome bloke on the back? Your lawyer? What is it then, a thriller?'

'How did you guess?' Adam lowered his voice. 'How long has this been going on?'

Derek glanced at his watch. 'Oh . . .'

'What's your bloody secret anyway?'

'No secret. I just happen to have been born looking like a rich Jewish accountant – '

'Donner and Blitzen!'

'Whose name, as it turns out, was Donner-and-Blitzen. Ah!' The bedroom door had opened and a very pretty, fair girl came out. She was wearing a cotton shift with a floral pattern and she was barefoot. 'Carol Richardson – Adam Morris, the famous – Excuse me, but what have you done lately?'

'Don't you know?' Adam said. 'You're supposed to be my accountant.'

'Oh of course,' Derek said, 'the famous Cayman Islands Trust. May his children live so long.'

'I love your books,' the girl said.

'You can't be all bad. That's a marvellous thing you're wearing.'

'She designed it.'

'Of course she designed it. *Did* you design it?'

'Sure,' Carol said. 'It's very simple.'

'I ought to go,' Adam said.

'He's always frightened of admirers.'

'I never had one before.'

'Poor little rich bastard.'

'Derek, incidentally, did you get that last tax thing I

asked Sandra to send on to you? It was all red and inflamed.'

'Forget it,' Derek said.

'Have you done anything about it?'

'I'll slip him a little dropsy, a little backhander, everything'll be fine.'

'Ha ha. Seriously, what do I do?'

'Pay it.'

'*All* of it?'

'That's the way they like it. Or you could pay half and spend the other half in the Scrubs.'

'I really have to pay the whole bloody *lot*? I shall be writing movies for the rest of my life. Can't we appeal?'

'We did appeal. We lost.'

'Why?'

'We didn't have a leg to stand on.'

'I don't know why you stay in this country,' Carol said. 'You could live anywhere.'

Derek said: 'Would you believe that my brother here – you have met, haven't you – ?'

'How do you do?' Carol said.

'How do you do?'

'He used to think it was wrong for people to work for other people – '

'Balls.'

'You thought it was wrong to tip waiters,' Derek said. 'He used to say thank you instead. And then he wondered why he never got his soup till everyone else had their coffee. So one day he saw the light. It was half past four on a December afternoon. They had to switch it on to find his soup.'

'Lies, all lies.'

'Of course,' Carol said.

'You were a Red.'

'I still am,' Adam said. 'I still believe – '

'Kids in private schools. Socialist, my fanny – '

'You wait,' Adam said. 'Just wait till you have 'em.'

'I'm not having 'em,' Derek said.

'Forty in a class. Afraid to play in the playground. Teachers who don't correct the work – '

'I quite agree with you Bryan. I quite agree with you.'

'We sent Tom to a Primary School. We sent Rachel. We sent both of them. Fiasco. On the other hand if I could get the Revenue off my back, I'd be perfectly willing to lead a really simple life.'

'You can't, so just carry on sending them to private schools, running the Merc, spending your holidays in the South of France – '

'They're not holidays.'

'Sweating over a hot secretary by the swimming pool – that may be your idea of work, it's everybody else's idea of a holiday.'

Adam waved Derek down and turned to Carol. 'That's a really lovely thing,' he said.

'The left one's a beaut,' Derek said.

Carol said: 'He's a big tit man, your brother.'

Adam said: 'Where can I get one? I mean – do you sell them? That's to say – '

'Isn't he wonderfully articulate?' Derek said.

'I'll give you my address,' Carol said. 'Got a pen?'

'Under my very nose!' Derek said. 'Oh well, I suppose there's room.'

'Oh,' Adam said, 'it's a proper shop.'

'Fairly proper,' Carol said.

'I was thinking for my wife,' Adam said, standing up. 'She's got a birthday.'

'Give her my love,' Derek said. 'Under plain cover, of course. I'd like to send something more useful, but – '

'Well, I'm off,' Adam said. He held out his hand to Carol. 'Nice to have met you.'

'Thanks for the book,' Derek said at the door. 'I'll treasure it. All the way to the bookshop.'

'They won't have it back,' Adam said. 'I've signed the bugger, which renders it instantly worthless.'

'You swine. What's it all about actually?'

'Some rotten little Jewish accountant.'

'Oh,' Derek said, 'everybody's story!'

'No, actually, remember when I went to see Stephen Taylor that time?'

'Stephen Taylor,' Derek said, 'Stephen Taylor … The man in the wholesale roast chicken business? The English answer to Colonel Sanders. What about it?'

'The fascist,' Adam said. 'The book's about him, in a way.'

'About this nice young Jewish feller goes down to see if there would have been a good job going for him under fascism – '

'You'd turn the Brothers Karamazov into a joke, wouldn't you?' Adam said.

'The brothers Karamazov, so what were they? A couple of Russkies got lucky in the circus business. Stephen Taylor. You hoped he'd like you, didn't you? The great man. What a toady you are, really, Ad, aren't you? When you've finished being cheeky to Sir, you can't wait for a kiss on both cheeks.'

'Derek Morris – critic and clairvoyant and what else begins with c?'

'Cheers, Ad. I've got work to do in the bedroom.'

'Cocksman,' Adam said, 'that's it.'

'And Karamazeltov to you, dear brother.'

iii

'He had a wife who, he could not help believing, loved him and he had children whom, to his surprise, he loved and who, to his even greater surprise, loved him. He was so used to travelling abroad that he would sigh when he had yet again to go to places which others counted themselves lucky to see once in a lifetime. He had everything that a man might reasonably desire. In the circumstances, what was more natural than that he regarded with envy those who had less than he did and that he resented the pleasures of his friends even more than he rejoiced in the misfortunes of his enemies?'

Barbara, wearing oatmeal slacks and a white polo-necked sweater, was lying on one of the twin buttoned chesterfields which faced each other across a broad marble table where stood a Michael Ayrton bronze of a man looking through a sheet of dark perspex at a bull. The radio was on the floor beside her.

'To such a man,' Adam's voice was saying, 'both gifted and favoured, a man who received more ha'pence than kicks, whom no one need suspect of being other than satisfied with his substantial lot, there was nothing so attractive as treachery. Deceit was a liberation for him, a liberty none thought him likely either to take or to need. Freedom and duplicity were one and the same. How could he change his life save in secret, out of sight of those who loved or envied him? He had everything. Of what then could he dream but of ruin, of rape, of death? There is no call to believe that Jack the Ripper did not have an extremely happy home life.'

'Adam Morris,' the announcer said. At the same moment the front door banged and Adam called from the hall. 'It's only me, dear. Jack.' He came into the room. 'How did it sound?'

'It sounded great,' Barbara said. 'I shall now go and cut my throat.'

'You don't want to do that, darling. What's your husband for?'

'I don't know what he's *for*,' Barbara said. 'I sure as hell know what he's against.'

Adam kissed her. 'If I wasn't a writer, I'd be the happiest man in the world, you know that.'

'You didn't see Ludwig on your way in, did you?'

'That fucking cat! Is he out screwing again? Talking of which, I went to see Derek after the meeting, take him his copy of the book. He's got a new girl. I wonder what his secret is.'

'Perhaps he can't keep the old ones,' Barbara said.

'He does keep them. He just has new ones as well. He sent you his love by the way.'

'Tom recorded your talk, if you're interested,' Barbara said.

'My own voice? Of course I'm interested. What've you been doing all evening?'

'Rachel's in a play, we've been doing her lines. She's a Siamese princess. She insisted on spending the whole evening like this.' She made oriental eyes. 'She said she couldn't remember what she had to say otherwise.'

'Any calls?' Adam said.

'And your golden goal time,' Barbara said. 'Three minutes eighteen seconds!'

'You're a bitch, Ba, sometimes.'

'The great man,' Barbara said.

'The great man? I don't remember calling.'

'Mike. Oh, and your mother.'

'How was she?'

'She was your mother.'

'She does go through that. What did he want? Did he say?'

'Mike? He said, Hullo, is Mr Morris there and then I said it was me, Barbara, and he said Oh, and I said you'd be back later and he said goodbye. Quite a long chat.'

'You scare him.'

'I don't scare him. I hate him.'

'That's what he's scared of,' Adam said. 'I really don't know why you hate him.'

'He's a fraud and a climber and a liar.'

'Oh is that all? It's thanks to him we can afford to hate him in comfort. Him and Bruno.'

'I hate them both. The way they've treated you.'

'OK, so they don't love me for myself, but then who does?'

'I do,' she said.

'And look what a bitch you are!' He put his arms round her and they looked at each other like people who had been married for as long as they had. 'If I didn't have you –'

'You'd be starring in the Arabian Nights,' Barbara said, 'with full harem and chorus.'

'I'm sure we could always find a little part for you, dear.'

'It would be, wouldn't it?' Barbara said. 'If –'

'I'll do the jokes, 'kay?' Adam said. 'I suppose I'd better call chummy.'

'I said you'd call him in the morning.'

'Or he can call me.'

'If you can wait that long,' she said.

'Oh damn it all,' Adam said, 'what do you want me to be?'

'Yourself?'

'That takes longer,' Adam said.

II

The front door bell was ringing. Christine, the Morrises' Irish housekeeper, was standing on the half-landing when Adam came out of his study. The bell rang again. 'Is anyone going?' Adam called.

Christine said: 'Shall I?'

'Shall *I*?' Adam said.

Christine came down the stairs with heavy steps and went to open the door. Adam glared at her, returning to his room slowly enough to see who it was before he shut the door. When he saw, he opened the door again and came out into the hall. 'Mike!'

'Am I disturbing you?' Mike said.

'Of course,' Adam said. 'Come in, come in. I was only halfway through a minor masterpiece of the narrative art. A thing like that can always wait, right? Christine, have we got some coffee for Mr Clode?'

'I'll make some fresh.'

'She'll make some fresh,' Adam said. 'She only does that for above-the-title people. Come in, come in.'

'That's new.' Mike pointed at a small Maillol drawing.

'No,' Adam said. 'We've had it well over a week.'

'You've certainly got some nice things.'

'Said the man with two Henry Moores and a Brancusi.'

'You're a lucky bastard,' Mike said.

'Christine,' Adam called, 'you might tell Barbara we're in here, if she fancies some coffee.'

'She went out,' came the reply from the kitchen.

'Oh. Is she coming back?'

'Lunchtime, she said.'

'How is she?' Mike said.

'Barbara? Terrific. Fine. And Jill?'

'That's partly what I wanted to talk to you about,' Mike said.

'Ah,' Adam said, rearranging the top copy of *A Double Life* on its stack.

'She's left me,' Mike said. 'Gone off with some sodding song-writer. Twenty-four years old. She's thirty-eight.'

'We're all thirty-eight,' Adam said. 'It's the only place to go after forty, isn't it?'

'She's only thirty-eight,' Mike said. He turned away as the coffee came in.

'Thank you, Christine,' Adam said.

'It makes me look such a bloody fool, for God's sake,' Mike began again. 'It couldn't have come at a worse moment. You've heard about this National Film Company?'

'Why, have you been gazetted commander-in-chief?'

'Well, I'm obviously in the running,' Mike said. 'Never marry an actress.'

'I'm not thinking of getting married at the moment at all actually,' Adam said.

'They'll all use it against me. The hypocrisy of this country.'

'Who will?' Adam said. 'Who honestly gives a damn?'

'The Ronnie Braithwaites of this world. He's not going to appoint someone who's being cuckolded by a bloody scouse schoolboy driving a white Rolls Royce. Never marry an actress.'

'No,' Adam said. 'I've got that down.'

'God, I envy you Barbara,' Mike said. 'You've got somebody reasonable, somebody reliable – '

'She doesn't look too bad sometimes either, properly lit, of course.'

'Barbara? She's beautiful. Do you know something? I sometimes think she doesn't like me.'

'Good heavens!' Adam said.

'I should never have married Jill in the first place.'

'Your big mistake was telling the colour supplement how happy you were,' Adam said. 'That's always the prelude to curtains.'

'She was a dream. A dream. The bitch.'

'Where is she at the moment?'

'Jill? In bed with her gap-toothed tunesmith, I presume. He strikes the hours, that one.'

'Will she speak to you?'

'What do you mean, will she speak to me? We're still great friends. The effing cow. She comes to see the boys. What the hell am I going to do, Adam? I'm fucking desperate, I really am.'

'I know,' Adam said.

Mike made a wry face. 'How soon can I have the script? Because – '

'I tell you what,' Adam said. 'Here's a draft outline to be going on with. Tell her to give it a month – be generous and forgiving, like you are when you've hired another writer behind my back – '

'And then?' Mike said. 'Adam, look, I never – '

'Save it,' Adam said. 'Tell her that you really think that you might work better together now – professionally – than ever before and that as it so happens there's a film just coming up – '

'She's heard that one before. She won't believe that.'

'Of course she'll believe it. We've all heard it before, haven't we? And we always believe it.'

'OK. So then – ?'

'So then you've got yourself a couple of weeks in which to discover that you've fallen in love.'

'Fallen in love? With whom?'

'Anybody,' Adam said. 'Call Central Casting. Having got somebody who really loves you and you really love – that can't take longer than testing a mattress or two – you then issue a firm public denial that there is any new romance in your life whatsoever – '

Mike said: 'Why on earth do it, if I'm going to deny it?'

'How else are you going to get people to believe it?'

'Look,' Mike said, 'what do you think I am?'

'One thing at a time, old son, OK? You deny you love this girl and you also deny that Jill's departure has anything to do with the arrival of a lovely new lady in your life – '

'People're still going to find out about her and baby-face – '

'I 'adn't finished, 'ad I, 'erbert? You will also deny that you find it pathetic and degrading that a grown-up woman on the rebound has to go and find consolation in the arms of a drug-sodden, teenage dwarf. Who is, of course, a charming person once you get to know him. A few days later you will be astonished and delighted to be asked to accept the direction of the National Film Company. "I never guessed this was coming," said an excited Michael Clode when I spoke to him late last night. Asked whether he had any plans for his friend Adam Morris to direct a film in the near future, honest, forthright Mike replied, "Who?" '

Mike grinned. 'You are a cunning bastard.'

'And you'll get the bill in the morning,' Adam said.

'But can I *do* it?' Mike said.

'You're the first person I thought of for the part,' Adam said.

'Tell me something. How do you manage to be such a cynical swine?'

'I put it all down to my happy home life, squire,' Adam said. 'Now. Did you read my book?'

'I've started it,' Mike said. 'I wondered if it would do for Jill. Could you make the girl American?'

'I could make her Serbo-Croat with a Canadian grandmother. That would account for them living in Hemel Hempstead,' Adam said. 'Of course we could make her American. Or Jill could play it English.'

'No one wants to know about England any more.' Mike stood up and brushed biscuit crumbs from his lap onto the Casa Pupo rug. 'If we do it, we should set the whole thing in America.'

'Maybe you should read it first,' Adam said.

Mike stood in the open doorway. 'I sometimes wish I'd stayed in Cambridge,' he said, 'do you know that?'

'What as?' Adam said. 'A traffic island?'

'You don't really like me, do you?' Mike said.

'Call me when you've finished the book,' Adam said.

'You don't know me really at all.'

'You're basically a simple soul who only cares for Byzantine icons and the main chance, right? Don't worry,' Adam said, 'you're among friends.'

'When it really comes down to it, do you know what really matters in life?'

'Are you buying or selling?' Adam said.

'You *don't* like me much, do you?'

'I don't like anybody much,' Adam said. 'Do you?'

'Why not? Why don't you like me?'

'Because you've made shit so attractive.'

'Shit?'

'Showbiz shit,' Adam said. 'You made me what I've got today. I wish I was satisfied.'

Mike said: 'If I get this National Film job we can really do the things we always wanted to do. You can be my conscience.'

Adam said: 'I don't want to play small parts.'

'I'm sorry if I've destroyed your integrity,' Mike said.

'My dear fellow,' Adam said, 'a little thing like that! I shall be up and about in a day or two.'

'Thanks for the advice anyway.'

'That comes easy,' Adam said. 'Just try borrowing money.'

'You'd let me have it.'

'Between the eyes,' Adam said. 'Sell the speedboat first.'

'She wanted it,' Mike said. 'I didn't. I always fall over when I water-ski.'

'Shut up,' Adam said, 'and steer.'

ii

'And very pretty too,' Adam said.

'Oh that's strictly stage one,' Carol said.

'That's the stage I like,' Adam said. He went back to the rack of kaftans. 'I think that's the one to have, don't you? Or do you think – ? I really wouldn't mind having them both.'

'Have them both.'

'I'll tell you what,' he said, 'I'll have them both. I always think one should have two of everything, don't you?'

'If you can get away with it. Hilda – ' Carol called. 'Could you come?' Hilda was a young girl in trousers, with a bun and a mouth full of pins. 'Mr Morris is having these two, if you'll put them in a box.'

Adam wrote a cheque and handed it to Carol. 'How did you come to meet Derek?' he said.

'He's my accountant, isn't he?'

'He seems very good at finding girls, I must say, my brother.'

'Perhaps girls are good at finding him.'

'I come of a triste generation, Carol. You did well to come a little later in our island story. Do you know, I have a friend, an *ami de collège*, who once told me quite seriously that even after he'd got married, he still found other women attractive? He thought it wasn't physically possible.'

'And is it?' she said.

'I think so.'

'People make themselves very unhappy, don't they?'

'If they can't find anyone else to do it for them.' Hilda came back with a box, nicely tied with a big pink bow. 'That's smashing,' Adam said. 'Thank you very much. Well – I'll – '

'Do you want some coffee?' Carol said. 'I generally have some.'

Adam looked at his watch. 'I really ought to go and look at those Persian bronzes that no one who claims to be cultured can afford to miss,' he said. 'Yes, I'd love some coffee.'

'Did you always expect to be successful?'

'Yes,' Adam said, 'and in spite of the signs to the contrary, I still do.'

'Derek says he's always known. That you'd make it.'

'Oh well, he can be jealous of me if I can be jealous of him.'

'What's he got that you could possibly want?'

'Freedom?' Adam said.

'You can do anything you like. Milk and sugar?'

'In moderation,' Adam said. 'Then why don't I?'

'You tell me,' Carol said.

'I do,' Adam said. 'In one volume after another. Few of which are ever reprinted. Success!'

'What about your films?'

'The money's nice.'

'I love money,' the girl said.

'Seriously?'

'Of course. You work hard, what's wrong with it?'

'I feel guilty,' Adam said.

'Maybe guilt's just one more of the things money can buy.'

'Maybe. But that's hardly the full story.'

'And what is the full story?'

Adam took a photograph from his wallet and handed it to her. 'Part of the full story,' he said. 'I always carry it.'

It was a cropped segment of an old photograph: a small boy, wearing a cloth cap, with his hands up. 'You?' Carol said.

'Me? No. Nothing to do with me. That's some six-year-old Yid on the way to what's good for him. Me? I was eating bread and Marmite at the time – hated it – and learning amo, amas, amat.' He took the picture back from her. 'This is the after-life as far as I'm concerned, Carol. Nothing happened to me at all. I've had a charmed life, I really have. I don't really feel guilty about the money. I feel guilty at being alive. At being so nice, so *agreeable*. I'm a lot nicer than I want to be, hard though that may be to believe.'

'I don't feel sorry for you.'

'Then why am I telling you all this?' he said.

'You lead the life of Riley.'

'Yes, and somewhere that bastard's leading mine.'

'What do you want to be?'

'A thorough-going shit,' Adam said. 'With no con-science, no memory, an immunity to syphilis and a mind that got to Linear-B twenty minutes before that bastard Ventris. Dumas *père* with a vasectomy, Flaubert without the pox and Cary Grant with a good script. I should also like to get a bit more top spin on my second service. How soon can you have that ready?'

'What do you want from life, for God's sake?'

'I'll start with a written apology,' Adam said. They both laughed and the girl touched him on the hand, she found him so amusing. 'Tell me,' Adam said, 'who staked you in this place? It really is nice.'

'Nobody,' Carol said, 'I saved.'

'What did you do?'

'Modelled.'

'Fashion?'

'And the other,' Carol said.

'What's that?'

'The other? Sexpot stuff, you know.'

'And how was that?' Adam said. 'To do?'

'Triple rate, it was OK. It was fine.'

'Didn't bother you?'

'No.'

'But you don't do it any more?'

'Don't need to. I did a centrefold job, you know, and I had to sign a contract saying I wouldn't do any more for a year and by then I was set up.'

'So somewhere or other,' Adam said, 'you're lying around with a staple in your navel?'

'Absolutely,' Carol said. 'I hope she likes them.'

'Who? Oh. The kaftans! Yes. She will. She will.' He put down his cup and picked up the box. 'Well, I must give my well-known imitation of running. I promised to have a drink with a literary lady, who happens to run a book programme on the Beeb. Funny how you remember old friends like that, just when you've got a book coming out. Thanks for the coffee.'

'Warn me next time you're coming,' Carol said, 'and I'll get some cream.'

He grinned and looked back at her from the top of the stairs. She was looking at herself in the long cheval mirror in the window.

iii

'I never actually met anyone who'd done it before,' Adam said. 'Very strange. I mean, you're standing there with this girl, wondering in a vague way what she looks like without her clothes on – I mean, in a purely academic sociological sort of a spirit, you understand – and then you get told that she's already available in the large family size in a well-known magazine. A hundred and twenty quid an hour for taking her clothes off. She also happens to be sleeping with my brother.'

'You have had a troubled afternoon,' Anna said.

They were sitting in the calculatedly charming bar of the new London hotel which Anna had rather surprisingly nominated for their meeting. Anna had a whisky and Adam a whisky sour. 'Another one?' Adam said, pointing at Anna's empty glass. Anna nodded. Adam looked round for the waiter. 'I've been meaning to call you for ages,' he said, 'and now, of course, I feel like a showbiz shit – '

'Do you?' she said. She was wearing a purple sweater and a long black skirt. On the back of her head was a knitted hat with a pom-pom, somehow self-mocking and rather saucy. 'Why do you?'

'Obvious reasons,' Adam said.

'Those are the ones I can never work out.'

'That's because you did a thesis on Jane Austen. It's

spoiled your capacity for the really vulgar things in life. Life for instance.'

'It's not the capacity that's missing,' Anna said. 'It's the opportunity.'

The waiter arrived at last. 'Same?'

'Can I have a double?'

'A double please,' Adam said. 'They are small, aren't they? A single's when they forget to wipe the glass, isn't that what they say?'

'I'm an alcoholic, you know,' Anna said.

'I know,' Adam said. 'I saw it in the paper.'

'I am.'

'Don't be silly.'

'I'm not silly,' she said, 'I'm an alcoholic.'

Adam said: 'That's absurd.'

'Oh I know it's absurd,' she said.

'Anna?'

'That's right, Anna.'

'Why?'

'I like it,' she said.

'You're *not*,' he said.

'Tell me why you're a showbiz shit. Are you laying lots of starlets and people?'

'No. Of course not.'

'Ken does it with lots of people,' she said. 'Why are you a showbiz shit?'

'Because I asked you to have a drink and because I had a motive.'

'Oh, are you going to seduce me?'

'Unfortunately, I said I'd be home for dinner,' Adam said. 'Do you realize I've known you for twenty years?'

'What was the motive?'

The drinks came. Anna was very thirsty. Adam said: 'My book's coming out in a couple of weeks.'

'I don't get.'

'The obvious again, that's why. I'm hoping to remind

you subtly and without too much overt solicitation that I'm hoping for a nice large review, preferably of the kind that will not leave the handle of a dagger protruding from between my shoulder blades.'

'Ken gets girls on his Credit Card,' Anna said. 'Did you know you could do that? He calls it shagging the Chancellor.' She put down her glass. 'I'd like another one of those.'

'Look, Anna. Don't overact just for me.'

'I'm quite used to it,' Anna said.

'Um,' Adam called, 'I'd – ah – like a, another double whisky, please. One.' He looked at Anna. She looked back at him without shame or hope. 'How long has this been going on?' he said.

'A while.'

'A month? A year?'

'I expect so.'

'Have you seen anybody?'

'What for?'

'Help,' Adam said.

'I don't want help,' she said. The waiter had brought the drink. 'This is what I want.'

'How does Ken feel about this?'

'He doesn't know.'

'Doesn't *know*?'

'No.'

'Don't you think he should?'

'I don't care whether he knows or not.'

'What about the children?'

'*They* know,' Anna said.

'Anna, what've you got to be unhappy about?'

'I'm not unhappy,' she said. 'I drink.'

Adam said: 'I always admired you so much.'

'Are you withdrawing you favours, you mean?'

'The amount you've read – I always feel that I haven't really read anything – and you've read everything. You've even read *Clarissa*.'

'Want to buy some books?' she said.

'I seem to have hundreds,' Adam said. 'Just not the right ones somehow.'

'Do you still make a lot of money?'

'Fair,' he said. 'I'm not complaining more than fifty per cent of the time. I do OK.'

'Because can you lend me a hundred quid?'

'A hundred quid.'

'Just till the end of the month.'

'It is the end of the month,' he said.

'Next month.'

'What's the trouble?'

'No trouble,' she said. 'I just need a hundred quid. I'll pay you back.'

'I'm not worried about that.'

'Then can you?'

'Have you thought about a psychiatrist?' he said.

'They don't lend people money.'

'Anna, suppose I gave you a hundred. What do you need it for?'

'I'd like another drink,' she said. 'Please.'

'Anna, I can't – '

'Waiter – ' she called. The waiter nodded. She smiled at Adam. 'You can have an Arts Feature programme all to yourself, OK?'

'I don't want that.'

'Then why are you buying me a drink?'

'I wanted to see you – and – well, I've made my confession. I like you. I – Is it Ken?'

'Is what Ken?'

'Started this.'

'Ken doesn't like me.'

'Doesn't like you! He's proud as hell of you.'

'My tits are too small.'

'I don't want to hear things like that, not from you, not from Anna.'

'A hundred quid isn't a lot to you, is it? It's peanuts.' She had a few peanuts in her hand – there was a dish on the table – and suddenly she flung them into her mouth. She started to choke. She choked and choked. Adam banged her on the back. She took a sip of her new drink. 'That's better.'

Adam said: 'Anna, look, there isn't any problem about a hundred quid as such.'

'A hundred quid as such is all I want.'

'You need help,' Adam said.

'And that's the form I'd like it to take.'

'I care about you.'

'Then is it a deal?'

'A *deal*?'

'Do you want me to take my clothes off?' she said.

'What do you think I am?'

'Because I'll take my clothes off.'

And she began to. Dear God, she began to. She took off her bobble hat and pulled her sweater over her head. Adam said: 'Anna, for Christ's sake – '

'Doesn't bother me,' she said.

'Anna, stop it. Sit down. I'll give you the money. Gladly. It's not the point, but I'll gladly give it to you.'

Anna put her sweater in her lap. She was wearing a rather grubby strapless bra. 'It's hot in here,' she said.

An assistant-manager, in black coat and striped trousers, was looking over at them. 'Anna,' Adam said, 'put your sweater on.'

'Don't you find it warm?'

'*Please*,' Adam said.

'I lost what tits I had with Harriet,' Anna said. 'And they never came back. They went and they never came back, my little pretties.'

Adam said: 'You're worth a hundred – ' He winced and shrugged and took out his cheque book.

Anna said: 'I couldn't have cash, could I?'

'I haven't got a hundred on me,' Adam said. 'I can let you have twenty.' Anna put out her hand. 'Look, Anna, for Christ's sake –' Adam put the money in it. 'I mean it goes without saying, but there's no question whatever – I mean to say, I'd sooner not be mentioned on the box at all than feel –'

'Of course you'll get mentioned.'

'I don't want any sort of – special treatment,' he said, 'just put it in the works, I mean, and let it take its chance –'

'I shan't do anything to it,' she said.

'Because that would be an awful betrayal.'

'Of everything that Cambridge taught us? Tell me something. What do you like to do best?'

'In what sense?'

'Sex.'

'Come on,' he said, 'I'm going to take you home.'

'What will your wife say?'

'Your home.' The waiter came very promptly at Adam's signal. 'I've got the car.'

'A novelist with a car,' Anna said. 'Just what I've always wanted.'

The Mercedes was parked on a meter, but that had not prevented someone from smashing the rear light as he pulled out. 'What kind of a fucking bastard does a thing like that?' Adam said.

'Will it still go?' Anna said.

'Of course it'll still go,' Adam said.

'You can always have it done, can't you?'

He drove her to Kentish Town in a poor humour.

'I'm sorry about the book,' she said, as she got out of the car.

'Sorry in what sense?' Adam said.

'I got the sack.'

'You what?'

'From the Beeb,' she said.

'You didn't.'

276

'No,' she said, 'I resigned, didn't I? To have more time to devote to this book I'm probably never going to write. I got the sack.' She leaned into the car. 'Shall I tell you something? Up books.' She turned and walked up the narrow garden. A child was looking through the bay window. Anna waved. 'Mummy's home,' she said.

iv

'Where's Tom?' Adam said.

'He's got whatsername upstairs. I'm afraid this steak's not what it was. Whatever it was.'

'She kept wanting another drink,' Adam said. 'It looks terrific. Has Tom eaten or is he eating her?'

'He was hungry when he got home,' Barbara said, 'so I fed them both.'

'What really goes on up there? Do you think he's got her bra off yet?'

'She doesn't wear a bra,' Barbara said. 'They talk about Nietzsche mostly.'

'You think I shouldn't have given it to her,' Adam said. 'The money.'

'I haven't said a word.'

'That's how I can tell,' Adam said.

'It's your money.'

'I don't think of it as mine.'

'Yes, you do,' she said.

Christine came down the stairs from the hall and walked, with ostentatious tact, across the kitchen to the refrigerator. 'Sorry if I disturbed you,' she said as she went out with a yoghurt.

'Madam's got her You've-Got-Five-Minutes-To-Be-Out face on this evening,' Adam said. 'What's the trouble with her?'

Barbara said: 'It's been one of her Why-Didn't-You-Say? days. Why didn't I say I was going to make the beds, do the sprouts, clean the fish, wash the kitchen floor, take Rachel to get a new hockey stick – '

'A new hockey stick?'

'She broke the other one.'

'If Madam's one of the things money can buy,' Adam said, 'you can keep it.'

'She makes you feel good when she brings you your coffee in the morning,' Barbara said.

'Makes me feel *what*?'

'Of course she does.'

Adam put on his Irish accent. '"Oh good morning, Adam, how are you today?" "I'm fine, Christine, how are you?" "As long as things are fine for you, that's all right then." "What's wrong, is something wrong?" "My lover's gone back to his wife, the father of my unborn child has gone back to Australia, I've had to postpone my abortion because my mother's dying, my sister's on the streets, and I never really wanted to do domestic work at all, I wanted to be a novelist like yourself, not that I've ever read any of your books and would you care for some more soggy biscuits with that?"' Adam looked at Barbara, who was managing not to smile. 'It's one thing to employ Humpty Dumpty,' Adam said. 'It's another to be drowned in yolk every morning.'

'Why don't you get rid of her?'

'You really don't want any help in the house? You really don't?'

'I want help,' Barbara said. 'I just don't want *that* help.'

'Like the producer said when he gave the screenwriter the Bible to adapt for television, "Take what's good and forget the rest." You think I should have just told Anna to pull herself together, show a little moral fibre and good afternoon, do you?' He took Barbara's hand. 'I'm bloody lucky. I had to help her.'

'When are you seeing her again?' Barbara said.

'I'm not seeing her at all. Not in the sense you mean. I don't fancy Anna.'

'You did.'

'Ba, she's lost her job. She's lost her tits. She's no fun to be with. Frankly I can't see why this isn't one extramural friendship that you're not encouraging with all your wifely heart.'

'If you make her much more unattractive, I don't see how you'll be able to resist her. Think what a kindness it would be if you did take her to bed. The ultimate handout.'

Adam said: 'I've been as faithful as any man in my particular line of business – maybe not in thought and word – but in deed, indeed in deed, for God knows how long, and you still talk as if I was the greatest woman-chaser since Casanova hung up his boots.'

'His what?'

'Ba, I gave her my word. I don't want anything out of her, I promise you, and just as well, because unfortunately there's nothing she can give. Not even a fair wind to *A Double Life*. Please believe me.'

Barbara cleared the dirty dishes. 'I believe you,' she said.

'Then why don't you *believe* me? I don't fancy Anna. I never have. In fact what the hell am I doing messing around with her anyway?'

'Trying to prove something to your old housemaster, presumably.'

'Presumably,' Adam said. 'Do you know, for years I used to dream that he'd caught us in bed together? You and me. Even after we were married. I used to swear I'd never seen you before in my life.'

'And you send Tom to a public school,' Barbara said.

'A public school with a difference,' Adam pointed out. 'They've got no chapel and they don't teach them anything.' He stopped and looked at her. She looked back at him with a sort of delicious, trusting suspicion. He leaned forward and kissed her. 'If you knew how much I really relied on you,' he said, 'you'd be disgusted. You really would. I love you, Ba.' He touched her breast with his finger-tips. 'What about bed some time? Oh don't worry: not until you've put the cat out, sorted out the kids' clothes for the morning, done your face and elbows and whatever else you do, and put on that bloody nightie that looks like it was supplied by the armoured car company.'

'Thanks,' she said.

'You can't be *offended*. That was as transparent a declaration of love as any married man is ever likely to make. At least, to his wife, I mean.' He took her hand and twiddled her wedding ring. 'Won't it really come off?'

'No.'

'You could always have an operation.'

'On BUPA, of course.'

'Of course,' he said. 'If there's one thing I'm not in the least ashamed about, it's having enough money not to have to wait my turn. I know what you're thinking. Jew.'

'I have never thought that in my *life*,' she said.

'I'm joking. I'm joking. I *am* joking, aren't I?'

'How can I tell?' she said. 'You're not laughing.'

'If there's one boat I never want to be in,' he said, 'it's the same boat as everyone else. They'd all want to stand around and watch me row.'

'You and your outboard motor.'

'You know I don't really think it means anything, don't you?' he said. 'Being a Jew. Not a thing. A birthmark, that's all. My little kosher strawberry patch. I draw attention to it first to avoid embarrassment. I'm not even very interested.'

'My name is Barbara,' she said. 'I've lived with you for twenty years, remember?'

He put out his hand. 'Care for another twenty? You can have first service.'

'You still think of me as the enemy sometimes, don't you? Be honest.'

'My loyal Arab.'

'Loyal *camel*.'

'The girl who gave a new meaning to hump the hostess. Ba, are we quarrelling? I mean, are we?'

'*No*. We're indulging in your favourite sport, aren't we?'

'Wanna bet?' Adam said.

'A frank, honest, serious, cards-on-the-table discussion in which you have all the best lines.'

'Well,' Adam said, 'who's the writer on the show? Anyway, are you sure you haven't got a few of those cards up your sleeve?'

'It's true, isn't it?'

'True? Shall I tell you something? Why not? We have the best marriage I could possibly imagine. I mean, that's just the half-time score, but I thought you might like to know. Now shall we go out and see a lousy movie?'

'Too late,' she said.

'You know I don't ever seriously expect to be anything but married to you, don't you?'

'Of course.'

'Complacent cow.'

'*Complacent*?' she said. 'What's the good news?'

The telephone rang. 'Here it is now,' Adam said. 'We've won a major prize.' There was a wall phone just inside the kitchen door. 'Chinese laundry . . . Yes. Of course it is. What's happened? Ah. Oh. When? I see. I'll be right along.' He replaced the telephone and came back and stood behind Barbara, his hands on her shoulders, thumbs down. 'My father,' he said.

III

Lionel Morris lay in his coffin in the bedroom of the flat in which he had lived for over thirty years. Adam and Derek sat in there with him, waiting for the undertakers to come to take him, and them, to the cemetery. They could hear the murmur of voices from the other room, together with the odd shaft of laughter, quickly quenched. The mirrors in the room were draped. The photographs and the two-sea scapes had been turned to the wall.

'He always used to say other people had had a good innings,' Adam said. 'Do you think he had a good innings?'

'They'll be here soon,' Derek said, from the window.

'I dread this,' Adam said.

'Oh really?' Derek said. 'I'm looking forward to it, myself.'

'You don't have to do the chat,' Adam said. 'I'm sure I shall get it wrong. Muttering stuff in Hebrew. Christ, what's it got to do with anything?' He looked into the open coffin. 'He would have got it right all right. He doesn't give us long, does He?' He glanced up. 'Do You?' He looked into the coffin again. 'Did you know him? I didn't know him. I hated him, I loved him – I suppose I loved him – but I certainly didn't know him.'

'I knew him,' Derek said.

'Was he good, was he bad? Who was he, what was he? I don't know, I sit and write all day . . . '

'Oh,' Derek said, 'are you a writer?'

'I'm a writer, yes, and I don't know myself any better than I did him. We make ourselves up most of the time, don't we?'

'I don't,' Derek said.

'He seemed so strong. I remember once we were backing round in some lane – '

'I remember.'

'You can't,' Adam said.

'I remember. He lifted the bumper up, didn't he? – and I don't know, it's not possible really – but it seemed as if he lifted the front wheels right out of the ditch and onto the road again.'

'I once said to him, we were having some sort of argument, I don't know, about Barbara – he ended up really liking her, you know that? – I said to him, "You're lucky, you're so sure of yourself. You know what's right and you know what's wrong and you know exactly what you're going to do about it." You know what he said? He said, "If you only knew ... " Knew what, do you think? I mean, what was so odd was, it sounded as though he really had a secret. It was a challenge almost. You know how he could look. "If you only knew ... "'

'Everyone has to have a secret,' Derek said. 'Something they never tell.'

'Being an accountant, you naturally don't believe in complete honesty.'

'Being a client,' Derek said, 'do you?'

'We never really talked about anything seriously. Him and me. I mean we talked *seriously*, but never about – I don't know – *life*. Life? I never knew him.'

'Well, it's a little late now.'

'It doesn't bother you, does it?'

'You always have to kick the scenery to prove it isn't real,' Derek said. 'Me, if they say this is a room in the palace, as far as I'm concerned it's a room in the palace. He was my father. He went off bang at a certain moment in a certain place and here I am. The result. Why? What for? What was he really like? Why should we ever expect to know the answers to things like that? He was my father. I sometimes think you believe in God more than he ever did. He didn't believe at all necessarily. He didn't have to. He lived in the world.'

'He took it as it came, and it came and it went. I don't

believe, for God's sake. The way the world is? I absolutely refuse to believe.'

'That's what I mean. You want a better deal. An improved offer.'

'He always wanted me to go to Hebrew classes. Oh well, at times like this I suppose one might as well say something one doesn't understand in a language one doesn't speak as say anything else.' The front door bell shrilled. 'I wanted them to change that bell ever since we first moved into this place,' Adam said. 'I'll go.' He reached into his pocket and pulled out a black skullcap. 'Action stations.'

ii

Adam was up as soon as he heard the out-of-tune whistle of the paperboy. He went downstairs with a sort of hesitant haste. The papers were there, their folded ends sticking through the letter box. He glanced up. 'Shema Yisroel,' he murmured and tugged them free. It was publication day.

He sat on the bottom stair and opened *The Times*. He had hardly looked before he was fumbling at the *Daily Telegraph*.

Barbara said: 'Well?'

Adam held out *The Times*. 'Brilliant, but.'

She came and sat beside him. 'He *loves* it,' she said.

'He loves it *but*. This man loves it.' He gave her the *Daily Telegraph*. 'Woman, sorry. Ever heard of her? I haven't, but she's got a great future.' He fingered the *Guardian*. 'Can't possibly have three in a row. Oh well, nobody reads this any more, do they?' He turned and saw that Barbara's face was streaming with tears. 'What's the matter with you?'

'I'm so happy,' she said.

'You are, aren't you? You're really pleased!'

'Of course I'm pleased,' Barbara said. 'We shan't have

to spend the next week speaking in whispers and waiting for the master of wit and irony to come out of mourning.'

Adam said: 'Lionel would've liked to see the *Daily Telegraph* say I had a touch of genius. You could keep Matthew, Mark, Luke and John but the *Daily Telegraph* ... Gospel!'

Tom said: 'What's going on?' He was in his pyjamas which were both new and already too short for him. He was fifteen, tall and strong.

Barbara said: 'Your father – '

'How do you do?' Adam said.

'How do you do?' said Tom.

' – has been hailed as a genius.'

'A *bit* of a genius. Don't let's exaggerate.'

'Oh the book,' Tom said, 'of course.'

'Nice of you to remember.'

Tom sat down and took the papers from his mother. 'He didn't like the scene in Paris,' he said.

'Thanks for noticing,' Adam said. 'He liked everything else. Read on, you campus bum.'

Tom said: 'Well done, Daddy. It might even sell.'

'Oh no,' Adam said. 'The publishers'll see to that. Of fifteen bookshops questioned, eleven said "Never heard of it", three said "Who?" and the fifteenth – one of a Large National Chain, which should be pulled as soon as possible – said that because of a lack of public demand they no longer sold books in their bookshops.'

'Who's this Veronica person?'

'Fascinating girl,' Adam said, 'brilliant girl. Never heard of her.'

'She likes this other one as well,' Tom said.

'Some bloody thriller. It should've been reviewed under Other Rubbish. She's losing her grip, our Veronica.'

'Sounds interesting,' Tom said.

'Well,' Adam said, 'there we are. Another publication day come and gone at – eight thirteen a.m. precisely. Come on, let's go and celebrate. Let's open a new packet of Muesli and some gold-topped milk. You can have it out of my slipper.'

'Yucch,' Tom said.

'West Ham supporter,' Adam replied. 'I know, Ba: you go back to bed – I'll bring the champagne up.'

'Are you feeling all right?'

'Do it, do it. When the man offers, do it. It doesn't happen often.'

'Done,' Barbara said, and scampered back up the stairs.

'I say, darling,' Adam called in a public voice, 'have you heard about this new book everyone's talking about? *A Double Life*? *A Double Life*.'

'I'd sooner have one than read about it,' Barbara said.

'Get your own bloody breakfast.'

Tom was already helping himself to Sugar Puffs and brown sugar. He had the paper propped against the packet. 'Veronica likes everything,' he said.

'She wants to see her name in the ads,' Adam said. 'Are you really reading Nietzsche?'

'Yeah. He's good fun.'

'Good fun?' Adam said. 'Are we thinking of the same bloke? Kraut, on the short side, somewhat mentally disturbed in his later years . . . ?'

'Yeah,' Tom said. 'Wrote Batman.'

'*That's* why he lived in Switzerland,' Adam said. 'We didn't rate him a real philosopher.'

'We? Who's we?'

'Wittgenstein and I. At Cambridge. We were rather against all that storming and dranging. We thought philosophy ought to be patient and unravel people's mental blocks. Trouble with doing that is, once you've unravelled them, their heads fall off.'

'Do you reckon he was anti-Semitic?'

'Isn't everyone? He was just anti, wasn't he? He hated everybody. That makes him one of us, really, doesn't it?'

'I don't hate people,' Tom said.

'What hope have you got of growing up into a worth-while person if you go around liking people? Wise up, kid. Turn nasty while there's still time or you may just end up happy and then what'll you do for an encore? What *are* you going to do in life actually? Have you decided?'

'No,' Tom said. 'Have you?'

'You're absolutely right,' Adam said. 'Careers, I spit on them. Only you've got to do something. Oh shut up. OK, I'll shut up. Take that upstairs. OK, OK.' Adam picked up the breakfast tray and went towards the stairs. Christine came down, in her dressing gown, just as he reached the bottom step.

'Oh,' she said, 'why didn't you call me? I could have done that.'

Adam stood there, drunk with success, and looked into that bland, lazy face and did what he had long dreamed of doing. He let go of the tray with both hands. It fell at Christine's feet in a cacophony of crockery. 'It's all yours,' he said.

Christine turned and ran back up the stairs.

'Slightly unnecessary,' Tom said.

iii

'Where is she now?' Barbara was drinking her coffee and eating cereal off a freshly laid tray.

'Packing, I think.'

'I must say it's a very subtle way of giving people notice.'

'I guess I blew my stack,' Adam said, 'you know? I shouldn't have. I'd never have done it to Himmler. Not and splashed gold-top milk on his nice new jack-boots. "Ah," I would have said, "Herr Obergruppenführer! Ve vos just talking about you. Milk and sugar?" Poor Christine. Should I go up and grovel?' They heard steps on the stair. 'Too late, here it comes.'

There was a knock at the door and Christine appeared with a suitcase. 'I think I'd better be going now,' she said.

Adam said: 'Have you had any breakfast, Christine?'

'I don't want any breakfast.'

'You can't just go like this.'

'I know when I'm not wanted,' Christine said.

'Oh,' Adam said.

'I've folded the sheets.'

'Christine,' Barbara said, 'aren't you taking rather needless offence?'

'That's what I think,' Adam said. 'I did apologize.'

'Some things can't be apologized for that easily, can they?'

'True,' Adam said, 'but I managed it.'

'I haven't been happy for some time,' Christine said.

Barbara said: 'What about money, Christine?' Adam found his wallet and pulled out a £20 note.

'I was paid on Saturday,' Christine said. 'I'm quite satisfied.'

'Oh, take it,' Adam said, thrusting the money into her hand. 'Or I'll drop another tray on you.'

'If it makes you feel better,' she said.

'Jack Benny where are you now?' Adam said. 'Christine, it doesn't make me feel better, but it'd make me feel worse if you didn't have it. It's yours. Please. And well earned.'

'Goodbye then, Madam,' Christine said.

'What about mail?' Barbara said.

'Oh I'll – I'll let you know, Madam, when I'm settled.'

'I'll hold it here, shall I, until?'

Adam reached for the suitcase. 'Let me carry that down for you.'

'I can manage.'

'I hate to see women carrying anything,' Adam said. 'Unless it's a breakfast tray, of course.'

'I shall miss the children,' Christine said.

'And they'll miss you,' Barbara said.

Adam put the case down at the front door. 'Hold on a minute,' he said. 'You haven't had a copy yet, have you?'

'Copy of what?' she said.

'The book. *A Double Life.* You must have one. After all, think of all that coffee you poured into it!' He ran into the sitting room, scribbled 'To Christine, without whom . . . ' in it and brought it back to her. 'There you are, still wet.'

'There's no call,' she said.

'Oh come on, you must have one,' Adam said. 'The price of coal these days. There's an hour's warmth in a thing like this if you burn it carefully. Besides, I've written in it now, I can't give it to anyone else. Take it, go on.' He put it under her arm and she opened the door. 'Come and see us,' he called. 'Collect your letter-bombs, won't you?'

'Hypocrite,' Tom said. He had come up from the kitchen.

'Nice of you to say so,' Adam said.

'Aren't you?'

'You must be this son I've heard so much about.'

'Didn't she have enough to carry?'

'O K,' Adam said, 'now shut up about it.' He went on upstairs.

Barbara said: 'Now what are we going to do about tonight?'

'Oh Christ,' Adam said. 'Derek and Carol. What do you think?'

'We'd better have them here,' she said.

'Would it be a bore?'

'I don't mind,' Barbara said. 'I shall just have to cook all day, that's all.'

'Well, that's settled then,' Adam said. 'You wanted her to go, didn't you?'

'I wanted her to go,' Barbara said. 'I just didn't want her to go today.'

'I'll help,' Adam said. He bent down and put his arms round her. 'What have you put all these clothes on for suddenly? I thought we were having breakfast in bed. I haven't had mine.'

'You have a son and daughter who have to go to school, remember?'

'What about having breakfast after that?'

'You'll be on the telephone,' she said.

'Balls I will!' The telephone rang. 'You did that,' he said.

iv

'It worked like a charm,' Mike said.

'She's coming home to your loving arms, is she?'

'Sorry?'

'Jill.'

'Oh, I see what you mean,' Mike said. 'Well, not exactly.'

'Oh.'

'Your advice, I meant. About falling in love.'

'Oh that.'

'I've found my anima figure,' Mike said.

'Your what?'

'How old are you?'

'Never mind that,' Adam said.

'You see, forty-two is a crucial age for men.'

'Really?'

'A decisive watershed.'

'Good heavens.'

'And Jill was absolutely right.'

'Is this her theory?'

'It's well known. It's well known. We've talked this all over, the four of us.'

290

'Oh, there are four of you now, are there?'

'Jill and Freddie and Frankie and me.'

'I've heard of you and Jill,' Adam said. 'Who are Freddie and Frankie exactly?'

'Freddie La Costa – the song writer, I told you about him – '

'Oh, Freddie La Costa. The millionaire dwarf. Of course, of course.'

'Fascinating character,' Mike said. 'Fascinating.'

'Really?' Adam said. 'And has he grown as well?'

'Brilliant,' Mike said. 'He's quite tall.'

'Ah.'

'He really put me in touch with this whole – well, it's a different approach to life entirely – '

'Oh I'd like one of those,' Adam said, 'but they do come expensive, don't they? And with V A T . . . And what about Frankie? Who's he?'

'She,' Mike said.

'Now you're talking.'

'She's – '

'The anima figure.'

'She came to an audition,' Mike said.

'You had *auditions*?'

'For a play I'm supposed to be doing for Peter. If we can get the casting. I think it's probably going to fall through.'

The drawing room door opened and Barbara came in with coffee.

'Oh darling,' Adam said, 'I could have done that.' He leapt up just in time to grab the tray from her as a gleam came into her eye. 'Phew!'

'Barbara, *darling*,' Mike said, 'how are you?'

'Hullo, Mike.'

'Why've you only put out two cups?' Adam said.

'I just work around here,' she said.

'Nonsense,' Mike said, '*nonsense*. We'll share a cup. You know I've always been mad about you.'

'I'll get another one,' Adam said, hurrying out of the room.

Barbara said: 'How's Mike?'

'Well, I'm just tremendous,' he said.

'Have you seen Adam's notices?'

'Yes, I'm really pleased,' Mike said. 'It's tremendous.'

'It's a really good book,' Barbara said.

'He's a clever sod,' Mike said, as Adam returned with the third cup. 'Well that didn't give us much time!'

Adam said: 'Mike's got a new anima figure.'

'Oh really?' Barbara said. 'What's it made of?'

'Flesh and blood,' Mike said. 'Name of Frankie Jessel.'

'And what else is new?' Adam said.

'We're all going to do a musical together, that's the idea. I'm very high on it. A rock Odyssey.'

'Oh lovely,' Adam said. 'What about this National Film thing?'

'Junked,' Mike said.

'*Junked*?'

'Postponed, under review, being reconsidered.'

'Oh, you mean junked,' Adam said.

'The four of us are all going to California next week to talk to the Studio.'

Barbara said: 'What about the book?'

'Book?'

'Adam's book.'

'Yes, what about that?' Mike said. 'Really good news, that. Incidentally, Ad, did you see the piece about that thriller by that woman? It sounds really just the sort of thing we might get together on after *Home Sweet Homer*.'

'*Home Sweet Homer*,' Adam said.

'It's only a working title,' Mike said. 'Only you like doing thrillers and it really sounds like the basis of something interesting.'

'What about *A Double Life?*'

'It's too good, Adam. It's just too good. You know what we always say – '

'I know what you always say,' Adam said.

'You need a lousy book to make a good movie. You're too bloody good.'

'Nice of you to come round.'

'I'm bloody grateful,' Mike said. 'You really said the right thing at the right time.'

'Forget it,' Adam said.

'He will,' Barbara said.

'I've changed, Barbara,' Mike said. 'I know you have some hostility towards me, but I understand. I understand. You'll find I'm going to be very different from now on. I'm going to enjoy myself. I'm not going to get into any more emotional hassles. Life's too short.'

'I love that fancy philosophy,' Adam said. 'Wittgenstein, thou shouldst be living at this hour. What wouldn't *he* have done with an anima figure?'

'So anyway,' Mike said, 'everybody's happy.'

'If you are,' Barbara said, 'we all are.'

Mike finished his coffee and stood up. 'Think about that thriller, Adam. Try and get hold of a copy if you can. Just a hunch I've got.'

'With a good tailor,' Adam said, 'it won't show.'

'If I can get some interest going on the Coast, I'll give you a call on some agent's phone, OK?'

'Is Bruno in on your rock Odyssey?'

'Bruno?' Mike said. 'Bruno who? So anyway, listen, God bless. I hope the book sells a bomb. And thanks a million.'

'A million?' Adam said. 'What's that after tax?'

v

The Right Honourable Ronald Braithwaite was making a party political broadcast. The Morrises had Christine's

Sony Colour TV on the divider between the kitchen and the dining area. 'What is it, after all,' Ronnie was saying, 'that we all want from life? When it comes down to it?'

'To look at you, mate,' Adam said, 'a nice young sailor, I should think, wouldn't you?'

'The good life? Of course we want the good life. But we also want a fairer society, a more equal society – '

'With a Ministerial car and driver waiting at the door,' Adam said. He was easing the cork from a bottle of champagne as Barbara came down with Carol and Derek. Bang! He poured the wine. 'This is the kind of equality I like,' he said.

Barbara was wearing one of the kaftans Adam had bought at Carol's. It wasn't her birthday for another fortnight, but Adam could never resist giving her things ahead of time.

'We want a society in which privilege counts for less than hard work, in which advantages matter less than skill, in which decency prevails over opportunism. The era of I'm All Right Jack – '

'He's up to date, isn't he?' Derek said. 'It must be all of 1962, by his watch, I should think.'

' – simply won't do any more,' Ronnie said. 'The government is determined, against all the vested interests, against all the specious arguments, to see a Britain in which the idea of us and them is banished forever, in which inherited wealth and the pressure groups of the fortunate and the unprincipled can no longer easily speak of the national interest and think only of their own. We want more schools, not more bingo halls, more hospitals, not more office blocks, more athletics and recreational facilities, not more betting shops and strip joints.'

'No more betting shops or strip clubs?' Adam said. 'He's just lost the next election.'

'But where is the money coming from?' Ronnie wanted to know.

'Why is he looking at me?' Adam said.

'From those, above all, who can afford to pay.'

'Dull, dull, *dull*,' Adam said, killing Ronnie's image. 'How sick and tired one gets, does one not, of being hectored and lectured, threatened and generally told off by *ces princes qui nous gouvernent?*'

'Well, here's to you and Carol!' Barbara said. 'And to your Majesty, of course.'

'Yes,' Adam said, 'this is terrific news. I think you're both mad, but that's another story. "Which I shall not fail to tell when the moment comes," he added in Churchillian tones. Derek, I thought you weren't ever going to get married?'

'It's only a sort of – well – it makes things simpler,' Derek said.

'That's what we all say.' He clinked glasses with Carol. 'I thought you were going to be my anima figure.'

'Oh, is that off then?' Carol said.

'Sisters-in-law can't be anima figures, can they? Breach of the kinship laws.'

'We're going to eat now,' Barbara said.

'First eat,' Adam said. They went to the table where a home-made *terrine* sat in one of Bruno Lazlo's Christmas presents. There was black bread and *chola* in a Spanish basket. Adam lit the candles. 'Shema Yisroel and all stations to Jerusalem South. Carol my dear, as head of the family, I take great pleasure in putting you on my right, my child.' The phone rang. 'Excuse me.'

'Jesus Christ,' Barbara said.

'No,' Adam said, 'Hilary.'

'His agent,' Barbara said.

'Terrific,' Adam said. 'Fine. That's marvellous. No, of course I don't. No, right. Off you go. Absolutely. Talk to you tomorrow.' Adam returned to the table. 'Ladies and gentlemen, at this moment in time, I am pleased to inform you that we are rich beyond the dreams of bingo halls.'

'Someone's bought the film rights!' Barbara said.

'Someone has bought the – Polish rights,' Adam said. 'The Polish rights. Money, money, money! Zloties, my darlings, zloties in all directions. What is the Polish for *A Double Life*? We may never know, but we shall have the zloties to prove it!' He sat down and raised his glass to the company. 'A party political broadcast on behalf of those present. Good luck. Call no man happy till he's dead. And the man who asks the question deserves to get the answer. I give you: Zloties.'

'Zloties!' they said.

'Next year in Brest-Litovsk!' Derek said.

Tom put his head round the door. 'What's all the noise about?'

'Future generations,' Adam explained.

'Won the Nobel Prize?'

'That's for pudding,' Adam said.

'Anyway, I'm on my way.'

'Say goodnight to your aunt then,' Adam said.

'When did this happen?' Tom said, shaking hands with Carol.

'Not for a bit,' she said.

'Goodnight, Mummy,' Tom said, 'don't worry. Derek, still counting other people's money?'

'Cheeky.'

'Keep on with the writing then, Dad.'

'Nice of you to say so.'

'I'm on my way then.'

'Then piss off,' Adam said. 'Tom – '

'For God's *sake*.'

'There's only one piece of good advice fathers can give – '

'I hope it's short,' Tom said, 'because I'm going to be *late*.'

'Don't do what I did.'

'Don't worry,' Tom said, waving.

'I didn't do so badly,' Adam said.

'He's a man,' Derek said.

'He is, isn't he? I wonder when it'll happen to me.'

'Keep on taking the pills,' Derek said.

'No choice, have I?' He smiled at Carol and then at Barbara. '*A Double Life*! I should have such luck.'

Barbara said: 'Maybe I'm your anima figure.'

'Very nice to meet you.' Adam held out his hand. As Barbara took it, he lifted hers to his lips and kissed it.

'He still kisses your hand?' Carol said.

Adam looked over at her. 'You have to start somewhere,' he said.

vi

'*They asked him how he had managed for so long to lead a double life. He replied that nothing was easier. As long as he could keep just one chamber of his castle locked and its contents safe from scrutiny, Bluebeard was model husband, reliable father and responsible citizen.*'